GIRL WITH A KNIFE
A STORY OF LOVE AND VENGEANCE
IN COLONIAL AMERICA

BOOK ONE
ASSAULT

JAMES T. HOGG

ALL NIGHT BOOKS

Book and cover design by Alexia Garaventa
Printed in the United States of America, 2023

Paperback ISBN 978-1-63226-107-6
ebook ISBN 978-1-63226-112-0

Published by All Night Books
www.allnightbooks.com
www.jamesthogg.com

This book is dedicated to three generations of my family:

- My mother, who pushed me to be a writer when I was a kid in high school who just wanted to watch television instead of creating anything.

- My wife, Ann. Without her, my life would not be good.

- My daughters, Kim and Bethany Stachenfeld, and my son-in-law, Andrew Clayburn, all of whom gave me input and guidance in crafting the story.

GIRL WITH A KNIFE
A STORY OF LOVE AND VENGEANCE
IN COLONIAL AMERICA

BOOK ONE: Assault

BOOK TWO: Defense

BOOK THREE: Devastation

BOOK FOUR: Recovery

BOOK FIVE: Redemption

CONTENTS

A WORD FROM
THE AUTHOR ABOUT THE
BOOK YOU ARE READING
—AND A WARNING

In the interest of literary integrity, I will disclose that although this story is my best effort to set a story in the late 1600s, to be completely honest with my readers, I must admit that I did not follow the rules of the time with complete perfection. Although I hope the story is consistent with the history, occasionally I took some liberties with what actually might have happened in Colonial America in favor of a more exciting and more readable story.

I need to give you fair warning, that my goal in writing this story was quite simple; namely, that the reader would be unable to resist turning the next page or starting the next chapter. For this reason, I am warning you that this is a hard-to-put-down story, in multiple volumes, and it is rare that anyone who reads the first chapter can escape being sucked into the plot and the characters. So I urge you not to start reading at a time when you have a major project due at work or a major paper due at school, as you just might find yourself blowing an important deadline.

When you are done, I hope you will have enjoyed reading it as much as it thrilled me to write it.

James T. Hogg

MAJOR CHARACTERS IN ORDER OF APPEARANCE

BOOK ONE
ASSAULT

Passatan	Chief of Sagawanees in 1677
Katakuk	Son of Passatan
Tamawah	Son of Katakuk
Nununyi	Sagawanee woman with bow and arrow
Gilbert Menon	Mercenary
John Jones	Mercenary friend of Gilbert Menon in 1677, sheriff of North Hinkapee in 1692
Betsy Jones	Wife of Sheriff Jones
Thompson Downing	Founder of North Hinkapee, circa 1670

Miles Downing	Son of Thompson, husband of Martha
Martha Downing	Wife of Miles, maiden name Scrabblestone
Pat Downing	Twin son of Miles and Martha
Matt Downing	Twin son of Miles and Martha
William Brown	Minister of North Hinkapee church
Jane Carlin	Widow farmer and mother of Tommy
Tommy Carlin	Farmer, son of Jane, suitor of Faythe
Robert Wentworth	Farmer
Lucy Wentworth	Wife of Robert, maiden name Palmer
Faythe Emily Wentworth	Daughter of Robert and Lucy
Chloe Wentworth	Younger sister of Faythe
Elmer Smith	Employee of the Downing family, nicknamed "The Rat"
Earl Carver	Lawyer for the Downing family
Liggett	Hired head man of the Downing family
Handel Lewis	Widower blacksmith
Perkin Massey	Proprietor of the Towne Tavern
Philip Alderson	Doctor
Ahanu	English boy raised by Sagawanees
Paul Josephson	Proprietor of the Inn at Bearminster

1677, SAGAWANEE LAND

INDIANS

"She can't come with us," said Passatan, chief of the Sagawanees. "Only my warriors will be with us when we kill the White Men."

"Father," said Katakuk. "If only you could have seen her with the bow and arrow. She bested all of—"

Chief Passatan interrupted, holding up a palm to his son. "I know of her prowess with the bow and arrow, and I've seen it many times, but there is much more to a death battle with the White Men. A man who loses has an honorable end, but a woman—you know what they will do with her and to her. She is your friend, and maybe more someday when the time comes. But this is not to be." He looked at his son meaningfully but not unkindly. "This talk is over."

Nununyi saw the look in Katakuk's eyes and knew the answer before he spoke. He shook his head and looked down.

"It's not fair," he said.

Nununyi gazed at Katakuk—in his late teens and just coming into his full prowess as a man. He was tall and strong and lean, with muscles like the boulders carved smooth by the rushing icy streams, with a firm, flat stomach and long dark hair that he bound behind with a strip of leather. He walked with a litheness that spoke of inner strength, too. He would develop power and eventually leadership of the tribe. When Katakuk took the mantle from his father, all would be well.

She admired that he was proficient in all weaponry, including the tomahawk, the knife, the spear, the musket, and even the sword he took from a White Man in battle. He sometimes prevailed over even the mature men in hand-to-hand combat. She smiled a little as she thought, too, of the bow and arrow. Their people were known for that. He routinely bested others his age in marksmanship.

But he had never come close to Nununyi with the bow and arrow. No one could. Yet for some reason he had no jealousy that Nununyi outshone him in this. Instead, Katakuk carried great pride in her achievements. Katakuk recalled a recent conversation with his father, and his mother too. "Father. Mother. You should see her. Even the best of our men cannot come close to her with the bow and arrow. Nununyi with a bow and arrow is like watching a panther roam through the forest. It is beauty."

Chief Passatan and his wife looked meaningfully at each other at the time. *Is our son in love?* the chief wondered, *and with a warrior woman at that?* He restrained himself from smiling, although this time he really wanted to. Chief Passatan almost never smiled, as he felt it inconsistent with being chief, but he had feelings, and a deep love for and pride in his son. Katatuk was quite aware of this and close-to-worshiped his father. So, despite Katatuk's disagreement with his father's decision, he would not go against him or undermine him; it was not his way.

Katakuk and Nununyi had been together since even before they could remember. At first it was just play, but then as they had grown up Nununyi had over time shown reluctance to do what women were supposed to do—cut up animals, cook, take care of babies, and deal with whatever the men didn't want to do.

Even as a baby she had been fascinated watching others with the bow and arrow. And it was one of the first things she had learned as a young child, a labor of deep love from the start. Indeed, Nununyi neglected pretty much every woman's duty she could, to the dismay and annoyance of her mother and the other women, all so that she could have time to fashion her bow out of a young sapling of just the right timbre, with the string made of the tendons of a deer or other animal, and then keep it well oiled and clean. She joined the boys at the side of the stream, fashioning arrowheads out of stone pieces of just the right sort, and she gathered the perfect feathers that would guide the arrows in their flight. All could see that nothing transported Nununyi into joy more than when she let loose an arrow to fly to its target.

At first it was a novelty that the little girl child worked with the bow and arrow, but before she was even nine years old, she was bringing home game she had shot, and tribe members became more and more impressed. Later, she was at first decently competitive and then winning contests with adult men, and everyone began to be in awe. After her eleventh birthday, Nununyi never lost a single match. It seemed as if she never missed, and so it was.

But archery in a competition is one thing, thought Chief Passatan as he stirred the last of the embers in the community fire that evening. *Tomorrow, many of us will die in battle. I myself might not be coming back. And I will not have a woman with us, distracting my son.*

"Good night," said Katakuk to Nununyi, holding her slim hand between his own as they prepared to part. "I have great sorrow that you are not coming." He hung his head.

"Thank you, Kata," she replied, using the affectionate nickname she had given him when they were toddlers and she had been unable to say the full name. "It is of no importance," she insisted, with staid indifference.

Katakuk tilted his head and furrowed his brow as he studied her. *What is she thinking?* It meant everything to Nununyi to join with the men in the battle. She had told him many times before that she had been born to let fly her arrows to defend her people.

Perhaps she was saving face, then. He gave her the respect she needed, saying only, "Someday, when I am chief ..."

She nodded and then said, "good night," gently withdrawing her hand from his.

Someday, he thought, as he walked away, *she will be my wife and she will be with me in many battles. Together we will kill the White People and drive them away. And she will also bear me sons who will be warriors.* Over the years the two had moved from being inseparable childhood companions to finding themselves a young man and a young woman, with feelings for each other that had grown in intensity over time.

Nununyi had at first not overtly revealed her feelings to him, even with his hints and encouragement. Katakuk realized that Nununyi preferred to be a puzzle to be solved—like the smooth carved wooden knots his grandfather had made for the amusement of them all. She refused to be an obvious conclusion. He had tried to return this conceit by doing his best to be a puzzle himself and keep her guessing. So he flirted with other girls from time to time, but he felt awkward and silly doing this, suspecting that Nununyi knew full well what he was about.

Finally, they had kissed, only that one time, and only a few nights ago. But that kiss had meant everything to Katakuk. He was indeed in love and now he could keep no secret of it from her.

She's so beautiful, he thought, breaking off his musing, but then lingering on her beauty.

Her dark black hair and brown eyes framed a face that had only two expressions—impassivity and a smile so lively that it lit up those around her. She was small, so he had to bend down to kiss her, but her body had whipping power, explaining or resulting from her kinship with the bow and arrow. Although she was not at all vain, she spent a great deal of time with her hair, always braiding it and tying the braids together in back—it was anathema that her hair might get into her face and interfere with a shot. He dwelt a moment on the thought of her light, sinewy body that was yet fully that of a woman—and he squirmed with the thought of what it might be to be fully united with her.

Yes, Katakuk was in love with Nununyi; there was no doubt about it. And Nununyi was in love with Katakuk, although sometimes she wondered if she loved him more than she loved her bow and arrows. She thought about this now and then: *I am in love with the man Katakuk, but my bow and arrows, they* are *me.*

Nununyi nodded when Katakuk gave her the news, knowing full well everything Katakuk was thinking. She had expected this result and was completely at peace. She knew exactly what she was going to do.

WHITE PEOPLE

"Jonesy," said the big, bearish Gilbert Menon, the affectionate name rumbling deep in his voice, "it's gonna be quite a dust-up tomorrow, isn't it?"

John Jones, the smaller of the two and known for his stiffness, nodded matter-of-factly. "Yes it will." Their spies had brought word that the Indian attack was imminent.

Both were in their early twenties, and the lumbering Menon was surprisingly swift in his strength. He was inordinately proud of his beard, his one touch of vanity, and he cut it every day, peering with his bright blue eyes into a shard of mirror he kept carefully wrapped in a pocket. He was otherwise careless of his appearance but always looked at other men as if he were measuring them up, which he was.

He's a good man to have by you when it's touch-and-go, thought Jones, glancing at his friend.

John Jones was of moderate height and "not thin or thick," as an old man had once described him. He was a creative and devastating fighter and had killed many Indians in the eternal skirmishes, most of them with Menon at his side—they were mercenaries for the settlers. Jones's hair was brown and he typically wore it long, though every few months when they emerged into a town he would find a barber to cut it short, and then he let it grow out again when they retreated back to the wilderness. His stiff personality was external, marking him as a man not to be trifled with. Inside, however, he was a man of passion and even love. He just had not found his soulmate yet. He knew he would … someday.

The two men were now veterans of many "dust-ups," as they called them, with the Sagawanee Indians. They were too young and foolish to be really afraid of anything, and their good luck gave them not the slightest doubt that they would prevail in any battle.

Jones looked around at the score of other men they would fight alongside this time, all armed with muskets, spears, swords, knives, and some even with Indian tomahawks. They were a fearsome and fearless fighting force. The Town of Hinkapee had hired them through their leader Harriman Keep-Safe to drive off the Indians who had been harassing them consistently, and with increasing bloodshed—the death toll had risen on both sides.

Harriman Keep-Safe was a ruthless and pitiless man. He felt the best way to drive Indians away was to kill them, and as brutally as possible. After battles, he personally saw to it that any who were wounded died slowly and in the worst possible way. "Mercy" was not a word he knew. Jones shook his head at the thought—*nothing good comes of it when a brutal man is in charge.*

"What do you think about it?" Menon had asked Jones one time after a particularly bloody battle. They were kindling a little campfire to roast a hunk of meat Menon had carved out of the leg of a horse that had fallen in the skirmish.

Four warriors had been wounded and left lying on the ground by their fleeing brothers, and they were struggling to breathe or to hold in their internal organs. Harriman had thrown two of them, alive, into the fire, watching impassively as they burned and screamed until death took them. The other two Harriman had tortured slowly and carefully. It had been clear that no one was to interfere.

"That way is not for me," said Jones with a shudder in spite of himself. He threaded some meat on a stick and held it over the flame.

"Me, neither," said Menon. "They're just people like us. There's a story I'm not sure I've told you. One time I was in a spying party and I got near one of their villages. I saw two of them. It was a boy Indian and a girl Indian, and he was talking to her. I couldn't hear what he said, and I wouldn't have understood it anyway, but clearly he was, you know, trying to talk her into doing what we all want to do with a girl. But she was cool with him, as girls can be. She smiled and giggled, but she turned him down. I knew right then that it was God who had put me there."

"God—why God?" asked Jones.

"Because he wanted me to know that Indians are people like us."

"I never thought of it that way," said Jones, nodding in agreement. "But it makes sense." He had never liked killing anyone, although he was a natural. It was too easy, and that worried him.

"I guess we should turn in, Jonesy," said Menon. "Indians think they're so wise, but they always attack in the darkest part of the night, just before sunup. They think we haven't figured that out."

"Yes," replied Jones. He found himself inspecting the long knife that was always at his side. Without even thinking about it he had taken it out of its worn leather sheath and was running his finger ever so gently along the ever so sharp blade. It was special to him, a gift from his father. It had a handle that he found easy to grip, and the right weight for easy and facile use. And the blade was unfailingly sharp. Before a battle he found himself communing it. He shook his head to throw off the knife's spell, *Menon's right, it's time for some shut eye.*

The group of twenty Indians crept up on the White Men's camp, which was quiet and dark. *Good*, thought Chief Passatan. *They are asleep, and we will catch them unawares.* He nodded to his left and to his right, where his son Katatuk sat on his horse, every bit the man he was becoming. All of them rode forward without hesitation, fearless in the faint starlight.

Indian chieftains did not lead from the rear, but instead from the front; accordingly, Chief Passatan offered the benediction of his heart: *I am proud of my son.*

This was his last thought before a musket ball tore through the top of his head, and he slowly, oh so slowly, fell to the ground. His horse, now riderless, followed the other horses and men forward in a rush at the sound of the shot.

No, the White Men's camp had not been sleeping after all. They were waiting, and it was a grim beginning for the Sagawanees. Three more warriors were quickly dispatched before the rest had dismounted and—armed, vicious, and fearless—struck out to take the battle to the White Men secreted in the trees.

The White Men's advantage lasted only moments, because a musket fired, betrayed with sound and smoke the location of the shooter, and there was certainly no time to reload before the Indians closed with each musket man.

The battle was intense, every man fighting for his own life and to end the life of his adversaries. The Indians asked no quarter and gave none, either, and the White Men returned the savagery upon their foes. Screams of triumph mingled with death cries, as swords, knives, tomahawks, spears, and musket balls found their marks.

Katakuk had seen his father fall and thoughts ran through him all at once with the shock. *What now shall we do?* he thought in a panic. *Am I now chief? What of the battle? Are we losing?* But then there was no time to think, and he closed with an angry, enormous White Man who bore down upon him.

Katakuk ducked under the path of the White Man's spear and rolled forward, coming up strong and hard with his knife. The look on the White Man's face—his last expression, in fact—was surprise at the quick slicing of Katakuk's knife up through his chin and into his brain, killing him instantly.

Suddenly, Katakuk, looking for his next opponent, was seized from behind and a knife came up to his throat. Instead of fear, he felt only sadness. *I will leave now, having been chief for but a brief moment,* but it was not to be. For some reason, the knife that would have left him bleeding like a slaughtered animal did not strike. Instead, the man holding the knife slumped to the ground.

Katakuk had a moment for a grim smile when he saw what had happened. An arrow had pierced the man in the head, an arrow with such vehemence, accuracy, and force that it had actually come out the other side. *Nununyi!* In a flash he knew why she had not been upset at Chief Passatan's forbidding her to come to the attack. She was coming anyway, and he felt a split second of pride and a thrill. But there was no time for reflection—another White Man was rushing upon him.

Arrows were flying from somewhere as another, and then another, and then another of Harriman Keep-Safe's men went down. Keep-Safe traced carefully the direction of the arrows, and then concluded where they were coming from. He had one more musket shot left, and he took a chance and shot it into the trees where he could see the outline of the archer. It was a lucky shot and found its mark—the body jerked and fell.

I'll see about that one later, he thought, pulling his hatchet from his belt and running full tilt against another of the savages. No more arrows flew thereafter from that location.

The battle was over just a few minutes later, when the Sagawanees' new chief gave the sign to his remaining fighters that it was time to leave. Although almost twenty Indian warriors had come to the battle, only seven were left, all of them wounded in some way. Katakuk's body was whole, but his spirit was worse than wounded. *I died*, he thought, *or came close to dying. But Nununyi saved me.* And where was she?

Katakuk pulled his horse under cover and bound it to a tree, then whisper-called to Nununyi in the direction from which she had shot the arrow that had saved his life. But all was silence in the woods. He crept out among his warriors—*my warriors now!* he thought, overwhelmed at the prospect that he was now chief. *Am I ready?* Gripping the shoulder of one warrior to ask about Nununyi, then staring into another's face with what he hoped was an impassive plea for news of her, Katakuk felt panic for Nununyi. But he could hardly begin his reign as chief showing panic for his loss, so with as much steel as he could muster in a whisper, he roused his men for retreat.

As they rode away silent, into the trees, his heart sank as waves of grief washed over him.

Father, oh Father, what a terrible day! he wailed internally and wordlessly. *Oh, Nununyi. My Nuni.*

But there was no time for grief. They had clearly lost this battle and now they had to get away with the few who were left—as their chief, he must care for them.

In seconds the Indians had melted off into the trees, found their horses, and galloped away.

Jones also thought that his troop had lost the battle. Out of their twenty men, almost ten had been killed outright, and of the ones remaining, almost all had severe wounds, which would no doubt claim at least two or three more of them. In the end it was the typical result of an Indian battle. It was a war of attrition that never ended.

He and Menon had been fighting back-to-back, protecting one another from being struck from behind. It was Jones's idea many months before, but Menon had taken to it instantly, and it had worked well in every battle. This day they had each dispatched an Indian warrior, Menon with a sword and Jones with his knife, their muskets long since discharged and thrown aside.

Menon and Jones, however, had only superficial cuts and bruises. They would need some medical attention when they got back to Hinkapee, but they'd soon be fighting again. Such was their fortune.

"You!" shouted Harriman Keep-Safe at Menon and Jones. "Gather up the wounded Indians and bring them here. Near the fire."

Jones wrinkled his nose in disgust. He knew what was next. He looked around the camp and counted three Indians wriggling in the dirt. He looked at Menon, who shook his head.

"A quick death?" Menon asked.

Jones nodded. Together they walked over to the first Indian. He had a stomach wound and his entrails were leaking out of him. He had only minutes to live, no matter what. Jones's eyes met the other's for just a second. Was it hatred or respect that passed between them before Menon's sword came down, severing the man's head from his body?

Harriman was shouting, but they hurried to dispatch another warrior, quickly and painlessly. "I'll have no part in torturing anyone," growled Menon.

Jones nodded wearily. Then suddenly, and even to his own surprise, he was saying, "This is my last battle. I don't want to do this anymore."

Menon shrugged. "Fine with me. Then what'll we do?" But then he stiffened, and Jones heard the same rustling in the bushes. "What's that?" Menon whispered.

They cautiously parted the leaves and branches to see what was making the sound, and Jones caught a glimpse of deerskin, long black hair, and a graceful bow still clutched in her hand where she lay.

"It's a girl Indian!" he exclaimed. "She must be—must have been—I guess … the one that shot down three of our men."

"Must be," said Menon. The dawn was moving from gray to rose and they could see the girl's body was still. But she had made the noise, and the blood was pulsing out of her. "I've never seen anyone so beautiful," he murmured.

Jones laid his hand on her warm cheek. She was still alive, but she wouldn't be if Keep-Safe knew about her. What horrors he would wreak upon her!

The men looked at one another. The two had become such close friends they almost thought as one.

Menon had knelt next to her and looked up at Jones and said, "Will you help me?"

Back among his people, Katakuk had to carry to his mother and the rest of the people the news of Passatan's death. As they'd retreated from the scene of battle, the warriors had retrieved the body and reverently draped it over a horse, and a warrior was chosen to trot alongside—he would soon escort the fallen chief into their midst. At dawn, the silhouette of burdened horse and man became visible to all Passatan's people, who were waiting to receive him. Most had lost fathers and sons and husbands and brothers, but all had lost their father, their chief, Passatan.

Katatuk's mother covered her face when she heard the news and then walked into the forest to be alone with her thoughts, remembering the man she loved.

And Katakuk had lost Nununyi. None at home had seen her, none had spied her beautiful body among the fallen at the site of the attack. As soon as he could decently do so, Katakuk had returned to the scene of battle and scoured the woods. There was no sign of her, nor of her bow.

But in the White Men's campfire were human bones.

1692, NORTH HINKAPEE

IN CHURCH

By nine o'clock every Sunday morning, the meeting house of North Hinkapee became a church and was well filled, so much so that many had to sit outside on benches or chairs that they carried with them, or even on the ground. Thompson Downing, founder of the town, had envisioned this problem decades earlier, so he instructed the builders to design one side of the meeting house to be able to be thrown open so that even those outside could see to the pulpit. In winter, everyone would cram into the building, thankful for the warmth of the bodies, though the less fortunate were forced to stand in the back and two or three deep around the edges.

Today, though, the latecomers who had to stay outside were not sorry for it, nor sorry to wait for the Downing carriage so that worship could begin. It was a glorious June day, an opportunity to rest from their labors of the week. Little girls made daisy chains, and clover ones, right where they sat in the lush grass, and little boys dug their fingers down into the rich soil to draw up wriggling worms, while their parents shushed them and brushed off their hands, striving in vain to make them hold their hands quietly in their laps.

The meeting house—or church on Sunday—was simple, like all the Puritan churches of the time. There was no soaring spire nor distinctive architecture, and certainly no statues nor paintings nor even expensive stained glass. Instead, the building was functional, a symbol of simplicity and a rejection of those Christian practices that led to feelings of spiritual passion and excess. A Puritan church looked a bit like a courtroom, and so it functioned on occasion. But its main purpose, making the Word of God central, was characterized by the raised pulpit that allowed everyone to see and hear Minister William Brown.

Though the church building was meant to symbolize the pure virtues of the Christian faith, it was actually a point of pride for the residents of North Hinkapee. Thompson Downing had included the people in his vision, helping them consider that they had all, together, carved their world out of the hard wilderness. And when they gathered for town business, and—most importantly—for worship, they shared that pride all together.

They were all waiting for the Downing carriage, for only when the Downings arrived could they begin. As the sole church leader in North Hinkapee, Minister Brown was proud to be one of the most influential persons in the township, of course behind the Downings.

Despite his outward piety over now almost twenty years, and his career promise to be devoted to the Lord God, Minister Brown could not help enjoying the good things in life, including fine food and drink, and women, too. At first he had simply been unable to control his urges. This had led to the loss of his previous ministry, and he had come to North Hinkapee for a new start.

For some time he had wondered if there were a canonical inconsistency between enjoying improper worldly pleasures and being a respected minister. It had troubled him at first, but after a time it ceased to bother him. He reasoned that God would certainly forgive these trifling indiscretions as a *quid pro quo* for all the good work he did with such passionate devotion. *The Lord's work*, he assured himself. Accordingly, he could easily be a fervent steward of the church and a preacher of God's will one moment and a lecher the next. It wasn't a problem.

Minister Brown was in his early forties and knew he still retained the good looks he had been born with. He was quite tall, which gave him an imposing presence, especially in that raised pulpit. He had an aquiline nose, down which he could look at the congregation to good effect, his eyes blazing in his dark complexion. And he wore his hair unusually long and flowing over his shoulders. He thought the few threads of silver in his hair made him attractive in a Jesus sort of manner, although even he had to admit to himself that there was no obvious connection between Jesus and silver hair.

For some years after his arrival in North Hinkapee, his sermons had missed the mark with the congregation. He was just too intellectual. He could tell from the eyes glazing over before him, and the many eyes actually closed, that to these farmers in North Hinkapee his sermons were uninspiring, even boring. It had taken some time for him to realize, and eventually accept, that for this audience he had downright oratorical infirmities. For a long time, he simply couldn't manage to rouse his congregation. The villagers in those early days fanned themselves in the summer and rubbed their arms in the winter, and almost no one was paying attention to him.

But all that changed when he started to talk more about the Devil, about demonic possession and witches. Indeed, he noticed over time that whenever he mentioned witchcraft or the temptations and sinuous deceptions of Satan, the audience paid rapt attention. This attention increased even further if he managed subtle prurience in the stories he told.

Almost everyone was terrified of witches and the Devil, and they looked for help from the authority of an ordained minister. Those who felt it was all hogwash were bright enough to fear accusations, for even one who didn't believe in witches could easily be hanged or burned as one. News of this sort from other towns, told in Briarcliff, reached even North Hinkapee.

Minister Brown had therefore shifted to these themes for virtually all of his sermons, and now everyone expected it and crowded into the church not just from duty or fear but from real interest. What would he deliver in this sermon?

The fear of the Devil had power, and it was so easy to inflame that fear. It was dark at night, and the woods were scary. Terrible things happened that could not be easily explained, so a supernatural explanation gave at least one kind of comfort at the death of an infant, the sickness of a whole herd of livestock, an Indian attack, or a ruined crop. Minister Brown's reputation as an expert in witchcraft helped his occult explanations ease one's grief or, better yet, threaten misfortune for one's enemies. Without actual hard-core facts, the word of a minister of the church was, to some, akin to the word of God.

Minister Brown loved that authority, though he had to maintain an appearance of humility—and the seeming reverent chastity of a single unmarried preacher certainly added to that impression.

From his seat at the front of the meeting house—the simple structure that served all the town's public gathering needs—Minister William Brown looked over the gathering congregation, conveying to any who caught his eye the message that he was watching. He would nod slight approval to those who had more status in the town and look right over the heads of the others. His genuine smiles, though, were usually only for the Downings, particularly Martha Downing, for whom he found himself in the grip of an almost uncontrollable lust. She was so bedazzlingly attractive that he found himself tongue-tied in her presence, often wondering if she could read his thoughts, which of course she could.

Where are the Downings this morning? Minister Brown wondered, looking through the doorway at the end of the center aisle of the meeting house, looking further down the road to the little rise where the Downing carriage would appear before too long. Then the day's worship could begin.

MARTHA DOWING
PREPARES
FOR CHURCH

Martha Downing was taking her over-deliberate time at her d.
table, adjusting her demure Sunday bonnet just so and smoo
her carefully tailored bodice for the effect she wanted. Her sh
prominent breasts seemed to defy gravity—it helped that she l
put her sons out to a wet-nurse at their births. She dressed alwa)
as fashionably as current society would allow, in a manner befitting
the matriarch of one of the wealthiest families in the Colonies. She
might wear the sober russets and deep greens of the other Puritan
women, but hers were the finest fabrics from England, with a weight
and drape that made clear she was a cut above the rest. An obvious sexuality radiated from her, even when she wore the most penitent of clothing, as when she wore mourning for her father-in-law,
Thompson Downing, for a full year after he'd died a decade before.
Her dresses then were black, but sumptuous—rustling, gliding, rich
black, setting off the flaxen hair that peeked out of her cap designed
to show more of her hair than cover it.

At last it was time too, and Martha strolled out to the carriage where her husband, grown sons, and the driver and horses that had been waiting the better part of an hour to speed the family to church.

All was right with Martha's world.

FAYTHE WENTWORTH SLIPS OUT

As everyone squirmed on their benches, wishing the hours-long service was already underway, Faythe Wentworth took opportunity in the restlessness to leave her place and get into the side aisle. On one level, she told herself that she *just* wanted a big dipper of water from the well outside; however, on another level what she *really* wanted was an eyeful of Tommy Carlin.

Staying crouched a bit as she sped down the aisle, she slowed and caught Tommy's gaze and his big grin that said, "Good for you, making a break for it!" She felt her face go hot, and not because she was sneaking out of church. Faythe had recently turned seventeen years old and knew things were changing for her. She'd always been good at darting around to avoid attracting attention to herself while getting where she wanted to go. But now she was growing up, and she needed to act more like a woman.

She tripped lightly down the steps and threaded her way among the villagers standing and sitting outside; then she headed for the town well a few dozen steps away. She wondered whether a *woman* would flirt with a boy in church. *Or is he a man?* Tommy was seventeen, too. *I guess he's a man?* She liked him, and she'd found herself thinking about Tommy Carlin a lot lately.

Faythe had known Tommy the whole four years her family had been in North Hinkapee, and they'd run around wild together with other children—mostly boys. But of late she realized that there seemed to be something new about him. *Or maybe*, she mused, as she drew up a bucket of water from the well, *there's something new about me.* Since she had begun having these feelings, she had spoken to him only a few times, and with parents around, so the conversations were awkward and somewhat perfunctory. How nice it would be to run around in the woods with Tommy again.

Faythe's mind went to places that it should not be going as she hung the dipper on its nail over the well, and she dawdled among the trees before returning to the meeting house. What would it be like to kiss him? Dare she think of it—even to be married to him and raise her own family? What would that be like? *What would—well—things beyond kissing be like?* She felt a womanly stirring inside herself, something she hadn't felt before, and she shivered a little, though the late-morning sun was hot. *Would he want a wife who is as tough and strong as he is?* Her parents had both told her on many occasions that she was strong, that she was different. Her father, Robert Wentworth, had trained her to fight like a boy—to be strong and quick, and Lucy Wentworth had approved of the training of their daughter. But Robert and Lucy were not like most of the parents in North Hinkapee. Would a man want a woman like her?

Then Faythe's thoughts veered in the opposite direction, as she kept an eye on the road that led to the Downings' farm. Their carriage was coming down the hill and would be there soon. But she still had a few minutes to herself.

"Fiddlesticks!" she said aloud, but under her breath lest anyone hear. "Why should I get married in the first place?" she murmured with some annoyance in her undertone, snapping twigs in her strong hands. Even if Tommy were the best husband in the world, she'd still be under his thumb. She wouldn't be free to make her own decisions anymore. *And how could I take care of my sister? Chloe will always need me!*

She walked back to the meeting house and picked her way through the people again, then quietly went up the few steps into the building and back up the side aisle.

No way marriage makes any sense, not to any man. But she had to admit that Tommy wasn't like most of the boys—men—she knew. He was more like her father, a man worth marrying.

She sneaked a glance at Tommy, or at the back of his head, full of reddish-brown curls, as she slowly crept by. She slipped past her sister Chloe and took her place by her mother—musing over Tommy's dimpled cheek, his expressive eyes and the mouth that always seemed to be smiling at her, inviting her to kiss him strongly. And there was something about those broad shoulders, the lean yet bulky muscles of his young arms strengthened by years of hard farming work—what would it be like to be encircled in those arms? That wave of womanly feeling rushed through her again, and she felt hot, somehow.

She shook with a wave of imagined guilt. *I shouldn't be thinking about this kind of thing ... in church!*

THE DOWNINGS ARRIVE

Ahh, here they come, Minister Brown thought as the carriage pulled up before the meeting house and the outside crowd parted. He rose from his heavy wooden chair with a warm smile that caused everyone to look over their shoulders, for it was the signal that the Downings were arriving. He strolled slowly down the aisle, setting a fatherly hand upon a child's head here and there, nodding to the severely stiff Sheriff Brown and his wife Betsy, who both smiled back politely but without enthusiasm, and he offered a cooler smile to the Wentworth family.

Minister Brown noticed Faythe as he strolled by. But Minister Brown never met Faythe's eyes. Last time he had done that he had drawn back in quick surprise, almost as if he had been stung by a bee. Though there was no reason for the feeling, he found himself angered for a reason he couldn't define. Despite his resolve not to meet her eyes any more, inadvertently his eyes moved to Faythe's, and her eyes shot beams at him like the glory of one of Ezekiel's terrifying angels, and Minister Brown looked away hastily. He scarcely noticed Chloe, who was clinging to Faythe's hand and was partially sheltered behind her dress.

Robert Wentworth, the girls' father, smiled mildly back at Minister Brown, and sat tall and as respectable as he could in his threadbare Sunday best, his light brown curls sprung out about his head, his eyes bearing the sadness of a hound's. His plain but smiling dark-haired wife Lucy affectionately held his hand between her own. No matter how rough things were for them, Lucy and Robert were always on their best behavior in public and always went out of their way to have a good word for everyone. These relative newcomers to North Hinkapee—as of several years back—were "the real thing," Minister Brown knew. They were the kindly, hard-working sort, and it gave even the cynical Minister Brown a warm feeling to see a wife and husband who so obviously loved each other.

Minister Brown continued down the aisle and soon he had arrived at the foot of the steps of the meeting house.

"Why good morning, Miles," he called, greeting the patriarch of the Downing family with special respect as Miles waited to help Martha down the carriage steps. Miles Downing was, to all public intents and purposes, clearly the man in charge. Among other things, Miles Downing was the man who managed the Village Payments that ultimately paid the minister his salary.

"And hello, Patrick and Matthew," he said to the two young men—the two strapping sons of the Downings—who came around the carriage after having disembarked on the other side.

"Hello, Minister Brown," replied Pat, holding his hat to his chest in respect. Matt just nodded and almost smirked at Minister Brown, making not so subtle his contempt by keeping his hat on all the way into the place of worship. Minister Brown almost suppressed his wince over these two, who were always causing trouble one way or another. Pat overall seemed to be a rather good-hearted sort, but he was invariably intertwined with his brother Matt as a participant in whatever misdeeds Matt could find for the two of them to do.

And, finally, Minister Brown bowed his head to Martha. "A pleasure to see you this morning, Martha," he said cautiously, careful to keep his eyes well above the level of her body, though he imagined that her jutting breasts would be straining against the bodice she would have had tailored purposefully to emphasize them. Martha nodded back to him expressionlessly.

Elmer Smith followed closely behind, as he'd ridden in on the back platform of the carriage like a footman. He was generally seen with the Downing family or rushing around doing their business for them. It always seemed to Minister Brown, and to just about everyone else, that Smith had his nose up the behind of Miles Downing, but there was no purpose in making note of it, and possibly some danger in speaking of it. Most people just did their best to politely avoid Elmer Smith. His nickname of "The Rat" suited him perfectly, with his long nose and overbite, and his skinny, scurrying ways.

As the Downings proceeded up the aisle to take their accustomed row three from the front—their box pew always reserved for them—Minister Brown waited at the steps, noting that for all their desire not to have the processions of the papists, North Hinkapee Church did have a ritual.

Near the steps and just outside on a stump was Handel Lewis, the enormous bald blacksmith, who towered so far over everyone that he almost seemed to be inside, up on the meeting room floor. His four motherless children were arranged on a quilt beside him, and he dandled the fifth, a baby, on his knee. Minister Brown held back a smile when he confirmed that Handel had chosen his spot on the open side of the meeting house, casually close to the widow Jane Carlin, who had managed a back bench inside with her son Tommy. Everyone in the town knew Handel had eyes for her—everyone, it seemed, except Jane Carlin herself. But Handel was a timid giant too shy to plead his case, so nothing had yet happened to fulfill his dreams.

Minister Brown turned and surveyed the congregation from the back as he slowly moved forward, the Downings taking their time to file into their box pew—the only one in the building, for others

34

had only benches. Minister Brown clasped a firm, friendly hand on the shoulder of Dr. Alderson, who was there with his family sitting near the front.

There was no formal arrangement for seating in the church, but the poorest families were nearly always seated outside, though a couple of benches near the back kept some appearance of equality before God. To effectuate this arrangement without obvious favoritism, Minister Brown had years ago taken to standing at the entrance to the church as the congregation arrived. He would nod and shake hands with everyone, and his nod effectively directed the person inside or outside, depending on where there was room. The Downings, of course, were always directed inside—to their own box pew—and the likes of the Wentworths and Carlins outside, as Handel Lewis was today. No one ever objected to this. There was a certain harmony and flow about it.

But the Wentworths and the Carlins had arrived early this Sabbath, and Faythe Wentworth had pulled her father's hand toward a bench inside. Minister Brown had smiled and nodded indulgently at Robert's and Lucy's tentative gaze at him, and he'd held out a hand to welcome them to the privilege. The girls had giggled a little and Chloe swung her feet under the bench, and Robert sat perhaps a little straighter.

Minister William Brown climbed the two steps to the platform, turned with a swirl of his robes to enter the pulpit, and climbed the two steps within that structure, too, so that he truly embodied his authority in the assembly of saints. He held his arms up, and the wide black sleeves of his robe fell down to his elbows, revealing the brilliant white of his shirt sleeves, bleached and pressed by one of the girls of the town.

"Beloved, we are gathered here this day to worship the Lord our God," he called out in his impressive voice, "for He is mighty. Let us begin with a hymn from the psalter, Psalm 37, which begins thus: 'Fret not thyself because of the wicked men, neither be envious for the evildoers. For they shall soon be cut down like grass, and shall wither as the green herb.' Now please stand and join me as we sing these words together …"

A SERMON ABOUT
TEMPTATION
AND THE DEVIL

After many long songs and prayers, the longest with Minister Brown humbly kneeling before his chair as an example to the congregation, it was time for the sermon. Minister Brown rose to his feet, held a hand up to the congregation to seat them as well, then he walked up to the pulpit with what he thought of as an appropriate stride, rising above them all as he took the steps to install himself behind the lectern. Finally, they had come to the part he and his congregation always waited for.

"Mr. Richard Brewster was a goodly man," he began with a flourish. "He went to church on Sundays. He said grace before every single meal. He plowed his fields. He did his work. He had him a wife and three sons. And he was faithful to his wife. Indeed, this man was unswerving in his devotions to the Lord God. Although he could read but little, and he owned him but one book, that book was the Bible itself. Richard Brewster was a tribute to what all men should be.

"But then one day he went hunting, and in the late afternoon just as it was starting to get dark in the woods, he came upon an old woman. To his surprise, he saw it was one of his neighbors, a Mrs. Jenkins, who had been living alone since her husband died. What was she doing alone in the woods at nightfall?"

Minister Brown could see his attentive congregation wondering, too, so he continued, quite pleased with himself:

"At first she seemed just the old woman he had always known. But as he came closer, she began to grow taller and straighter, and before his very eyes she grew younger and younger. He watched in amazement as the old woman became a beautiful young woman with a shapely form that was a delight to the eyes, in the way of a seductive woman." Minister Brown tried not to smile when he said this. He knew just how far he could go without going over the line.

"To his astonishment and fear, Richard Brewster noticed that a glow shone about her. And then she smiled at him.

"She said, 'Richard, it is good for me to find a good, strong man like you. Indeed, how be you?'

"Richard was stricken. He couldn't speak. Something was wrong. This was devilment or witchcraft, and he knew it. As I told you already, this Richard was a good man, and he knew this wasn't right. How could an older woman become young before his eyes—without devilment?"

Minister Brown opened his eyes wide in questioning and slowly shook his head, spurring others in the congregation to shake their heads as well.

"He should have fled home right away, but instead Richard Brewster spoke to her. He said only, 'I be fine,' answering her question in innocence. But then he added an obvious question: 'But how is it you become young before my eyes?'

"'Come with me,' she said, 'and I'll show you.' She beckoned her hand and Richard, without thinking, took her hand and followed her."

One simple farmer in the congregation half rose to stop the metaphorical Richard Brewster from his fatal misstep, and Minister Brown knew his congregation was now hanging on every word.

"Richard followed her for a short distance, but then he came to himself, at the last minute, and shook his head as if to say 'No.' He broke her hand's grip and without another word he went home, his heart beating fast."

That simple farmer nodded with satisfaction—Richard Brewster had chosen the better part.

Minister Brown, having left them all with the image of Brewster hurrying home, letting three beats of silence carry the impression into their hearts, continued.

"Richard Brewster thought he was free, thought he had been tempted by the Devil himself, who had sent a witch to suborn him. But Richard Brewster had resisted."

Minister Brown stopped right there again and looked around at everyone. "But Richard Brewster had made a crucial and eventually fatal mistake, although he knew it not. He indeed went home to his wife. But he was nevertheless bewitched." An older woman in the congregation gasped audibly, her hand over her mouth at the thought.

"It took several days, but Richard Brewster came to realize that he no longer found his wife pleasing. This was a terrible thing. Indeed, it is a terrible thing for a man and woman living together to not be able to consummate their union." At this, the more chaste in the congregation, perhaps those with difficulty consummating their own union, looked down with some slight embarrassment.

He cleared his throat and mumbled, "A terrible thing," shaking his head sadly. "This was an affliction, and for some reason, Richard did not tell his wife about his chance meeting with the woman in the woods. Why was that?"

The question hung in the air and the congregation was rapt.

"Although I know many things as a servant of the Lord God, I do not know the answer to questions of that nature. Richard was a good man. He had as yet done nothing wrong, but he was ashamed somehow to tell his wife. Nor did he tell his good minister. He kept it to himself, and he grew in dissatisfaction with his wife. He was bewitched indeed.

"Days went by. Richard kept thinking about the woman in the woods. He saw her in town, but then she was just Mrs. Jenkins, as she always was, just an old woman. Had this really happened, or had he dreamt it all?

"That very night he had seen her in town, he fell asleep and had a dream in which the woman had come to him, had sought him out. He sprang awake."

His congregation couldn't admit it, but they were entranced. But since the titillating tale came from an impeccable source, they had permission to listen to something otherwise forbidden—dreams of women, bewitching …

"Richard Brewster felt a calling in that dream. He was being called to the woods. Of course, he would not go. But even as he had determined not to heed the call, he found himself dressing to go out.

"He had lost all power over himself, all control of his actions. So he went outside, obeying that force within him. And of course, Mrs. Jenkins was waiting for him in the woods. It was obvious now what was to happen."

Minister Brown sneaked a look at the Downings in their box pew, and he saw the usual amiable interest from Miles and general disinterest from Martha, which he found unsettling.

But Minister Brown was too clever to go too far, so he said, "We are in the Lord's house, and I cannot say more of the specifics"—to the obvious disappointment of everyone on hand. "However, let it be said in somewhat veiled language that after that night Richard Brewster could no longer say he had been faithful to his wife. He was not." Minister Brown shook his head sadly.

"He went to the woods the next night and the next, each time with a different story in his mind and conviction that each night would be the last. But it wasn't. It couldn't be, not any longer." Minister Brown leaned over the pulpit and lowered his voice. "Has any man here—or woman—found it so? That 'the last time' was not the last?"

The eyes of some of the congregants went wide; others held very still while cutting their eyes one way or another.

"And it wasn't long before Mrs. Jenkins brought her friends. Other witches. Yes, of course, Mrs. Jenkins was a witch. She was sent by the Devil to tempt Richard Brewster away from his path of virtue to a path of sin.

"A coven was there one night, an entire congregation of witches, and at this point the Devil himself appeared, in the shape of a man dressed all in black, and, needless to say, quite terrifying. Richard Brewster found himself speaking the Devil's tongue, although no one had taught it to him. And eventually he was given a book to sign. It was a book of parchment, like any book, but the words in it were written in red, glowing, fiery ink with a black quill. It was The Devil's Book indeed," said Minister Brown in a tone now hushed. No one was talking or fidgeting; all of North Hinkapee were staring at him.

"Yes, it was The Devil's Book. At first Richard Brewster refused to sign. He did not sign that night, nor the next. But every night he was drawn back to the delights of the gathering in the woods, and eventually he could not resist any longer, and so he signed him his name. And he signed his name with blood pricked from his own finger with the Devil's claw. And as he wrote his name in blood, it transformed and shone in red fiery ink just like all the other words.

"Richard Brewster now belonged to the Devil. And he was a witch himself."

William Brown, minister of the North Hinkapee congregation, paused a long time now, to let this sink in.

"All of this happened," he said quietly, "because a good man made a simple mistake. Instead of running, as fast as he could, from the Devil's apparition, he spoke to it, reached out and touched it, and was thereby entrapped."

Then his voice changed abruptly, as if coming back from the story to the present world.

"We here live in modern times. We have good lives, although hard lives, here in North Hinkapee. Unlike other places we have heard about, we haven't had an outbreak of witchcraft here, because we are so strong in our faith. Look about you at how we are all—all your neighbors and friends and our benefactors the Downings themselves—all are here worshipping God in this wonderful and beautiful church!" He stretched out his arms to embrace his congregation.

"But we must be exceptionally vigilant at all times. The Devil is out there. He will come for you. He will. He will come for everyone at one time or another. And you must be ready to send him packing."

With a few more words of exhortation and the decoration of a verse about the roaring lion their Enemy was, Minister Brown finally finished. He was very pleased with himself. He had done exactly what he wanted to do. He sneaked a peek over at Miles Downing, who nodded to him approvingly. He tried to catch Martha Downing's eye, but to his disappointment she wasn't looking at him and didn't seem to be paying attention anymore.

Overall, the morning had gone well. He looked forward to his usual Sunday night dinner at the Downings'. He would undoubtedly receive some praise for his fine sermon. He tried not to smile but instead to look appropriately grim and concerned.

LUSTFUL THOUGHTS

For Matt Downing, it started the first time he saw Chloe Wentworth—really saw her. Until recently she had just been a little girl—a "kid"—but suddenly she was growing up and looking like a woman for the first time, but still with that innocent, wide-eyed baby face. It was in church when this transformation happened in his consciousness, and his body immediately responded, which made it even more embarrassing and nearly impossible to hide, no matter how he crossed his legs or held his coat before him.

And still worse, he was with his mother at the time. And his mother had looked at him oddly when she noticed his attention on the girl. Martha was intuitive, and had a quick premonition to pay more attention, but she was distracted and the thought passed. She would remember this much later.

However, the problem for Matt was unsolvable. Matt was eighteen years old and Chloe was a mere twelve, maybe "almost thirteen" by now. It would be a stretch for a marriage, and Matt wasn't interested in that, anyway. The Downings were the wealthiest and most powerful family in the town of North Hinkapee, whereas the Wentworths were little more than peasants. What rose up within Matt when he saw her was not a vision of having her at his hearthside, raising his Downing heirs, but having her, having at her—against her will seemed even more exciting—in a barn somewhere, or in the deep woods.

But Matt couldn't get Chloe out of his head. She had matured into an almost-woman very early, too early. Her breasts were much too large for a child of her age. And the curves of her body were those of a fully-grown woman. Any adult man who looked at her could surely feel the heat of attraction, although of course no ordinary North Hinkapee man would admit anything like that. They must all look at her and pretend they just saw a child, but no one could hide that this girl was going to be a beautiful and extraordinarily desirable woman. It was just happening all too fast.

Better yet, from Matt's perspective, Chloe Wentworth was all the more appealing because she was completely oblivious to all of it; she was just too young for that sort of thing. But that didn't stop him from daydreaming about having his way with her. At first it was just urges, solved by abusing himself, as the minister called it. Then it was daydreaming. But now even at night he dreamed of himself and Chloe, and he wondered if that were a sign from the God Minister Brown said revealed things in dreams.

The more nights that went by with Matt growing in frustration, the more these dreams grew violent. Chloe would run from him, but in the dream Chloe was crying and terrified, and that was even more exciting. Matt would chase her down and then he would "get her." At this point Matt would awake sweating violently and very aroused, or he'd find he'd already soiled himself.

Then one day Matt had his dream start to move in a slight way towards a terrible reality.

It was a beautiful summer-like day in late April, cool but not too cool. The fields were barren, still, with the farmers starting work for the growing season, and the woods were full of game trying to forage in the new growth, so Matt and his brother Pat had gone hunting. Though other men worked during the day, Matt and Pat did not have to, so they'd had a leisurely afternoon enjoying the weather but not seeing any game. Their stomachs were rumbling for supper, so Matt had just about decided to call it a day, as the dusk was closing in.

They were standing in the blind his father had built some years before and left in the land the Downings had leased to Robert Wentworth. The legalities were irrelevant as long as they were undiscovered. The trespassing hunters were concealed in the blind, with the tips of their guns sticking out, and if they were motionless, they would be completely invisible to the animals. When the deer or turkey or rabbit came into range, wham!

From a distance, Matt and Pat were easily identifiable as brothers, though they were not identical twins. Both were muscular, fair, giants over six feet tall with straight blond hair and watery blue eyes. But there the similarities ended. Matt stood tall and straight while Pat had a perpetual slouch. Matt was charming and winsome, but with an edge, while Pat was reserved and quiet. Matt was what was thought to be "manly," while Pat was better at daydreaming and enjoying his solitude. He liked working with his hands on the farm, though he didn't have to, and he even liked reading, though books were quite scarce and a priority only to their father—their mother didn't much care for them. The twins were inseparable, but it didn't seem to be based on love between them. They just seemed to be together because it made sense.

Matt suddenly saw, a dozen paces away, the curly-blond-haired Chloe, in a yellow dress, but she could not see them within the blind. And she was alone, it seemed.

Pat had been growing impatient and whispered, "Matt, we should get home. It's starting to get dark and there's nothing to hunt today. When can we go?"

Matt murmured back, "Soon," and then he grasped Pat's shoulder and pointed toward the girl, then held his finger to his lips. Matt was always in charge and Pat just went along. He would wait as long as Matt wanted him to wait.

Matt had told Pat something of his obsession with Chloe Wentworth. "Matt, you've got to give this up," Pat had responded, but Matt couldn't, or wouldn't.

In this moment, dazzled at the prospect, Matt spoke without even realizing he was speaking: "We could get her, you know."

"What do you mean?" whispered Pat, though he knew exactly what Matt meant.

This was because Matt spared no detail in explaining his fantasies to his brother. This included incredible specifics regarding his one night in a house of prostitution. Indeed, no detail was left out as Matt described to Pat everything that had occurred.

Not that long ago Martha had become impatient that her boys were overly focused on lustful pursuits. She had suggested to Miles that perhaps it was time for their *father* to take them to the unimaginatively named Inn at Bearminster to complete their growing up into manhood; however, Miles seemed skittish about it, so eventually Martha arranged for Liggett, one of the men who worked at the Downings' farm, to do this errand. True to the boys' character, Matt had been all too eager, while Pat had been too afraid. Although both boys accompanied Liggett to The Inn at Bearminster, only Matt consummated the planned evening.

So Pat's stomach did flip-flops as he considered his brother's intentions towards Chloe. *Could he be serious?*

Matt held up his hand for silence as Chloe passed them, twirled once, and continued on the path toward her home. Once she was out of earshot, Matt spoke again, more normally.

"We could get her out here in the woods. No one would know. She plays out here all the time with her sister, pretty far from their house. All we'd have to do is get Faythe away from her. Then we'd have our chance."

"We?" Pat replied.

Matt said nothing as he was focused on the girl far down the trail.

"Matt, you're crazy," Pat said.

Matt gave Pat a look indeterminate but conveying several things: "I'm in charge, not you," and "I'm just fantasizing here, so don't break my mood."

Pat cast his eyes downward.

"We'd stay in the blind," Matt said in a deliberate way, entranced by his own plan. "We'd wait till she came about here"—he pointed to a spot on the trail. "Then you'd jump out and say 'Surprise!' While she was startled, I'd jump out from behind here"—he pointed again—"and grab her. We'd have to bring a towel or something to stuff in her mouth to shut her up. Then we could do whatever we wanted."

Matt called up his dream of what she would look like stripped naked before him. The prostitute he'd looked at for hours that night had had saggy big breasts and a somewhat wrinkled belly, but Chloe, so young, would bear her breasts high and tight, her belly soft and completely smooth.

Oh, this would be a wonder, he thought. That it would be completely, crazily *wrong* was not lost on Matt, but he had found that, at least so far in his relatively young life as a Downing, when he did what he wanted to do, things somehow worked out in the end. He was not unduly troubled by this way of thinking. And besides, right now it was just fantasy—wasn't it?

Pat looked at Matt and tremulously asked, "Matt, you're not serious, are you?"

"Of course not," Matt retorted with contempt. "Pat, you're such a whiner. I'm just joking around."

"Even thinking these thoughts is a clear sin," said Pat. But Matt gave him the look again, and he said no more.

So Matt tried again, and this time the message, delivered with just a look, was a little friendlier, inviting a conspiracy, as if to say: "Come on, brother, I'm not serious here. If I can't confide my closest feelings to my brother, who can I talk to? Be here for me—I need your support."

Pat suddenly stilled himself, causing Matt to do the same. Matt looked out to the trail and saw Faythe, vigilant, looking around. She seemed to sense that something was off, but even though she looked straight at the blind, she couldn't see either brother, for they were trained by their hunting experience to remain motionless and soundless when the prey was alert. *So Chloe was not alone after all.*

Finally, Faythe seemed to shrug off the feeling and moved off in the direction Chloe had gone, calling her name.

Matt identified Faythe as Chloe's guard dog, and Matt was Chloe's hunter. Faythe was an obstacle to getting what he wanted—he wanted Chloe Wentworth.

Once the older girl was out of sight, the brothers extricated themselves from the blind and started to head home. As a fruitless attempt to possibly distract his brother from his fixation, Pat casually offered the observation, "Faythe is much prettier, isn't she?"

Pat knew that Matt could never "get" Faythe, even with Pat's help. The athletic Faythe was too strong and would put up too much of a fight. It would never work.

But the distraction attempt went nowhere. "No," said Matt, his eyes fixed in the middle distance, his imagination fixed on Chloe. "Chloe's the one."

Pat started rubbing one hand down his other arm and then switching, always a sign he was nervous. Sensing his brother's discomfort, to deflect the tension, Matt laughed and punched his brother in the arm. "Let's get back."

Matt knew on a deep level that he couldn't control himself much longer when it came to Chloe. Events were going to take shape one way or another. In a strange way he was just in the grip of a force that he couldn't control or, maybe, he mused, it was a force he just didn't want to control. *And why not?*

A WORD FROM
SHERIFF JONES

The service being over, Minister Brown climbed down from the pulpit and seemed about to wish everyone a good day before making his way to the Downing box pew to greet them specially, as was his habit. But then he seemed to remember something and held up a hand and said, with appropriate deference, but with the clear indication that he himself was in charge, "Now our good Sheriff Jones has some words for us, no doubt his usual monthly warning about the risk of Indian attacks."

Sheriff John Jones—former Indian fighter—stood up, a little groggy from trying to ignore the ridiculous demon-filled sermon without just falling asleep. He found William Brown a level below despicable, and he could see right through his oozing personality. The preaching was hogwash and the sheriff was consistently amazed that a good part of the congregation seemed to eat it right up. He shrugged and walked forward.

Sheriff Jones's job was a trying one, although not obviously so. There were petty squabbles in the village every now and then, but these were typically easy to settle with a gentle word and a bit of humor. But the job was difficult because he must always manage the constant worry about the Indians. An attack could not only kill villagers the sheriff was responsible to protect, but it would fracture the harmony and quietude that had prevailed without interruption since Thompson Downing had formed North Hinkapee and established an unusual form of diplomacy with the Sagawanee Indians.

Things had been not exactly friendly, but at least not unfriendly, with the Sagawanee Indians for the years since Downing's first overtures of friendship with the young Chief Katakuk. However, as John Jones had explained in his first meeting with Thompson Downing at the tavern in Hinkapee in 1677, the Indians likely regarded all the White People—English, Dutch, German, or mixes of people in different settlements—as an integrated group. So, no matter how North Hinkapee's citizens behaved, if another group of White Men slaughtered some Indians, the Indians would counter-attack—not necessarily on the perpetrators, but on those who were vulnerable to attack, those who were by extension also guilty of the slaughter.

Jones had only two flintlock muskets and a shorter-length pistol, and other citizens of North Hinkapee had similar weaponry. With even this pitiful armory, Sheriff Jones somehow had to protect the entire town. Yet there was no real way to actually protect a town from an Indian attack, for the Indians did not follow English means of warfare. Instead, they flowed quietly into a place like flood waters creeping across the landscape from a swollen river. All the people of North Hinkapee could really do would be afterwards—to seek revenge after the attack had claimed the lives of townspeople. And once that started, revenge upon revenge would ruin them all.

Every several weeks Sheriff Jones would speak to the congregation, after Minister Brown was done, since that was the most convenient way to gather as many as possible at one time. Jones would remind the people of the plans for what to do if there were an Indian attack. Since there had never been an attack in anyone's clear memory, his vigilance and words largely fell on deaf ears these days. It was not that people refused to listen; it was just that humans, like chickens in a coop after the fox has left, just don't find worries imminent unless they are, well, imminent. He thought ruefully of the irony that the villagers would listen with rapt attention to the prurient details of Minister Brown's idiotic ramblings but considered the sheriff's warnings old folktales, and they scarcely paid attention to information that might one day save their lives.

Sheriff Jones was no great orator and was rather stiff in his delivery, as one might expect. He started in his usual way: "I know we've been lucky so far that we haven't had an attack in North Hinkapee in many years, but that luck won't hold forever. We've got to be ready.

"If, and *when*"—he looked out at them while holding his hat respectfully against his chest—"*when* there is an Indian attack … And don't get me wrong, there will be one. It is just a matter of time." He paused for effect, but there seemed to be no actual "effect" on the congregation, which seemed to be just waiting for him to get done. He sighed.

Sheriff Jones had a critically important message and he wanted to get it across, but when he spoke in public he tended to ramble, losing authority as he lost his grip on his hearers. He was much better in one-on-one situations, when he connected with people and earned their respect for getting right to the point.

"Depending on where the attack takes place, the right thing to do is to stay protected in your home and shoot your guns from there, shoot as much as you can.

"This—the sound of the guns—will let me and everyone else know what is going on. And everyone who hears such a thing, you do the same, whether or not you see Indians. The more gunshots we hear, the more we'll all know we're under attack."

He stooped over a little to shift his address from the men to the rest.

"Then you women and children, you *stay* at home while your menfolk go to battle, and don't dare open the door, no matter what! Even if the Indians burn your house down, you don't leave. You got that? It's better to be burned to death than to suffer what the Indians will do to you in an attack."

As these words sank in, Sheriff Jones shuddered a little at the memory of the brutal Harriman Keep-Safe, who had more inventive ways of torturing people than Jones had ever seen the Indians use. As Thompson Downing's diplomacy had proven, the Sagawanees, like the people of North Hinkapee, just wanted to live in peace. Jones wished them no harm; however, he had seen firsthand that the Indians, when in attack mode, were extremely resourceful and dangerous.

He felt that he must deliver this message particularly strongly this day, on account of his wife Betsy's sixth sense, which she kept well-hidden. A healing woman with herbs and these powers of sight could easily be thought of as a witch, with dangerous consequences. This risk would be less pronounced if that woman had a husband; however, there was no reason to take chances. Accordingly, Betsy Jones revealed her sixth sense only to her husband, and it was only last Sunday morning that she told her husband that she could feel a dark cloud bearing down on North Hinkapee. In this, Sheriff Jones reached the obvious conclusion that the dark cloud would be from the Sagawanee Indians. *Where else?*

He continued. "You men, in the event of an attack, we will start by grouping here right in front of the meeting house. You'll need to ensure your families are safely shut in, then bring every pistol and musket you've got."

Sheriff Jones looked out at the congregation, wondering if anyone at all was listening, but then he noticed Betsy staring at him with loving, shining eyes. She was listening to every single word and looking at him with unhidden pride exactly as she always did. It gave him some strength. *The love of a good woman is a powerful thing*, he thought for a moment, trying hard not to smile back at her.

FAYTHE THE FIGHTER

Faythe Emily Wentworth left the meeting house that Sunday noon with the dignity of all her seventeen years. Was she beautiful? Perhaps not in the classic sense, as she did not have the generous curves that telegraphed her suitability as a mother, but there was something bewitching about her, something that made men who looked at her take a second look and wonder to themselves. She clearly wasn't like any other woman they had seen before.

Faythe had a long and smooth neck and long, black hair from her father's Irish heritage. Her face was quite pretty to look at, with an artistic nose that seemed it might break easily. She was slender and supple, like a strong sapling. She moved with speed and grace, and hidden strength.

But it was her eyes that distinguished Faythe Emily Wentworth. Indeed, the intensity of Faythe's green eyes was hypnotic. If a man or even a woman looked into them too long, the result might be a loss of speech, as her spirit carried a kind of lightning current of understanding in the place of words. Some people didn't like this feeling, and for a reason they couldn't define, they found themselves almost angry about it, certainly uneasy. Minister Brown certainly fell into this group. But few ever looked at Faythe just once. There always needed to be a second look, to understand what had transpired in the first look.

As Faythe wandered home behind her family, thinking her own thoughts as she slowly followed the path through the woods, she found herself hearing again the words of Sheriff Jones. She admired the man, but she found his words annoying. *I can shoot a gun as well as most of the men. Why would I not be with the men shoulder to shoulder, fighting whoever needs fighting? When the time comes, people will be surprised how I will handle things.* Her thoughts turned to a fantasy of her repelling raiders and intruders, delighting in the surprise on the faces of the men who would watch her in action.

Faythe's thoughts and dreams were unusual for a young woman of her times, but to her they were as natural as carrying wood for the fire. And though the people of North Hinkapee knew little of what stirred below the surface in Faythe Emily Wentworth, one thing was immediately clear to everyone, and to Faythe herself as well: Faythe did not easily fit in.

INTERLUDE

THE TALE OF NUNUNYI CONTINUES

Nununyi stirred, a fluttering feather of memory explaining the great pain in her chest, as if a mighty man had swung the trunk of a small tree to strike her down. She had fallen, thinking, *So this is death? It's so peaceful. So beautiful.* Nununyi had fallen to the ground ever so slowly and saw moonlit earth come up to meet her face as she hit the ground. And then she was gone …

Pushing aside the terrible pain in her chest, she thought, with something akin to panic, *Where is my bow, and where are my arrows?*

She stirred and made to move, but the pain made clear that her body was broken. Then a voice said words she could not understand but that were clearly intended to be soothing. She opened her eyes and a face came into focus. It was the terrible face of a bearded White Man. She fell unconscious again.

When next she woke, the White Man was gently cleansing her face with a warm, wet cloth and she lay within a wooden lodge. She was oh, so thirsty. The White Man seemed to be able to read her thoughts. He raised her up enough that she could sip water from a tin cup. She was too tired, too sick, and too thirsty to wonder why this White Man was keeping her alive or what his intentions were. She drank and drank and drank, and he refilled the cup three times.

"So beautiful," the man whispered to himself—though it was not until she'd learned his language sufficiently, many moons hence, that she recognized what he always murmured to her: "So beautiful." It sounded a little like her name—"beautiful Nununyi"—and she turned the words over in her mind.

She would not meet his eyes but turned her own to the room in which she lay. Against the wall leaned her bow and her quiver half full of arrows. She was comforted.

She awoke the next day and felt alert for the first time. She could not move even a little without intense pain, but she was awake. The White Man was clearly communicating with her, or trying his best to do so. He pointed to himself and said "Menon. Gilbert Menon." Then he pointed at her with raised eyebrows clearly inquiring.

"Nununyi," she whispered back after a long pause.

"Noo-noon-yee," he said slowly. He gave her a big smile. "I won't hurt you," he said, but Nununyi had no idea what that meant.

As the days passed, she healed slowly. Nununyi became able to sit up and eventually to hobble around, leaning heavily on Menon's arm, until she could sit outside in the summer warmth and breezes.

Menon slowly taught Nununyi English words so they could communicate just a little. He had fallen in love with her when he had first gazed upon her after the attack; and every time he looked upon her he found himself loving her even more. The young woman was beautiful in face and form, but in her full power completely deadly—she fascinated him and, for reasons he couldn't identify, this stirred his passions. He hoped that when she recovered she would not leave him. But he could see that she looked at him with intense distrust.

It is no wonder, he thought. *The last she knew, we were trying to kill her people and she was trying to kill us.* What could he do about it? Could this somehow change? Could this warrior woman come to look upon him favorably?

After two weeks, Nununyi was able to walk with only a little assistance. *Time to take the chance,* thought Menon. He led Nununyi outside and helped her sit on the bench where she had been warming herself in the morning sunshine each day. Then he brought to her the bow and arrows that had been leaning on the wall of the cabin all these days.

Her eyes lit up with delight, and she caressed them lovingly. Her happiness coursed through him, as well. He encouraged her to fit an arrow to the taut string, and she did.

Then he walked away about ten paces and turned. He looked her in the eyes, and then he got down on his knees, spread his arms wide, and nodded.

Even in her stiffness and lack of practice, Nununyi could easily have killed him straightway. She had her bow and arrows, and he was defenseless in his cloth shirt, offering his throat, his belly, his heart before her.

Nununyi contemplated the opportunity for a moment, but she concluded, *How could I kill the man who saved me?* She put the bow and arrow aside and looked Menon in the eyes. She did not smile, but it was clear that whatever was between them had turned to a different course, like a rivulet breaking off from the path of a river, breaking off to find its own way.

1675–1687, BOSTON

HERE COMES FAYTHE!

Faythe Emily Wentworth came into the world in Boston, Massachusetts, at three o'clock in the morning in the year 1675, as a storm raged outside the small window of the bedchamber. The midwife had managed to get there by grit, determination, and a desire not to let down Lucy Wentworth—all of this intention mixed with some luck.

The childbirth was mercifully not as bad as the storm, but difficult as these things usually are. But when Faythe lay in Lucy's arms, working at her first feeding, Lucy thought herself the happiest woman in the world.

"She's just perfect," the new mother said to her husband Robert, after the midwife left.

"Perfect," agreed Robert.

And indeed the infant seemed perfect, with bright and oh-so-big eyes that seemed both hazel and green and changed in the light, and a tiny rosebud mouth. Lucy often told her daughter that she knew immediately that Faythe was going to be "special."

Faythe was a fighter from birth. Even putting her down for the night was a struggle if Faythe was not in the mood to go to sleep. It was a bit like a wrestling match with a squirming eel, and it tested all of Lucy's patience and motherly skills. And the older Faythe got, the more difficult she was to manage.

As it was with many children, Faythe's first word was "No," but hers was an emphatic "No!"

At first Lucy and Robert could outwit her. They were, after all, the parents, but Faythe quickly learned to avoid their tricks on her way to more consummate and continuing obstinacy. For a while she was a trial to her parents and growing up to be a pretty awful child. But then one day, at just five years old, Faythe had her first epiphany.

The Wentworths were living in Lucy's father's comfortable home in Boston, and Faythe had taken a stand in the common room, defying her parents' will that she take a nap.

"No, no, no, I won't!" she raged, stamping her feet. "I don't need a nap!"

Although she was screaming and yelling, at the same time she was watching herself and wondering, "Why, in fact, am I doing this?"

Then she saw a look pass from Lucy to Robert. Faythe expected it to be a look of exasperation, at the trouble she was causing, but it wasn't, not at all. Instead, Lucy was smiling adoringly at the man she loved, and Robert gave her a wink back and a half smile. And neither of them was paying Faythe and her transgressions any particular mind.

Faythe was shocked. Then all at once she understood two things. First, Faythe was not actually the center of the universe. Her parents were looking at each other in a way that did not include her. And second, her parents clearly loved and enjoyed each other, but how could they enjoy the Faythe who was such a nuisance? Could they still love her, then?

Faythe wanted to be worth loving. All at once her screaming and stamping dissolved into tears.

Growing up was hard. Being Faythe was going to be so hard.

A fire burned in the little girl—she yearned to be sure of things, to take a stand, but she didn't want to be a bad person. Perhaps there was a clue in something Lucy said to her soon after: "If you look for the bad things in people, you'll always find them. But if you look for the good things, you'll find them, too. You get to make this choice—always you do—and sometimes seeing the bad will feel good and right at first. But in the end, you'll have a much better and happier life if you look for the good. You'll see this as you get older."

"Yes, Mum," said Faythe, for she was too young to really understand what Lucy meant, but she saved her mother's words in her memory, knowing they must be important.

Not long after her first epiphany, Faith's sister Chloe came into the world. It was at noon on a fine Saturday afternoon with the nicest of weather.

The stout midwife took charge of the household upon her arrival, ordering Robert Wentworth about and speaking sharply to Faythe herself, to shoo her out of the way. But she spoke to Lucy as lovingly as Lucy spoke to Faythe.

"Now, my dear," the woman said as she pressed her two fists hard against Lucy's back and Lucy groaned, "they say a woman's first childbirth is a fight to ease the birth canal. I well remember that fight that stormy night those five years ago! But the second and the rest will slide out smoothly."

And so it was with Chloe. The midwife kept saying, "See, it's all the easy way this time." Faythe wasn't so sure, as her mother seemed to be groaning and sweating a lot. Faythe stayed out of the way, as she'd been told, and wondered what might come of all this work.

At last the groans and calls of encouragement built to a high pitch, and then everything relaxed and the midwife was back to soothing words and a joyful tone that drew Faythe to the bedside. There her mother was smiling beautifully, her hair all loose and her face as red and damp as on a washday, when she hauled steaming dresses and linens out of the wash pot. And in her arms lay a tiny baby, wrapped up in a blood-smeared towel.

And what a stunning baby. Chloe was a beauty as soon as she was cleaned up. And quiet and smiling and content from the moment she entered the world. She had the bluest of eyes, the blondest of hair, and the sweetest of smiles. Later that day, when the midwife admitted Robert to the room, he gently kissed his wife on the forehead and did the same with the newborn, then backed up to a chair in the corner and called Faythe to sit in his lap.

Lucy, beaming at father and daughter across the room from her, said, "Once again, I am the happiest woman in the world."

Faythe toyed with the idea of being jealous of her new sister, but this thought vanished in seconds, and almost the instant she set her eyes on Chloe. Instead, Faythe quickly determined that one of her self-appointed roles in life was to help her mother take care of Chloe. Indeed, so strong was Faythe in this determination that it was as if Chloe had two mothers. Faythe was not necessarily particularly maternal, especially at such a young age, but Chloe had clearly been brought into the world to be her companion.

Lucy remembered coming home shortly after Chloe was born to see baby Chloe in Faythe's arms, with Faythe singing to her. Faythe was almost six years old and Chloe was maybe six months. Chloe was gurgling happily and trying to pull Faythe's hair. Faythe was rocking her back and forth and singing to her. There was something about the scene. Lucy knew it was a special moment and did her best to burn the image into her brain. She never wanted to forget it, and she never did until the day she died.

FATE IS UNKIND TO THE WENTWORTHS

For the next few years, the Wentworth family enjoyed a comfortable life in the home of Lucy's widowed father. Stanford Palmer, Faythe's grandfather, traded in luxurious foodstuffs that sold for outrageous prices in Boston. He had a keen sense of what to buy and when to sell it and usually profited quite well from the differentials. For the Wentworths it meant a steady supply of candied orange peel, Dutch cheeses, and pepper from India, while many in Boston lived on cod and potatoes.

"Don't ever forget, Faythe," her father reminded her as they enjoyed yet another sumptuous meal, "that you come from humble stock. We're grateful for these bounties"—he nodded to his father-in-law—"but we know how close we are to poverty."

Stanford Palmer replied, "What really matters is the riches of our souls, and after our lonely years, Lucy and I together, after her mother died, I rejoice at the full household we enjoy now."

Faythe's grandfather was a kindly man but formal. He didn't wrestle around on the floor with her as her father did. But when he gazed at his family, Stanford Palmer radiated love that surrounded Faythe as did her parents' love. And so Faythe knew the best of what people could be.

Along the way, awkward mother-daughter conversations arose from the fact that it was really hard to be a proper girl in the Puritan colony of Massachusetts. Lucy, as a proper mother, tried to instill in Faythe the virtues and expectations of her station, generally the idea that women were to be seen and not heard, and that the young should respect the authority of adults. As both a female and a child, Faythe would be doubly pressed down. Women were to be admired for their housekeeping and child-rearing abilities, primarily.

"Why, Mama, are the men in charge?" she remembered asking one day, while nestled comfortably in Lucy's lap after they'd read together a story about a prince who became a king.

"Why—why—that's just the way it is," Lucy had replied, fondly stroking her daughter's shiny black hair. Then she was silent.

After a time, Lucy seemed to come to a conclusion, and she patted the back of Faythe's hand on the book, and said, "I think that's what God intended. We women should be taken care of by the men, who are in charge of most things, except the household. That's where we truly run things."

Faythe wrinkled her nose and noticed, without understanding it, that she was trembling just a little, no longer quite as content and secure in her mother's arms. Lucy patted her hand again, reassuringly, and drew her head in to kiss the top of it.

"Seems funny to me," said Faythe. Her mother said nothing, which led Faythe to believe that this view of men-in-charge was perhaps open to question. This was a third epiphany for Faythe.

Faythe decided that she would be seen and heard as much as she liked, or at least as much as she could get away with. Lucy seemed to ignore it and Robert overtly winked at her, which just egged her on. Although the Wentworths were devout and God-fearing to a fault, theirs was simply not a typical family.

Over time, Faythe more firmly formed her particular view of the world in which she lived. It made no sense that the men were in charge, for they often seemed as dumb as posts. She became more and more certain that whatever God had in store for her, it would be on her terms. She would not strive to fit in. She cultivated the strong and quick-to-boil temper necessary, and instead of practicing temperance of her passions, she practiced intemperance.

To her surprise, even amazement, no one knew what to do about her. Her aggression often made the other side back down in shock or even fear. Women weren't supposed to act this way.

Perhaps God enjoyed the juxtaposition of the two sisters, for as the two girls grew up, Chloe became as timid and shy as Faythe became the opposite. From the time Chloe could walk she would follow Faythe around everywhere. Faythe was the center of her world, and Faythe loved Chloe as much as any mother loves her child.

But as different as Faythe was, she adored her mother. Faythe thought Lucy Wentworth was just about the best person in the world, having come to that assessment after considering all the people she had met in her life and making a careful comparison.

So many people turned out to be disappointments for so many reasons. Some were mean, some venial, some lazy, some not loving of others, some plain stupid, some sure the world owed them a living, and some quick to take advantage of others.

But Lucy was none of those things. She was always optimistic. She looked for the good in people, even in bad people. She was never rude or mean-spirited. A sure way to infuriate Faythe was to say or imply something remotely negative about Lucy. Faythe, at just ten years of age, had given a boy of a similar age a bloody nose for taunting her about her mother. The lad had nothing against Lucy, but he was testing to see what would happen if he pushed this point. With no warning, Faythe slugged him right in the nose, just as her father had taught her. The fight, if that's what it was, was over in a second, as with that one blow, the boy ran away bleeding and trying not to cry.

First time I won a fight with a boy, thought Faythe at the time.

So it was a household of love and good will in which Faythe spent her early years. Lucy and Robert, in addition to their passion for each other, had in common their reverence and trust in the Lord God. They believed that if they trusted in the Lord and did what was right, then things would just work out well in the end. Unfortunately, for whatever reason, it seemed that God had other plans.

Robert Wentworth enjoyed the work his father-in-law had given him, but he had decided that he wanted to be a farmer, as he was trained for nothing else, so he made plans to buy a farm by making seven years of payments to the current owner, after which he would own the farm outright. This transaction was signed in 1677, so the farm would be his in 1684. Robert would not be able to make the payments on his own, however. Stanford Palmer was willing to subsidize a large portion of the payments, which made the transaction viable.

But then fate was terribly unkind to Stanford Palmer, and thus to the Wentworths, when a ship from England on route to Boston sank, taking all the Palmer fortune to the bottom of the sea.

"I'm ruined," Lucy's father kept saying again and again. "I'm ruined."

And because Palmer was ruined, Robert was as well, for he was unable to make the final year's payment on his farm and it reverted to the original owner.

"My dear, I'm so sorry," said Robert to Lucy with tears in his eyes.

Many wives would have reproached their husbands, more so because of their own fears for the future. But Lucy hugged her husband instead. "Why, Robert Wentworth," she said, "we'll be just fine. You're a good man, and the Lord God will provide for us."

To add sorrow upon sorrow, Stanford Palmer, long used to the finer things and perhaps faltering in his faith in the first real economic misfortune of his life, declined in body and spirit in his financial humiliation as men came to carry away his furniture and other household goods in payment on his debts. He began taking doses of a physik he had imported from the Indies, and then taking more, until one morning Lucy found him passed on to the next life.

Robert and Lucy Wentworth, with their young children, were now alone in the world, saddened and wearied by tragedy. They had no income, no farm, and no real plan for what to do.

FAYTHE'S SECOND BRAWL

Faythe was only nine when her family suddenly faced a poverty that none of them had ever really known, although Robert remembered well enough being hungry with his dad as a small boy. The family moved their few possessions to the poorest part of Boston, where they shared one small, dilapidated room. Lucy and Robert went out every day looking for work or food or wood to burn, and Faythe, though only a child herself, had to care for her four-year-old sister Chloe for many hours at a time.

Faythe had strict orders not to leave the room to venture outside, so of course she did exactly as she pleased, and she promptly sallied forth onto the street, leading her sister by the hand, both of them huddled into blankets against the chill.

Faythe quickly fell in with three other children whose parents were equally impoverished—Emily, Billy, and another Emily, who was much smaller than the first Emily. "Big Em" and "Li'l Em," plus Billy and Faythe, roamed the streets, taking turns holding hands with the always quiet and virtually always smiling Chloe. The four became fast friends so quickly that after only an afternoon it was as if they had always known each other and would always be together.

But then there was Harold. He was a year older and had no friends, so he defined his existence by bullying Faythe's young posse. He pushed and shoved, delivering an occasional punch and constant demeaning looks and taunts. Faythe determined that completely ignoring him was the best strategy, and that seemed to annoy him much more than if she'd engaged with him.

Faythe's troop ignored Harold as best they could, doing their best to avoid him. When Harold came around, Faythe found her heart beating faster and she sometimes trembled. But it was not from fear. Instead, Faythe found it difficult to restrain herself from letting him have it. Harold must have sensed how dangerous she could be, for he had never actually pushed or hit her or little Chloe. Did he sense the hornets' nest behind those hazel-green flashing eyes and decide it was best not to stir it up? In a mild defense, the little group of friends sometimes called him "Hard-Nosed Harold" and other unflattering names, but they had a détente, and overall, life was not bad for them.

Then one day Big Em showed up with a new friend, who introduced himself to the troop as Jacob Levy. He was an immigrant boy whose family had just come over from Amsterdam, and he could speak only halting English. He spoke funny and looked funny, but the troop took him in right away, considering him exotic.

Jacob was soon a prime target for Hard-Nosed Harold, who, for whatever reason, found Jacob to be a severe annoyance. The troop rallied around Jacob, and Harold settled down a bit.

And then things changed, all in an afternoon.

"Jews are bad," said Hard-Nosed Harold suddenly and confrontationally, planting himself in front of the smaller boy. "My dad told me so."

Jacob said nothing. He just looked down at his shoes.

"What? Cat got your tongue?" Harold bit the words out with anger, and he gave Jacob a shove, and the new boy stumbled a step or two backwards. But that was not enough. Harold found something about Jacob just too offensive for a mere shove, so out of nowhere he seemed to grow bigger with his rage, and before anyone could do anything, Harold threw Jacob on the ground and pummeled him. The more Jacob cried out, the more Harold punched him.

Faythe, girl or not, could not stand the injustice. "Well," she said to herself, "the game is up for you, Mr. Hard-Nosed Harold."

"Look out for Chloe," she said to both Emilys and put her sister's tiny hands in theirs. Without another word, she strode forward and grabbed Harold by the arm he had raised to hit Jacob yet another time. With a hard pull, she yanked Harold backwards, and all at once he was sprawled on his back.

Harold was shocked and surprised at the attack, and even more surprised when he saw it was a girl that had thrown him down.

Faythe blazed her eyes at him in a deadly challenge.

But Harold was not afraid. He jumped up and glared right back at her.

"Listen to me, Harold!" she yelled out shrilly, her voice shaking just a little from fury, not the fear he might think. "That's it for you!" She stepped forward and swung at him with all her might, slamming her fist into his ribs.

Harold winced in surprise, but he was not disabled. He quickly hit Faythe back, full in the face, and knocked her down as if she were a boy, and a boy his own size. She half sat up, blood dripping from her nose, and he seemed to falter. Even a bully wasn't supposed to hit a girl.

His uncertainty allowed Faythe to get up, and she swung at him again, this time connecting hard with his arm, but it was a wild swing and revealed she didn't know what she was doing. Hard-Nosed Harold was a veteran of quite a few battles, and decent with his fists. Faythe had no idea what to do but, in the parlance of the times, she was a "game cuss," or in this case, a "game miss."

The next few moments of battle were hard-fought but decided very quickly. Faythe found herself lying on her back on the ground again, with some bumps and bruises and a very bloody nose. But she was not really injured. Harold stood there looking down at her, then he muttered, "Taught you a lesson" and stomped off.

Billy and Jacob, who had been no help whatsoever, helped haul Faythe to her feet, and Billy babbled that Harold wasn't so tough—"No pride in beating up a *girl*!"

Faythe whipped her head around to glare at him and, without a word, picked up Chloe in her arms, and Chloe, whimpering, wrapped her legs around Faythe and buried her head in her sister's shoulder. Though she staggered with Chloe's weight, Faythe marched with as much dignity as she could to get home.

"I got in a fight and I lost," was all Faythe would say after repeated questioning from her parents. She wanted a reputation for being tough, and "running to Mum" after a drubbing would hardly enhance that reputation. She just shook her head without speaking during the questioning, and at last Lucy and Robert gave up the inquest with shrugs.

As they sat at their meager supper of stale bread and hot water, Faythe calmly asked Robert, "Dad, can you teach me how to fight?"

Robert looked at her in amazement, then silence, his head tipped as he considered some things. Then, with a decisive little nod of his head, he ventured a fatherly edict: "Young ladies do not engage in behavior of that sort."

Robert looked at Lucy for the expected approval, but to Faythe's amazement, and surely Robert's, too, Lucy said, "Of course they do! When young ladies are attacked, they need to learn how to fight back to protect their honor and their families. Robert, you're a good man with your fists—it's high time you learned your daughter the same."

This was revolutionary! Faythe dabbed at her still-oozing nose with a wet cloth and looked from one parent to the other.

"Yes, ma'am," was all Robert could reply. He got up from the wooden box he sat upon, for they had no chairs, and he reeled slightly, perhaps from hunger, perhaps from surprise at his wife's position on his daughter's fighting predilection.

Faythe glanced at her mother, who caught her eye with a wink, and suddenly Faythe felt pride and hope well up within her, and a warmth their chilly tenement did not provide. *What will happen next?* she wondered. What a day it had turned out to be!

After pacing the small room, kicking aside a pallet the girls used as a bed, looking out the tiny grimy window, and scratching his head, Robert Wentworth returned to the table, where three young women awaited his next words.

"My da taught me to fight in the barnyard when I was boy—it seems so long ago it was really another lifetime." His voice was wistful. "And he was a good teacher and I a good fighter. But now I have no son myself to teach …"

He bent to take Faythe's chin in his large hand. "All right," he said to her. "Let's get on with it—up with thee, now." He pulled back his hand and dropped into a fighting stance, nodding for her to stand, too. Right there in that rude flat he gave Faythe the first of many lessons on how to protect herself. This was Faythe's second epiphany—that girls could fight.

The next day she was prepared, at least a little, by her father's instruction, and she was almost eager to meet up with Harold again. Sure enough, he was out on the street, and as he drew closer it was clear he bore more bruises than she had dealt him the day before.

He came straight up to her and said, "You're a girl, and sorry I hit you," in a low voice and without any preamble. Clearly his father had put him up to it, not to mention likely inflicting bruises for hitting a girl.

"And you're a boy, and sorry I hit you, too," said Faythe right back. Although she was a little disappointed there wouldn't be another scuffle, she knew her dad would be proud of her forgiving spirit.

Harold, looking down at his battered shoes, one sole flapping open as he worried it back and forth on the cobbles, finally said with obvious difficulty, "You wanna be friends? I could sure use some …"

After a pause, Faythe nodded. "Let's shake on it, then."

They shook hands, man to woman.

Harold, showing himself to be a bit of a gentleman after all, said to Jacob that he was sorry, and it took Jacob only a moment to realize that it was much better to be friends with Harold than to be his enemy—or his target.

And so it was that Harold joined the troop of Big Em, Li'l Em, Billy, Faythe, Chloe, and Jacob. The past was forgotten; they were all a pack now.

FAYTHE IS DISSATISFIED

For close to a year after her altercation with Harold that led, surprisingly, to a strong friendship, Faythe had secret fighting lessons with her father almost every night. Even if Robert was tired, she was invariably up for a scrounge in the family's one-room apartment.

"Come on, Dad," she would say. "Just one round. Or are you afraid ... of a girl?"

"I'm too tired," Robert would reply, feigning exhaustion, but seconds later his Irish brawling heritage would light up his clover-green eyes, and he would attack without warning, trying to bring her down.

This worked the first few times, but Faythe caught on quickly. Indeed, after a while Faythe found, to her complete surprise, that she almost liked the sensation of getting hit or having her head smack into the wall. Although Robert made every effort not to injure his rambunctious daughter, street fighting was a dangerous undertaking, and there were times he went pretty far, but Faythe never complained of the occasional bloody nose or bruises. There was no way she would just "cry like a girl" and risk one of her parents putting a stop to it all.

Faythe insisted that they practice, but Robert insisted that the lessons be kept solely indoors and completely secret. Puritan society would not bear with the public knowledge of a father teaching his young daughter how to fight. So the lessons proceeded, but indoors only. It was a Wentworth family secret.

Robert emphasized to Faythe the effectiveness of the element of surprise. "No one will ever expect a woman to strike first. And a fast and hard blow to the nose or the balls ... I mean the groin ... can be disabling even to a large man."

"Then," Robert advised, "you should run like the wind and get away."

Faythe wrinkled her nose. "I don't like the idea of running away."

"You can be foolish and fight more, or be wise and run away," said Robert, tapping his temple where his brown curls glistened with sweat from their sparring.

Faythe reluctantly acknowledged his logic but thought that, when the time came, she might not run away after all.

Eventually she began to feel a little frustrated. However roughly her father threw her around the apartment, he was never trying to harm her. And a street fight would be the opposite. Her opponent would be trying to disable her, to shut her down. How could she know if she was really learning how to fight?

Am I any good? Can I really defend myself? she wondered almost out loud late one night as she was lying on the pallet she shared with Chloe.

There was only one way to know, and that would be to get in a real fight. But how could she do it?

Asking her parents was not a good strategy, since the very question would alert them to Faythe's intentions. *It's better if they just don't know.*

But maybe Hard-Nosed Harold could help.

Harold was one of the few who knew about Faythe's secret lessons with Robert, and they had occasionally "tussled" for fun. So the next day she told him of her plan: "I want to get into a fight."

"Oh no," said Harold, holding up both palms against her mad scheme, his eyes darting back and forth, instantly realizing to his dismay that one way or another this was going to happen irrespective of his view on it.

"Oh no," he repeated, stronger now, hoping futilely that a strong protest would have the necessary effect, which of course it didn't.

"Oh *yes*," said Faythe, fixing him with her hazel-green eyes. She was used to getting her way with Harold, who was already more than a bit sweet on her, so he had no chance. She wore him down and wore him down, until finally he agreed.

"I guess we could go down to the docks ..." he finally said.

Faythe lit up with excitement. The docks were in a part of Boston that even Harold was somewhat afraid to go into. To the tough boys down there, the wrong *look* was often enough to start an altercation. Harold had gone a little white around the jowls, so Faythe put her hands on his upper arms and shook him encouragingly. "Let's make a plan!" she said.

"First off, you can't look like a girl," said Harold.

"I know," said Faythe. "I'll cut my hair and dress like a boy." Faythe was just 11, and her figure had not filled out, so a baggy shirt would hide things just fine, or so the two of them thought.

Eventually it was all arranged. Faythe left Chloe with the Emilys, who had figured out what was going on. Big Em expressed her views potently, saying, "Faythe, that's the dumbest thing I ever heard in my life!"

Li'l Em said exactly the same thing, but in a higher tone: "Faythe, that's the dumbest thing I ever heard in my life."

"Yes, to be sure, it is," replied Faythe, serene in her determination. "Now take Chloe for me."

Big Em sighed and Li'l Em did the same, and then Jacob showed up and tried his own style of low-key dissuasion, but by now they had all become accustomed to the fact that Faythe was, well, "different" from other girls and would do whatever she wanted. So they agreed to babysit Chloe while Faythe went off to get herself beaten up.

"I'll take care of them!" promised Jacob with a brave and definitive nod, at which Faythe and Harold exchanged both eye-rolls and winks. It had become funny in a way that Harold and Jacob had become buddies, with Harold being careful not to let his dad know that one of his friends was a Jew.

Harold and Faythe set off down the street that very afternoon, a relatively tough-looking bigger boy with a small and slender one with short-cropped hair, a cheap cap, and a baggy outfit.

FAYTHE'S FIRST
REAL BRAWL

At first it was all a lark to Faythe. She wasn't worried at all, and she waved her cap back at the girls and Jacob to give them confidence. But once she and Harold had left them all behind and got closer to the rough area of town, she started to have some doubts. *Is this as dumb an idea as it seems?* she wondered.

Yes, it was.

Her exhilaration began to turn into a feeling she really didn't like at all, a churning fear and a dragging dread. But there was no turning back now. It was better to be afraid than humiliated. So Faythe squared her shoulders and convinced herself that they were off on an adventure.

The men at the docks were going about their business unloading and loading boats, making a lot of noise with rumbling carts and grunts and curses, and there were all sorts of smells, some good ones like the aromatic pipes some of the men clenched between their teeth, and some of them awful, like things rotting. And there were dangerous, exciting smells—men's sweat.

Boys were running around, too, some of them busy doing work for the men, and others just loitering. Faythe was impressed that Harold seemed to know some of them, and they nodded back and forth. Harold was respected here. *So that's good, but what do they think of me?* She touched the brim of her cap and spat into the dirt as she'd seen tough boys do.

Harold told her he was looking for the right battle to pick. It had to be someone he didn't know. Eventually, he held up a hand to slow her in their stroll, and she saw what he saw—some seemingly appropriate adversaries. There were three of them. One was about Harold's size, one was sort of middling size, and one was significantly smaller, but still a bit bigger than Faythe.

"The little one's your mark," he said out of the corner of his mouth.

The boys were doing nothing at all, just standing at one side of the muddy street in the almost-rags that children in their own neighborhood wore. These boys, though, looked to be veterans of many fights. One had a black eye that had gone red and purple.

Harold stopped suddenly and challenged the smallest one with a snarl: "What are you *looking* at?" Faythe sneaked a peek and saw a look in Harold's eyes that was asking for trouble.

"Not … much," answered a different boy, the biggest boy, drawing the words out as if drawing a line in the mud and daring Harold to cross it. All the boys stood very still.

Faythe was standing next to Harold and appraising the three as her heart slammed rapidly under her ribs. She was sure they could see the beat. She knew all at once that the Emilys were right—this was just about the dumbest thing she had ever done. She considered just letting everyone know she was really a girl and that it was time to go home. But there was no chance for that now. So she tried to look tough to back up Harold. She stared at the three boys, one by one, looking them over with what she hoped seemed like a critical eye. Could they see her fear?

Harold turned to Faythe and pretended to speak to her. Then he turned back to the boys and said, "My friend Christopher here says he could kick any of your asses." He added, unnecessarily, "He's new in town and wondering who's tough 'round here."

Faythe felt her face go white with fear at that challenge, silly as it was, and it had the necessary effect on the others, too. The boys moved forward till they were ranged in front of Faythe and Harold—it seemed clear that Faythe would get her fight right then and there. She was looking at the smaller boy and contemplating what to do, but things didn't go that way.

All at once the biggest boy stepped in front of Faythe. "You're a little boy to have such a stupid wonder," he said. Then he repeated the words as a mocking taunt in a babyish voice, "Wonder who's *tough* around here!" He rolled his eyes and the smallest of the three giggled.

"And you're dumb as shit," said Faythe, trying to talk tough, even though her heart was racing. She had been planning to beat up the smaller boy. This boy was really—well, big!

The big boy moved suddenly forward and gave Faythe a hard shove in the chest.

She stumbled backwards, taken a bit by surprise, and to her annoyance she tripped over a stone. As she fell backwards she worried for a split second if he could feel that she was a girl under that shirt, but the thought dissolved in the thrill of the moment—she was in a fight!

She rolled over quickly and was on her feet a second later. Dad had trained her to avoid "going to the ground" with a bigger and stronger adversary.

She stood and faced him and he faced her back. *It's now or never.* She could tell by his stance he was not a trained fighter, but more like a tough kid who punched and kicked and bit. She put her fists in front of her face as her father had taught her.

Harold and the other two boys watched. For the moment there was nothing else in the world but the two contestants, everyone rapt. Harold shook his hands out nervously, as if trying to decide what to do, and she knew he was scared to death, too, even more than Faythe. He felt responsible for her, but she shook off that thought.

Faythe was on her own, just as she had insisted it must be done.

She moved slowly forward, circling the other boy. He charged forward again, intending to put this smaller boy down with one blow, but he wasn't prepared for a jab from Faythe that hit him square in the nose. And he wasn't prepared for the right cross that Faythe landed in the side of his jaw. He twisted to the side and almost fell, stunned.

None of them had seen anything like this before. There was blood dripping from the boy's nose, and his eyes were watering. Though Faythe had never been dealt a hard blow in the nose, Robert had accidentally slammed it a time or two, and her own eyes watered in sympathy at the pain.

"Ow!" he cried in spite of himself, but he had the sense not to add, "That hurt!"

Faythe pressed her advantage and was on the other boy in a flash, raining punches and kicks on him. It looked like the fight was going Faythe's way, until he grabbed her by the arm and practically hurled her over his shoulder and onto the ground.

Faythe fell heavily, her back slamming into the ground so that the wind was knocked out of her. She couldn't breathe while she tried to crawl to her feet. Meanwhile, the other boy, still bleeding and reeling from the Faythe's blows, was getting his breath slowly, too.

At last the two faced each other warily again. Thankfully, Faythe was able to breathe again, although she was gasping. She had also banged her shoulder pretty hard and had blood on her arm. Was that hers or his? She pushed away her thoughts of pain.

Only then did Faythe begin to hear the other boys, who were egging on their fighter and shouting advice. Faythe had her hands up, watching her opponent. She wanted to strike the boy in the face again. But he was clearly ready for that. He must have perceived his advantage on the ground, and he dove for her legs.

Faythe hit him in the head hard when he came in, but not hard enough to stop him from tackling her. The two went down and then it all went bad for Faythe. The boy was just too strong. He just kept grabbing her and hitting her. Faythe struggled like a vicious eel and fought back with all her might.

But finally she realized she was just lying there trying to cover her head while the boy slugged her. Then Harold was pulling him off, and the fight was over.

AFTERMATH OF
A BRAWL

If one counted the fight with Harold, Faythe was now "zero for two" in battles with boys.

To Faythe's surprise, there were no other fights that day. There was some sort of implied honor going on, and Harold did not have to fight the other boys. She had challenged a boy to a fight. There had been a fight, and she had lost fair and square. And that was it …

Harold let her lie there for a few more moments and then pulled her to her feet. She was dizzy, as she had been hit in the head quite a few times, and she was now sure that the blood was hers. Her lips were bleeding and so was her nose. And her ribs really hurt. She had been punched and kicked in the ribs quite a few times. She wondered if they were broken.

As she stood up, she wondered if she was supposed to shake hands. Harold apparently thought so. He said to the boy, "Guess you won … shake on it …"

Everyone seemed to have a sense that Harold was in charge, and the other boy, possibly surprised, put out his hand. Faythe, weakly, put hers out, too, and shook with the little strength she had left. He nodded at her.

Amidst her pain, Faythe was happy—indeed *very* happy, because she saw respect in his eyes. *I have been a worthy adversary*, she thought, smiling a little at the stories she'd read of knights in combat.

Now it was time to go home and face the grilling from both of her parents. Faythe would not make up a story but just tell the absolute truth and let the consequences come as they must. What would Robert and Lucy say? That Faythe had been taught to fight to protect herself from attack, and not to start brawls at the docks. She almost but not quite saw the humor and almost chuckled a little under her breath.

Through the pain, Faythe was too happy to care about the trouble she'd be in. She had fought a much bigger and stronger boy, and even though she had lost, she had followed the encouragement to "Quit ye like men," as the Apostle Paul would say.

As Faythe and Harold turned to leave, her opponent called out, "My name's Dill and my friends call me Dill." He twisted his mouth into a smile, showing where one of his teeth had once been knocked out.

This must be what passed for a joke among them, and the other boys, who must have heard it before—who probably heard it all the time—grinned.

Harold was still too nervous to really laugh, but he nodded and smiled appropriately. After a moment, Faythe replied, "My name's Fay—I mean Chris ... "

"You're tough," said Dill.

"You're tougher," said Faythe, trying to keep her voice low to sound like him.

"You wanna join our gang?" asked Dill, to the surprise of Faythe but not of Harold. "We're the toughest here and we do what we want. We could use some more fighters."

Faythe was figuring out how to reply when Harold answered for them both. "Yeah," he said. "I'm Harold. Harold Hard-Nose. Count us in."

Faythe looked at him with surprise, and Harold continued. "We gotta go now, but we'll be back." He offered his hand to Dill, who shook it.

Dill turned to his friends. "This is Nate and that's Brass. We call him that because he's got brass balls. Right, Brass?"

They all grinned and nodded at their new ... *friends?* Faythe's grin turned into a wince—she was in a lot of pain. The beating had hurt a lot more than when her dad had roughed her up. She was dizzy and thought she might pass out.

She didn't remember any more of the conversation, and eventually Harold led her away.

Although Faythe was in a daze, she could tell that Harold was proud of her.

And she was really proud of herself. She had done something no other girl would ever do, and she had lived to tell about it. Soon she'd have to face the music at home, but that didn't much worry her. It was better to ask for forgiveness than permission, after all.

The conversation was predictable at home. Lucy gasped at the bedraggled new version of her daughter. But she soon made sure Faythe was not permanently injured and then stepped back to see what she had to say about it.

Robert, however, was much more worried. "What happened? Who did this to you?" He asked who had attacked his little girl, and he grew in strength and rage before their very eyes, pacing the few steps across their small room. He was furious.

"Father. Mother," said Faythe calmly, hoping to modulate her father's emotion with her formality. "I've been fighting with Dad for over a year now, but that isn't real fighting. I had to try a real fight."

Lucy and Robert waited silently, wide-eyed, for what she would say next.

The story tumbled out. Faythe left nothing out and finally concluded, "So, Dad, even though I lost today, I now know I can really fight." She bowed in a gracious courtly way, as she imagined a knight might do. "And I thank you for the lessons."

And then she turned to Lucy. "Mum, I could say to you that I'm sorry, and I will if you wish, but this is something I just had to do."

There was silence as Lucy and Robert had to deal with the realization, not for the first time, that their daughter was making a declaration that she would live her life on her terms, and to the Devil with the consequences. Faythe was looking at them expectantly, proudly. She had not backed down to a bigger, stronger, and tougher boy, but she had "quit" herself like the woman she was becoming.

Robert opened his mouth a time or two to say something, but then seemed to think better of it, so he waited for Lucy to speak first. Finally, she did. "Good," was all she said, and opened her arms to embrace her battered daughter.

Faythe returned the embrace and found, to her eternal annoyance, that she had teared up. And then, when her father had made it a three-way-hug and Chloe reflexively threw herself into the pile, Faythe started just crying out loud. There were just too many emotions going on.

Ironically, despite the fighting lessons with her father, and many more afterward, Faythe would have little use for these skills for a long time to come.

THE BEGINNINGS OF NORTH HINKAPEE

THE INSPIRATION FOR NORTH HINKAPEE COMES FROM A YOUNG BOY

Thompson Downing never planned to form his own town. Instead, the inspiration came to him quite out of the blue. It was a fine spring day in 1674 and he was having a pint in the Hinkapee tavern. As he enjoyed his beer, he noticed an unusual youth who had the air of an Indian, though he was clearly of the same English origin as most everyone else in the area. The puzzle led Thompson to start a conversation.

"Boy," said Thompson. "What's your story?"

At first shyly, and then with more gusto when Thompson offered him a plate of food, the boy told him everything about his short life. His language was a little halting, as though English were not familiar to him.

The name "Ahanu," he explained, meant "he who laughs," and it was given him by the Indians when he was so young that he could not now remember what his original name had been. He explained that the name was in the nature of a joke, since "I am not a happy one," he said. Indeed, Thompson's expert reading of people concluded that this was a thoughtful and quiet soul—not so much at peace as detached and impassive in his demeanor.

Ahanu's English mother had been kidnapped by the Sagawanee Indians when she was already pregnant by her English husband. His mother had explained to Ahanu that she had found life with the Sagawanee preferable to life with Ahanu's father, so that even when she was freed she elected to remain with the Indians. So Ahanu grew up as a Sagawanee, mastering their language, and he learned the language and many of the ways of the English from his mother. But Ahanu never fit in with the people as his mother had.

When his mother died, the Sagawanees would not accept Ahanu into the tribe, for as a male, he always posed the danger that he might become a traitor to them in a battle, and revert to the White Man. But they didn't want to kill him, either. Accordingly, they deposited the ten-year-old boy at the edge of the Hinkapee village and rode away.

Ahanu was at first accepted as returned by the grace of God from the savages, and he was allowed to live among the villagers; however, after a period of time it turned out that no one really wanted to support him, and his father had long since passed away. So he supported himself by begging and cleaning things that needed cleaning. He was not trained for much else.

"A very interesting story, young man," said Thompson, fixing him with his uncomfortable gaze, which Thompson noted seemed to have no effect on the boy.

"You know their language—and ours," Thompson murmured to himself, his intellectual wheels turning in the silence, which did not seem to disturb the boy. Finally, Thompson said, "I have a job for you. Are you interested?"

"Yes, sir," said Ahanu.

Thompson nodded and smiled at the young lad. *It all falls into place.* He now had the wherewithal to build his own town and this young boy would help him do it.

For a moment Thompson considered a pause in his plan. He could also tell that there was something off about the boy—a character flaw. He considered briefly if it would matter and concluded it would not. *It does fall into place.*

It didn't take long for Thompson to find a location not far to the north. It was technically part of Hinkapee, but there was nothing there but forest. Since Thompson was willing to make some annual tax payments to Hinkapee, he was able to purchase the effectively worthless land to form his town, subject to the eventual approval of the Hinkapee authorities.

There was water from a winding river and land to be cleared for farming, not to mention the other necessities for a frontier town. But in order for the township to be viable, there was first the large—actually enormous—matter of making peace with the Sagawanee Indians.

Now, in the months after the attack that had led to the death of Chief Passatan, Thompson had obtained from Ahanu the information that the boy's childhood friend Katakuk was the new chief and a likely recipient of an effort at diplomacy. Thompson didn't believe that Ahanu was really *friends* with Katakuk, as Ahanu described the relationship, but that wouldn't matter.

So Thompson Downing simply rode off into the forest with Ahanu that day in 1678. This might have seemed foolish to some and brave to others, but for Thompson Downing it was merely a calculation of risk and reward that made sense to him. Thompson hoped that the Sagawanee Indians would be willing to speak with him, through Ahanu, rather than just kill him as a White Man alone in the forest. He brought three horses—one for himself, one for Ahanu, and one laden with gifts, one being the horse itself, the best of the three.

So it was that one day in the year after the tragic losses to the Sagawanee people, a scout came running to Chief Katakuk to announce the coming of two White Men, one of them being Ahanu.

The young Chief Katakuk called ten of his warriors to accompany him on horseback and settled himself on his own horse with all his chiefly dignity—his father's mantle over his shoulders—to receive his visitor. The chief knew already that Thompson Downing was the founder of a settlement nearby, a settlement not involved in the recent conflicts.

Chief Katakuk rode with his men to meet the White Men.

Katakuk was a young man still learning how to be a good chief, but the griefs of the previous year had taught him the futility and pointlessness of battle with the White People. No victory was worth the losses he had known—his father and the woman he loved.

Yes, he mused, *we killed many White Men in that battle only last year, but there are always more White People to take their place. And now I have no father and no Nununyi, either.* Almost his first decision as chief had been that he would do his best to minimize fighting with the White People. But at the same time, he knew he could not risk losing the confidence of his people, if they thought him a coward avoiding battle.

Katakuk had concluded that if he maintained outward statements of bravado but was cautious about taking action, he could creatively, cleverly avoid war. And if he did have to take action from time to time, he would take such decisive action that his ferocity would never come into question.

As the visitors came into the clearing in which Chief Katakuk sat awaiting them, his men behind, Ahanu raised his palm in greeting, and Thompson Downing did the same, and both men dismounted, indicating they posed no threat. Katakuk recognized that this tall man, his hair shorn close to his head, his face bearing scars of pox or some other malady, had so much dignity that his limp seemed to add to his magnificence. Katakuk raised his own palm in greeting, and the White Man's piercing gaze met his own.

Much passed between these leaders in a moment.

"Chief Katakuk," Ahanu began, "I bring before you today Thompson Downing, who has been eager to meet you. I serve as his interpreter, and I serve as a friend to both of you, to bring you together. Will you hear him?"

Outwardly Chief Katakuk betrayed no emotion, but he inclined his head oh-so-slightly to Thompson, ignoring Ahanu, who was merely a mouthpiece. Katakuk wanted to make clear he was willing to listen, but no more than that.

"I will hear him," the chief replied.

"Great Chief Katakuk," said Thompson in a strong and loud voice, awaiting Ahanu's translation. The boy had suggested to Thompson that being humble and overly respectful would be the most appropriate strategy, because he thought Katakuk would be prideful as a young chief. But Thompson, with his uncanny gift for reading people, had immediately seen the opposite in Katakuk's eyes, and concluded that exuding strength and power and directness would be more likely to succeed. Thompson always trusted his instincts in these matters, and for good reason, since he was never wrong.

"I bring you gifts and a proposal that will benefit us both," he said without preamble. Thompson got straight to the point and Ahanu translated.

Thompson knew that if Katakuk gave just a slight sign, the young warriors would easily slaughter them. He was determined to show no fear. Everything depended on the outcome of this conversation.

First Thompson nodded, and Ahanu led the riderless horse forward to Katakuk. With an inclination of his head, Ahanu said in Sagawanee, "My master brings you these gifts as a token of his good will. He is not like other White Men. I ask you to listen to what he has to say."

95

And so Thompson spoke, clearly and elegantly. "Chief Katakuk, we the White People respect you as a strong warrior who will never be defeated. However, it benefits neither of us to lose our young and strong men and women to endless strife when we can both benefit from an alliance."

Katakuk strongly agreed, but he made no sign, so Thompson continued.

"I have been establishing a new town, that will be different from the others of the White People. As you know, we have made no aggression against you or your people in the years we have lived in North Hinkapee. Instead of considering you our enemies, we will consider you our friends, and we will work together. We will promise no warfare against you if you will give us the same promise. And we will trade with each other. And all will benefit."

Thompson outlined more of his ideas but deliberately did not go into great detail. The proposal was clear enough. Peace instead of war. Trade instead of theft, murder, and suffering.

The young Ahanu earnestly translated all that Thompson said, rightly conveying the solemnity of the occasion—for if Katakuk ordered the death of Thompson, the interpreter would be slaughtered, too.

Katakuk made no answer for what seemed like a very long time—indeed, the silence stretched over several minutes. Finally, he answered, looking at Thompson, but thinking more meaningfully about his warriors assessing his actions. "I will consider your proposal," he said, and turned abruptly to ride off with his entourage, the laden gift horse trailing behind the last warrior, who held its reins.

As Katakuk rode away, he contemplated the role Ahanu had fashioned for himself among the White People. *I wish I could speak their language*, thought Katakuk, especially since he didn't trust the interpreter. It was not only that Ahanu was, after all, a White Man, for those differences had been minimal as they'd grown up together. But although Katakuk's impression of Thompson Downing was immediately positive, he did not trust the look behind Ahanu's eyes.

Although Katakuk would not agree to anything for a while, not wanting to appear impetuous, Katakuk had already decided to accept Thompson's proposal. The result would be peace in North Hinkapee, but with the maintenance of moderate aggression by the Sagawanees in other settlements of the White People. This would result in the maximum benefit and the minimum loss of life for his people.

Due to Ahanu's presence and bilingual fluency, Katakuk's wisdom and intelligence, and Thompson's handsome gifts and his pledge to be to the Sagawanees more friends than foes, it took just one more meeting in the forest to conclude the arrangement. Now North Hinkapee had a chance to thrive.

Over the years, a fair number of residents of Hinkapee started to relocate to North Hinkapee, as they concluded that living in a town free of the risk of Indian attacks was a much better plan than taking the risk of being slaughtered in their sleep in (Old) Hinkapee, as it was coming to be called.

1687–1692, NORTH HINKAPEE

ARRIVAL IN NORTH HINKAPEE

The Wentworth family finally left the Boston area in 1687 and drifted around New England, from village to town to bigger town, each time landing just enough work to feed themselves and barely get by. Although they were as friendly as possible and sought to do good for others they met, they always found themselves to be "outsiders" and not part of any community.

By 1688, the Wentworths had wandered into North Hinkapee, and they all liked the feel of the community—on the edge of the wilderness, but orderly and peaceful, with pretty farms and plenty of space for more. The sheriff, John Jones, had greeted the family as they drew their wheeled cart into the town one late afternoon, and after learning a bit of their story, Jones had urged them to his home for refreshment. By the time they finished the meal, John and his wife Betsy had welcomed the travelers into their home for as many days as they sojourned in North Hinkapee, and it soon became clear that if the Wentworths settled there, the Joneses could become true friends. Robert learned that a family called the Downings owned most of the land and ran things, and he and John Jones set out the next day so the sheriff could give Robert an introduction to Miles Downing.

On the walk over, Sheriff Jones explained the original plan of Thompson Downing, Miles's father. Thompson wanted settlers in North Hinkapee who would put down roots and build the town over the generations. To achieve this purpose, Thompson had, in a risky gambit, reached out to make peace with the warlike and dangerous Sagawanee Indians. Through an interpreter named Ahanu that Thompson had found serendipitously, Thompson had been able to convey his force of personality, his positivity, and his honor to the Sagawanees' young chief, Katatuk.

Accordingly, Katatuk and Thompson Downing had shaken hands on a non-aggression pact, which had permitted the Town of North Hinkapee to thrive, as its biggest risk to success had been resolved. More and more settlers, who had tired of endless bloodshed with the Indians, found North Hinkapee an oasis that permitted them, and the town as well, to thrive.

Sheriff Jones also took pains to proudly explain his role. "When Thompson came courting me, I made clear that he needed the law to be respected in order for the Town to thrive and I was not about to be 'his man.'"

This last comment caused Robert to look askance at Sheriff Jones, finding it odd that Jones would mention that point. Jones continued, saying, "So I have been the sheriff here for many years and can say this is as good a place as any to put down strong roots, for you, and for your family, too."

Sheriff Jones concluded by explaining that now that Thompson Downing had passed, his son Miles Downing was the heir to the grand plan—though John explained that Miles's wife Martha had much influence and might well be in on negotiations.

"I expect Miles Downing will be eager to have you homestead in North Hinkapee," John said. "And as sheriff, I am eager for that, too."

Sheriff Jones had realized, instantly on meeting them, that the Wentworths were perfect for North Hinkapee. They were a young family that would work hard and, once settled, would not want to leave, ever. He expected that the Downings would quickly come to the same conclusion.

Robert, for his part, was thinking that perhaps this far-flung town might well be a destination for his family. What better options were there?

At the Downings' fine home, Robert, well washed and groomed for the occasion, offered gentlemanly courtesy to the striking Martha Downing, and she led the men to her husband's study. John made the introductions and then set off back to town, leaving them to it.

It didn't take Robert and Miles long to come to a preliminary agreement, and then they went out to examine the most likely property, a portion at the edge of the Downing holdings and not a far walk to town.

"Don't know if a seven-year deal makes sense to me," said Robert, opening the negotiations. "I did that and lost the farm in the sixth year. It's just too long."

"How about six years, then?" said Miles. Although seven years was the standard term, Miles had quickly warmed to Robert, and Robert thought he could negotiate a better deal. Stanford Palmer had taught him some things about negotiating, making his own way in the world. Knowing what the other man needed was a key part of making a good deal, and Robert knew Miles Downing needed new settlers. Robert quietly breathed a prayer of thanks for his father-in-law as he squared his shoulders to reply.

"How about five?" asked Robert. "And a free year up front, since there is no farm to work. There are woods I have to clear and, well, being honest, I have no money to pay right now."

"Done," said Miles.

"And, well, Mr. Downing—"

"Really better if you call me Miles."

"Miles, I really can't afford to make the same mistake twice. I will need some other protections."

"You're a plain speaker, Robert Wentworth. What do you need?"

Robert sensed a weakness in this fellow Miles Downing and remembered Sheriff Jones's mention of Martha's role in the family en-
terprise. He wondered whether things would have gone so easily if
she'd come out to the property with them. It would be best to quickly
manage the terms he needed and try to establish solid ground in their
business relationship. Robert thought back to the gentle life he'd enjoyed in Boston before the family's reversals and longed for such peace
and solidity again. Perhaps once he'd proven himself as a prosperous
farmer, in the course of time, he and Miles could even become friends.

After further discussion, Miles agreed to give Robert a good axe
and plow from his own farm and to lend him the money and short-
term help from a farmhand to get started on building a simple cabin
and clearing for the farm. And he offered a cow to boot! Robert se-
cured the right to extend the lease for two additional years, without
payment, if there were a bad harvest that would have left him unable
to make the payments.

Miles told him that he was willing to offer these terms because
he liked the look of Robert. "If Jones vouches for you, that's good
enough for me," he said. Then, perhaps getting carried away in the
spirit of camaraderie, Miles admitted that it was a good arrangement
for him, getting someone clearing and working and ultimately paying for land he didn't have resources to develop himself.

"Well," said Miles. "Do we have a deal?"

"Rightly we do," answered Robert. "Rightly we do." He offered
his hand and Miles shook it warmly.

Robert looked Miles in the eye as they shook hands. *I like this fellow*, he thought. *He seems like a good fellow. I think I can trust this man.*
And Robert read in Miles's expression that he thought the same.
Each man had a responsibility to do business on his own behalf, for
the sake of his family, and each one could admire that motive in the
other. There might be difficulties in the future, but they would face
those difficulties as they came. Today they could hope for friendship
as well as business.

Miles said that the papers would be drawn up and sent to him in a day or two by the Downings' family lawyer, Earl Carver. He would have Lucy read this most important paper before he actually signed it. Robert had never been able to learn to read, despite Lucy's labors with him. "I think I just started too late," he'd said in resignation, lamenting his childhood poverty that had given him no opportunity to learn. He *had* learned to sign his name in a way that suggested he'd had some learning.

"And why don't you bring your family when you come back with the papers?" Miles offered. "Martha insists on making acquaintance with all our people ... with new settlers."

THE WENTWORTHS AND THE DOWNINGS MEET AT LAST, OR AT FIRST

Faythe had much enjoyed the Joneses' hospitality in the few days they had stayed with them. Betsy Jones had kept her huge kettle boiling to bathe them all and wash every bit of their clothing that had grown filthy from their life on the road. She even trimmed their hair and made over an old dress of hers into dresses for both Faythe and Chloe. Though Faythe had begun to develop a womanly figure, going hungry during those growing years had kept her smaller than she might have otherwise been, and Chloe was positively tiny. Their new clothing did not take much fabric.

What a pleasure it was to have a full belly and clean clothing! Faythe had been listless in all the family's wanderings, but she was feeling restored, ready to get on with whatever new adventure life was bringing them. And the next adventure was to be an outing to the home of the Downings, which her father had described as "broad and tight as a fine ship."

While the men negotiated the final details of their deal, Lucy and the girls sat with Martha Downing, Lucy offering gracious and friendly conversation such as she had enjoyed with friends in Boston in their comfortable years. Martha offered Lucy tea and ignored the girls, other than cutting her eyes disapprovingly at Chloe when the youngster started swinging her legs in the chair her mother had directed her to.

Mum would have offered us tea AND cakes, Faythe thought, taking a quick measure of Martha Downing and concluding she would never be a friend for her mum. So this was a business deal the husbands were making, and the women's task was to make small talk until it was done. Faythe settled in to endure the slow passing of time, looking about her at the rugs and polished brass ornaments and pewter such as she had not seen since Boston.

With a clatter of a back door and the thunder of feet on the floorboards, suddenly two big blond boys barged into the ladies' gathering. The first boy stomped in muddy shoes right across the carpet and stood before his mother, ignoring the guests, and the other boy lingered in the doorway. They seemed to be thirteen or fourteen, around Faythe's age.

The first boy was complaining about something, in a tone of command to his mother. She responded under her breath, with some annoyance, and then brightened to a stiff smile and introduced them to Lucy and waved her hand in the direction of the girls—"and her daughters." The first boy, Matt, just looked at Lucy Wentworth and then at Faythe and Chloe—not as people but as if he'd just been shown the new cows his father had bought. Faythe took an instant dislike to that one. The brother, Pat, nodded and half-smiled at them all at the introductions. *That one's better, maybe*, Faythe thought.

"Perhaps you boys might show the girls around while the men are talking and we women are getting acquainted?" said Martha Downing.

Lucy nodded her approval, and the four children left the room and then the house together, with Matt in the lead, Faythe close behind with Pat beside her, and Chloe trailing after.

Pat said, "I-I'm Pat," though he didn't seem able to ask Faythe her name.

"I'm Faythe. Pleased to meet you," Faythe replied, and the boy went crimson. "This is my sister Chloe," she said as Chloe caught up with them in the farmyard.

Matt had climbed up on a trough and balanced himself, towering over them. "This is my dad's farm," he said. "It's the biggest farm here."

Faythe said nothing but conveyed with her countenance essentially, "So what?"

"My grandfather settled the town, and now we Downings run things here."

Faythe nodded impassively and said nothing. Matt continued in this vein as he showed Faythe and Chloe around, Pat quiet and stumbling a bit as he tried to keep pace with Faythe. They toured the large barn full of many horses, the out-buildings with blacksmithing and other work going on, the mill on the small river nearby. "It's all ours."

Faythe continued to say nothing.

Her silence seemed to annoy Matt, and he said, "Cat got your tongue?"

"No," said Faythe and shrugged.

"Well, you don't say much."

"What's to say? You're bragging and I'm trying not to listen."

Matt flushed. "Not bragging. I'm just telling you how things are around here."

Faythe shook her head and gave a slight eyeroll.

This set him off. "You and your family will need to know your place here in North Hinkapee."

"And what place is that?" said Faythe, narrowing her eyes at him.

Matt stopped walking and looked Faythe in the eyes directly, trying to be intimidating.

She looked him right back in the eyes and took a half-step towards him. She was figuring out where to hit him—the nose or the groin. She knew from her father's advice how especially tender men were in that region. Their eyes locked, and from a distance it probably looked very strange, a girl and boy staring at each other.

Pat nervously said, "Wanna go see the chickens?" and Chloe overcame her shyness with excitement. "I do!" Matt and Faythe ignored them both.

Finally, Matt said, "One word from me to my dad and you and your ragged family will all be sent packing, back to where you belong."

Faythe moved forward again so that there was only a foot or so between them. Matt was a full head taller than she. "You're a lout," she said. "A boorish lout."

Faythe had heard a woman say this some time ago, to put a too-aggressive man in his place. She didn't need to use her fighting skills when she had other advantages.

Matt flushed. It was bad enough that he was being challenged, but it was worse that it was in front of others.

He moved forward and gave Faythe a shove in the chest, actually touching—*Accidentally?* she wondered—clutching at one of her breasts in doing so. Faythe was about to fly at him when all four parents suddenly came outside into the yard where the children were standing. Faythe checked her charge and gave Matt a venomous look and a slight hissing sound, but that was it. The introduction of Matthew Downing to Faythe Emily Wentworth was over.

Faythe forced her breathing to a normal pace as the adults approached, and she noticed Chloe trembling. The little girl's timid personality was becoming more evident over time, and the insecurities of their hunger and cold the last few years had not helped. Faythe dropped to her knees and wrapped her arms around her sister, who was shaking and staring at Matt, obviously struck with panic.

Faythe determined right then that at all costs she would protect her sister from Matthew Downing.

When the parents reached them, Lucy and Robert went straight to the girls and knelt beside them, seeking to learn what was wrong. Faythe was determined to handle the situation herself, so she made light of it all, claiming that Chloe had been scared by the Downings' large dog that had jumped out without warning.

Lucy held Faythe by the shoulders and studied her face, her own brow furrowed with concern, and Faythe saw Martha Downing watching closely, too, from a distance. Lucy was about to probe into what had happened, but her intuition told her that this wasn't the time, so she said nothing.

But then everything just dissolved into farewells and handshakes between the men and polite, cool words between the women. And then the Wentworths walked home together. Nothing more was said, but all three Wentworth women were thinking different things.

FAYTHE AND LUCY

The Wentworth family bent all their energies and good will into creating their new farm over the next few years. The work was backbreaking. Trees had to be cleared and the stumps burned, the fields plowed and countless stones removed, and their home built from the trees Robert felled with help from the Downing worker lent for the purpose.

Faythe loved watching her father thrive with all this work after the dispiriting years of their poverty. Robert Wentworth, by his nature, fell into tasks by starting immediately and moving forward relentlessly until a job was completed. Indeed, he seemed to gain energy from hard work.

Even in their rude log cabin, Faythe and all her family were very happy. It is said that wealth and power don't buy happiness. But being poor and not very important doesn't necessarily lead to sadness. Maybe things were getting better for the Wentworths, although as Robert pointed out ruefully from time to time, they could hardly have gotten much worse.

As time went on, things did start to get better for the Wentworths. The farm took shape, with first a house and then a barn, and then some small fields to cultivate. And friendships developed as well, with the sheriff and Betsy Jones, of course, and with similarly situated farmers who were also working off their lease debt to the Downings.

Although things were improving and clearly on the right track, Faythe didn't forget how she had felt during the hopeless times when her family was on a road to nowhere without end.

She remembered the meanness they had experienced.

Sometimes she remembered her mother's advice to look for the good in people. But certainly the past had not proved Lucy correct in her conviction that there was always good in people. Indeed, most people they had interacted with seemed to be out for themselves. Trusting, loving, and believing in others seemed to be a sucker's game. Faythe wondered about this enough that she even started wondering why she was wondering about it.

But although it was an internal topic of conversation with herself, Faythe never asked Lucy about it as the years passed. Perhaps Faythe was afraid of a possible answer whereby her mother might admit that she realized now that she was wrong all along.

Lucy and Faythe had made it a ritual in their new home in North Hinkapee to take a stroll outside for the lesser part of an hour at roughly mid-morning. They did this almost every day unless the weather simply made it unbearable to do so. Chloe and Robert knew this was "their time" and didn't interfere.

On a cool Monday morning in May, 1692, Lucy and seventeen-year-old Faythe were taking their walk, and Lucy said, "So it seems you've taken a liking to that Tommy Carlin?"

Faythe flushed a little and smiled. "Yes," she said. "I like him …" Her tone did not finish the sentence.

"You like him, but what?" asked Lucy.

"Well, I have something to say you might not like to hear."

Lucy looked at her as if to say, "You can always tell your mum anything."

So Faythe just blurted out, "Mum, I'm not sure if I want to marry."

"There's nothing saying you have to marry Tommy."

"I'm not talking about Tommy. He's just the kind I'd want to marry … I'm talking about whether I want to marry anyone … ever."

Lucy looked at her with surprise and concern. Any mother would assume that her daughter would someday find a man she loved, marry him, and become a mother herself. Even if the Wentworths were not a typical family, it would be a far stretch to consider Faythe remaining an old maid by choice. Lucy knew Faythe was *different*, but still assumed she would expect to find a good mate. Her brow furrowed.

"Faythe, may I ask you a question?" she said.

"Sure," said Faythe, wondering how she could defend this new idea she had been working with. After all, marriage would come soon, most likely, if at all. Once done it would be done, forever and always. She looked at her mother.

Lucy said, surprising Faythe with the apparent turn in the conversation, "I remember the day we met the Downings, when your father signed the paper for the farm. Do you recall that day?"

"Yes, Mum." *What does this have to do with marriage?* Faythe wondered, puzzled.

"When we came out to where you children were in the farmyard, you seemed to be in a right fury, and Chloe all afraid. But as you did not speak of it to me then, I thought to just wait. But I will ask you now. Did something happen that day, with those boys, that might have made you … or Chloe … afraid … of, well, marriage?"

"Ha!" cried Faythe, indignation pushing aside puzzlement. "I wasn't afraid at all! But Chloe was, and that Matt was pushing things with me I wouldn't put up with."

"What I mean," said Lucy, "is ... what was he pushing? Was he behaving in a way that was unseemly?"

Unseemly? wondered Faythe. And suddenly things started falling into place in her mind. *How incredibly intuitive my mum is,* she marveled with a fleeting thought.

She remembered Matt touching her breast, wondering again if it was an accident after all, and the impudent and unpleasant look on his face. And then she recalled feeling prickles in her breasts just yesterday at the thought of Tommy Carlin. Somehow it was all mixed up inside her and she was confused and enlightened at the same time. The ways she wanted Tommy to touch her were the ways she'd never want Matt to touch her. And whatever poor girl Matt married would have him touching her like that all the time—there ought to be a lot of girls who didn't want to get married!

"Well, sort of," Faythe said. "He pushed me ... in the chest. But that wasn't the worst of it. He was bragging about his farm and saying we ought to be kicked out of town, that kind of thing."

"Very well, then," said Lucy, thinking how important this conversation was. "I am afraid that there are a few men in the world who do not treat their wives well. Your dad and I do not want you to think ill of people, but we want you to be careful of such men as that. And we would never want you to marry such as that! You can be sure Robert Wentworth would never allow it!"

They walked a while in silence, Faythe resting happy in the assurance that her father was the sort of man she would want to marry, and maybe Tommy was that sort, too. *But ...*

"Mum, it seems to me that when a woman gets married, she's under the control of her husband. Isn't that right?"

"I'm not sure I'd put it that way, but, yes, the husband is generally in charge of affairs."

"Then why should a woman get married?" asked Faythe.

Lucy considered her answer and finally said, "There are a lot of reasons. Perhaps because a woman is safer under a man's protection than alone? Perhaps because two people working together can accomplish a lot more than either one alone? Perhaps because she might want to have her own children? And perhaps because she loves him and doesn't think about every angle? Love can make us forget the inconveniences of life."

Faythe digested these various reasons and said, "But it still sounds like she's taking a big risk. If she has a good husband, like you do with Dad, then it makes great sense, but if she has a bad husband, then she's in a very bad way."

Lucy shrugged and said, "Yes, that's true. This is why a woman must make a very wise and careful choice. It's the most important decision she'll ever make."

"How did you make the choice with Dad? Did you carefully think it through like you are saying?"

Lucy laughed and said, "Well, you know our tale, we've told it so much. We just *knew*."

They continued their walk, quieter than usual. Lucy was wondering whether she had achieved her purpose, and Faythe was now questioning whether not marrying was too strong a conviction after all. Tommy was certainly the opposite end of the world from Matt. It was surely confusing.

INTERLUDE

AN INDIAN WEDDING

Gilbert Menon's farm was less than a mile from the wayside Inn at Bearminster, a place not well settled but frequented by travelers between Hinkapee and Briarcliff.

Menon had put up a sign on the road reading "No Hunting—No Trespasing," and though Menon had been told by his visiting friends that the spelling was wrong, he said liked it the way it was, and so the sign remained. Behind the sign, a narrow path wended its way through the woods to his small, cozy cabin. The way was easy for a man on foot, especially his fellow mercenaries out tramping to find their old friend. It was more difficult for a man on a horse, and very difficult but just barely achievable in the best of weather for a wagon. Menon had few visitors, though, as he preferred.

Especially now, he thought, as he peeked into the bedroom he had given her and gazed at the sweet sleeping face of Nununyi.

Over several months, Nununyi healed and Menon did everything he could to court a woman he could scarcely speak to, a woman from another world. He assumed he had but a short time to win her over, for once she recovered, she would certainly return to her own people. *Why would she stay here with me?* They were an unlikely pair, but every day that passed for just the two of them in the woods, he grew a little more hopeful that his dream might come true.

With much practice, they were able to converse just a little, haltingly, and eventually Nununyi asked Menon in halting English, "Why save me? Why not die?"

He wanted to say, "Because God cast a spell over my eyes and my heart, and put before me the most beautiful and wonderful creature I had ever seen, and I fell in love with you the moment I saw you." But of course Nununyi wouldn't have been able to understand, so instead, after thinking long about it, he put his hand on his heart, looked at her meaningfully and earnestly, and then pointed to her heart.

Nununyi gazed at him, and then lowered her eyes. She understood perfectly.

The next day, Menon picked some long-stemmed autumn flowers from a nearby meadow and brought them to Nununyi, who seemed not to know how to respond. She had learned the word and dutifully said "Flowers," then looked up at him with a question in her eyes.

And the next day he brought her flowers again.

And the next day as well. That time his hand lingered on hers when she clutched the bunch of stems, and he looked at her and smiled. And for the first time Nununyi smiled—accidentally at first, but then not accidentally—back at him.

Menon's heart leaped within him; it seemed his courtship was going well. *Dare I kiss her?* he wondered.

The next day when Menon brought her flowers, he knelt down next to the chair she was sitting in, so that their faces were at the same level. Slowly, ever so slowly, he leaned closer to her, looking into the deep brown eyes that looked back at him with an expression he could not read.

She's going to let me kiss her! he thought, excited, but then he felt a blade poking into the flesh of his neck. He held still but looked down and saw an arrow held strongly in Nununyi's hand, restrained but warning against his throat. All she had to do was thrust her arm upward a little and Menon's life would flow out of him.

He drew back, rose to his feet, and went out to chop some wood, disheartened that his first attempt had ended in failure. *Still, Rome was not built in a day*, he mused. *I will give it more time.*

But the next morning when Menon awoke, he knew instantly that she was gone. From his cot in the main room he could usually hear her breathing, but this morning there was no sound. His eyes went to where her bow and arrow, her most precious possessions, had been standing for the months she had been with him. They were gone, too.

His heart was heavy at his failure. His kiss had scared her away. He sighed a ragged sigh. He was very sad, and lonely too.

Several miles away already at dawn, Nununyi was making her way through the woods now blazing their fall colors. She walked parallel to the road and away from the rising sun. Even though she was in a place she had never been before, she was able through what she had been taught to study the moon and stars and the rivers and trees in the dark, and now the sun in the day, to begin to find her way back to her people.

It was a few days before Nununyi finally made her way quietly back to the lands of her people, through the new town White Men had settled when she was a child, and it wasn't long before she picked up the familiar trails of the Sagawanees and finally made it to the edge of their camp. She had moved with great quietness each day of her travels and was confident that she had not been seen.

But as she approached her home, for some reason she stopped, shy, before entering the small village of their summer encampment.

At the rustling of the trees near the trail, she peered through and her heart stopped—it was Katakuk!

But he was not alone.

He was with another woman. A young woman. She recognized Watakee, a young girl with innocent prettiness. *More little girl than woman*, she thought with a pang of jealousy. As she watched, she saw to her shock that Katakuk first kissed the girl and then took other liberties with her. His hands possessed the girl and she responded in a way that made it clear she was his wife or his betrothed.

Nununyi was alone—he had left her for another. She felt pain in her much worse than that of Harriman Keep-Safe's gunshot wound.

At first Nununyi wanted to rush out of the thickets and announce herself, but if he could so easily cast aside her memory and find another, perhaps she was foolish to long for him.

Nununyi refused to cry, although she wanted to. *Crying is weakness*, she thought, but she realized in that moment that tears were nonetheless coursing down her face. She melted away into the forest.

"I seek your blessing to marry your daughter Watakee," said Katakuk solemnly to the father and mother of the pretty young Sagawanee girl, dark-haired and dark-eyed, who sat meekly on a log nearby.

Three months had now passed since Nununyi's disappearance and presumed passing. Katakuk's heart was heavy every time he thought of her, which was almost all the time. He knew he had to move past Nununyi, for the good of the tribe and for his own good as well. Finally, he achieved a level of inner peace at which he could love another as his wife, but Nununyi would always be with him, and hunt with him in spirit. *Indeed, without her sacrifice to the gods I would not be here at all.*

Although Katakuk was fulfilling proper custom in seeking the consent of Watakee's parents, the conclusion was foregone. What parent would refuse the chief? And as Katakuk was such an excellent choice of mate, what parent would want to refuse? It was a beautiful match.

After an appropriate mourning period for Nununyi, who had not even been Katakuk's actual wife, Katakuk had courted Watakee for several weeks. He had stumbled blindly through the expected rituals of becoming chief, his heart numbed and far from him in his grief over both his father and his beloved Nununyi.

"Will you be a good husband to my daughter?" asked the father solemnly.

"Yes, I promise to do that," said Katakuk.

"And will you protect her?"

"Yes, I will."

"And will you provide food and sustenance to her?"

"Yes, I will."

More questions were asked and answered; however, Katakuk found his thoughts wandering, as they always did, to Nununyi. *My heart is broken*, he thought. *If she had not been so headstrong, if she had listened to my father, she would be here now.* But then he added the heavy, wondrous thing he also knew: if Nununyi had not ignored his father's instructions, Katakuk would have died in battle. *She saved me with her beautiful arrow.*

He turned his thoughts back to the present. Watakee was not Nununyi, but she was an excellent choice for a first wife. She was well trained, obedient, and in their private time in the woods, she had shown clearly that she was an eager mate. And, of great importance, he thought, chagrined at the truth of it, she was very pretty, too.

Watakee's father was speaking. "Chief Katakuk," he said, "you have my consent and my wife's consent to marry our daughter Watakee, and we are honored to have our family join with yours."

Young Chief Katakuk bowed to Watakee's father and mother and then turned to smile at his bride, who smiled back eagerly.

It was almost a month after the date that Nununyi had left that Gilbert Menon found himself awakened by the soft sounds of a beautiful Indian warrior girl slipping into bed beside him.

1692, NORTH HINKAPEE

PLAYING IN THE WOODS

Faythe and Chloe liked to play in the woods. They had been lighting out from their family cabin most afternoons for several years, after supper on the long summer days, and though they were becoming more women than girls, they still called it "playing." Faythe humored Chloe in that, for Chloe seemed always to be a little girl in her mind and spirit, despite the changes in her body at twelve.

"Can I be a princess today?" asked Chloe.

"Didn't we do that yesterday?" said Faythe.

Chloe giggled. "But it's my *favorite* one. I'm in trouble, and you save the day like you always do."

Faythe sighed inwardly. Chloe wasn't growing up, and, looking intently at her sister, Faythe realized that maybe she never would.

Instead of the more mature stories the rest of the family enjoyed, Chloe invariably wanted to be told variations of the same story lines, about how Chloe would be married to a prince and live in a big house or even a castle, and Faythe would look after her and always be with her. Chloe didn't care that the stories were simple and unoriginal; all she cared about was being with her big sister, listening to the soothing sound of her voice. Then everything was fine and always would be. There was nothing to worry about.

"All right," said Faythe, trying to come up with a slight variation of the story line. "Once upon a time there was a sweet girl named Chloe. She had a mom and a dad, and she didn't know it yet, but she was really a princess …"

Chloe closed her eyes and lay back on the log she had straddled and awaited the tale. Life couldn't get any better than this for Chloe, it seemed.

Anyone witnessing Faythe's nurturing of her little sister might think she was the ultimate "little mother." No one could look out for Chloe like Faythe did. Yet for those who seemed able to take care of themselves, Faythe presented a much harder exterior.

"Mum," Faythe had said to Lucy on one of their walks, "what will happen to Chloe?" Faythe appreciated the adoration, but she was disturbed that Chloe had no direction of her own, always wanting to just follow Faythe around like a duckling follows its mother.

Lucy smiled and squeezed Faythe's shoulder. "I'm sure God has a purpose for such a sweet girl. It may not be obvious right now, but at some point"—and here she paused as if overtaken by doubts of her own—"I'm sure God will show us."

Sometimes the girls would play a hide-and-seek game that Faythe had made up and called "Rescue." Chloe was, of course, the one in distress. Chloe would hide and Faythe would search for her and then rescue her with some dramatic gesture like urging Chloe to ride on her back or pushing her up a good climbing tree and following after, so that they could sit far above the forest floor and call it their castle.

As Faythe told Chloe the usual story this June evening, up in a tree, she had an odd feeling that they were not alone, but she couldn't place it. Something just seemed funny. She looked around carefully but couldn't see anything. Just trees and the undergrowth and the path.

"Did you hear something?" she finally asked Chloe.

Chloe shook her head, so Faythe continued with her story until it was just beginning to get dark. *No more games tonight*, she thought. They really should get back so Mum and Dad wouldn't worry or be upset that their chores were neglected. With their father's work ethic, Faythe always made sure the chores were done, but the girls always fancied that they *might* not get done and that their mother would be vexed. As if sunny Lucy were ever vexed.

They clambered down the tree and started home, with Faythe leading the way and Chloe docilely following along, just a step or two behind.

Suddenly, the quiet of the woods was disturbed with a great crashing through the underbrush, and out jumped two big men.

One blocked Faythe's way.

"Boo!" said Matt Downing, his arms raised as if he were about to swoop her up.

Chloe gave a shriek and Faythe whirled to see Pat had grabbed Chloe's long braid that had fallen out of her cap. The child's eyes were wide with terror, her hands over her mouth.

"Yeah, boo!" echoed Pat a little more weakly, ending with a nervous giggle.

Faythe's heart was racing. She had been spooked, and by a couple of big dolts. She was furious with herself for not realizing that something was amiss. And she was even more angry that she'd permitted herself to be scared. She hated that emotion.

Fearlessly and furiously, she stepped forward, right into Matt's space, causing him to step back in surprise.

"What in heck are you oafs doing here?" she challenged loudly. "This is our property." She hoped the authority of her voice would belie her concerns, for she was suddenly aware of danger. They were alone in the woods with two large and strong young men, one with a terrible reputation and whose intentions were unknown.

After a moment's hesitation, when his eyes darted back and forth, Matt replied indignantly, "It isn't your property—it's ours."

"Not as long as we're tenanting here," said Faythe confidently, staring him in the eye. She had no idea of the law but figured Matt didn't, either. "And either way, what ill-mannered boors are you to jump out and try to scare us? Move out of our way."

Matt stood his ground and stared back at Faythe with some anger taking over the original mischief in his eyes. The way her gaze held him unnerved her—nobody else did that. He wasn't used to being pushed around by a girl, or really by anyone. He looked inclined to hit her, which would have been way out of line in North Hinkapee or elsewhere. Men didn't hit women in the new colonies—at least that's what his dad said.

Pat had dropped Chloe's braid and pushed her toward her sister for comfort. "Matt, we gotta get home. Let's go."

Faythe was almost sorry at the interruption, because her aggression was coming up to a quick boil. She was already rehearsing her father's instructions and gauging where she would hit Matt for maximum effect. It seemed that every time she was near Matt Downing she had that urge—planning just where to hit him.

Strangely, she was wondering whether, if she beat them both up, she might now be *two for two* in bouts with men.

Matt looked at Faythe, his lip curling in a contemptuous sneer, and as with their confrontation the first day they'd met, Faythe looked right back at him. There was again something powerful and unpleasant and unyielding going on between them as they stared at each other. Neither would give ground and neither moved. Pat was silent, and Chloe sniffled a little, both hypnotized at the gladiators before them.

Finally, after a long half-minute, Faythe concluded that two-on-one wasn't good odds, so she turned and grabbed Chloe by the elbow and started to push past Matt.

Matt moved to stop them, putting his hand across her onto Chloe's other arm, and Faythe grabbed Matt's arm and flung it, hard, back at him.

"You don't touch my sister," she growled, and glared at him again. She was inches now from initiating battle, and to the Devil with the consequences.

Matt was going to move forward, but at this moment Pat seemed to reach for all the strength of character inside himself and grabbed Matt by the elbow, dragging him back. He suggested again, more strongly, that it was time to go home. Matt gave Pat a furious look and gave Faythe a venomous one. Then, in a rare turn of events, he listened to his brother and followed him off into the woods, back towards the Downings' farm.

Faythe and Chloe walked home quickly, Chloe trembling and trying hard not to cry as she struggled to keep up. Finally, Faythe slowed down and turned to Chloe.

"Sister," she said, "let us compose ourselves before going on." Chloe nodded. "Let's take some deep breaths and calm down." So they did that. Then they sat down on a rock by the side of the trail. Things felt safer now, since they could see the outline of their little house only a few hundred paces away. At last Faythe stopped shaking. At last she was calm.

"Chloe," said Faythe, "I don't think we should tell Mum and Dad about this."

"Why?" asked Chloe, wiping her nose with her skirt and wringing her hands in her lap.

"If we tell them, they won't let us go in the woods anymore to have our special time, will they?"

"I guess not," said Chloe.

"So this has to be our secret," said Faythe. Chloe nodded again.

"Also," added Faythe, "I want you to stay away from those boys."

Chloe gave Faythe a comic wide-eyed look as if to say, "Do you really think I need you to tell me that?" They both giggled and relaxed with the release of tension.

"I thought you were going to smack that Matt boy," said Chloe.

"I almost did," replied Faythe fiercely. "He deserved it. He is not good."

Chloe agreed. "Chores now?" she asked. Faythe nodded assent and the two girls went the rest of the way home, Chloe clinging to Faythe's hand.

After their evening chores, dinner and family conversation, it was time for bed. Faythe looked at her sister peacefully asleep as soon as she lay down, and she felt concern rising in her again, concern she might not be able to share with their mother, now that she had a secret to keep. *What will growing up be like for Chloe?* Faythe wondered. It would be too easy for a bad man to abuse this precious innocent, who wouldn't know how to defend herself. Faythe loved Chloe so much; she wanted to shield her from everything bad in the world and make it so that only good things could come to her. Of course, this was impossible, and that made her sad.

Before falling asleep, Faythe felt her thoughts about marriage converging with her thoughts about Matt. She imagined the fate of the poor woman who might become his wife someday. How awful it would be. Now, she felt more strongly than ever that marrying would not be for her.

TOMMY AND FAYTHE
—TOMMY'S FIRST TRY

The next evening, Faythe was taking some scraps out to the chickens when she saw through the trees that someone was leading a horse toward their place. Her father saw him, too, and straightened up from his work on the gate to greet the visitor.

It was none other than Tommy Carlin!

"Evening, sir," Tommy said.

"Evening t'you, Tommy," said Robert. "What do we owe the pleasure to?"

"Mama had just too many strawberries from the garden," Tommy said in a strained, high-pitched tone that sounded odd, considering he usually had a nice, low voice. "She was gonna make them into pies, but there're just too many, and it's too early in the year for pies to keep, so she told me I should bring 'em here and you might find a use for them."

"Well, first, thank your mother for us," answered Robert. "It's a kindness, and we take it kindly. I bet the women inside would be pleased to see you, and to receive this gift."

Tommy was silent.

At the door, Tommy set down the basket and wiped his hands on his breeches and ran them through his hair before knocking.

A moment later Lucy opened the door and exclaimed, "Why Tommy, it's so good to see you! What brings you here?"

Tommy said, "I told Mr. Wentworth about the berries—"

Lucy enthusiastically welcomed him, and the berries, into the house. Faythe tidied her own hair out by the chicken house, and then made what she hoped was a jaunty entrance.

The basket of strawberries stood on the table, and around its three sides stood Tommy, Lucy, and Chloe in an awkward silence. Faythe took her place on the fourth side of the table for more awkward silence, and after a few agonizing moments, Lucy suggested that perhaps Faythe might like to show Tommy the new barn.

Faythe and Tommy eagerly took the suggestion and left the house and walked across the yard, Robert Wentworth waving to show he was watching carefully and at the same time pretending he was not watching carefully.

Faythe walked into the mostly built barn and Tommy followed. She made a pretext of showing him the stall for the old plow horse and the empty pen for the breeder sow they hoped to buy. Tommy nodded knowingly and tried to show interest. It was clear that he had something to say, but he was shy and it seemed awfully hard for him to speak. He cleared his throat several times.

Faythe found herself at a bit of an advantage and considered having pity on him. She almost said, "Tommy, seems like you've got something to say. So just come out with it." But she was enjoying letting him squirm, and so she said nothing at all, and the tension built.

Tommy kept clearing his throat, and the repetition was at first awkward and then funny. Finally, Faythe could hold back no more and she started smiling, then giggling, and then before she knew what was happening, she was laughing out loud.

Finally, when she caught her breath, Tommy spoke. He was very quiet, and Faythe said, wiping her eyes, "I'm sorry—I didn't hear you."

So he blurted out, "Faythe, I really like you. You're so beautiful. I can't think about anything else except talking to you. I'd like to—I'd like to court you if you'll permit it. And your father."

Tommy had run out of breath, he was so nervous, and though he had a lot of muscles and impressed everyone with his "presence," he seemed to have grown smaller and younger in his embarrassment. There was fear in his eyes.

"Well, why don't you kiss me, then?" said Faythe impetuously.

Tommy was taken aback. He stood gaping at Faythe, confusion and hope joining the fear in his eyes.

Faythe felt anticipation. What she'd dreamed of for so long was coming true just like in a story, and she was ready to get on with it. She had seen her parents kiss many times before and they seemed to enjoy it. She was waiting. She added, finally, to give him confidence, "It will be my first kiss."

Tommy gulped and looked around the fresh new barn as if seeking an escape.

Faythe wondered. *Maybe it's his first time, too.* Here he was, alone with a girl, and he seemed to have no idea what to do. He just stood there.

Faythe had finally had enough of Tommy's indecision. She stepped forward and put her face close to Tommy's. All he had to do was lean down a few inches and their kiss would happen naturally.

After a short pause Tommy did what was natural—and they had their first kiss in the barn, surrounded by the smell of the hay, the horse, and the implied smell of the pig that hadn't yet been purchased.

Faythe felt in herself something that she hadn't felt before. It was a sexual urging, stronger than what she'd felt when she looked at Tommy in church. Now she was connected to him at the lips—soft, generous lips—and it took her breath away. Her mother had spoken to her about this, of course, and had given her the ground rules. This new feeling was very powerful and exciting.

"So this was what it was all about?" she murmured to herself as they separated, a little breathless. He looked stunned.

She pulled Tommy closer, against her body, and he answered with another kiss, a deeper one accompanied with a quiet groan. She knew the origin of the insistent yet awkward firmness pressing into her waist, and she pressed herself against him, just a little, so he could not be sure if it were intentional.

At last the kiss ended and they stood apart, each looking at the other. Tommy seemed at a complete loss.

In the few seconds it took them to come back to their individual selves, Faythe considered whether she should let Tommy know that she expected she would never marry anyone, ever. But she said nothing. She wanted more of what they'd just had, and moments like these were too exciting to pass up!

There was really nothing more to say or do. So they walked out of the barn quickly, before Robert or Lucy might wonder too much about what was going on, as if they didn't know exactly what was going on.

They walked over to where he'd tied the horse, and Tommy turned to Faythe and said, "I hope I'll see you soon and, I—well, this is kind of awkward, but maybe you might not mention the berries to my mom if you see her."

Faythe furrowed her brow and Tommy continued. "She—well, she might not really know about it, is all. I might have made it up so I'd have reason to come on over here." He swung up onto the horse and waited for her response.

Faythe smiled back conspiratorially. "It'll be our secret, then," she said, but it was likely one of her parents would spill the beans when they saw Jane Carlin. *He must not have thought about that yet.*

Tommy started the horse down to the gate and waved to Robert Wentworth, who waved back and nodded. Tommy tipped his hat to Faythe and rode off into the now-fading evening light.

Faythe said to herself, *So, now I am officially confused!* However, she was pleased that she had handled things as properly as she could. He'd asked permission to court her, and she'd been very careful not to answer that question.

Robert was washing up on the porch when Faythe meandered back to the house, and he held the door for her, not saying a word. Inside, Chloe was giggling and Lucy was looking first at Faythe and then at Robert, who took his place next to his wife and squeezed her around the waist. Both of them looked happy and sad at the same time, Faythe thought, with tears glistening even as they smiled. Something significant had happened to the Wentworths that evening.

LOVE AND
THE CARLINS

As summer passed, Tommy was swept up in his passions. He was completely enamored of Faythe, but other than that one kiss in the barn, he had been unable to even get in the vicinity of the woman of his dreams. There were too many farm responsibilities for both of them.

As he had ridden away from the Wentworth farm that one miraculous evening, Tommy relived every moment of his first kiss. It wasn't as he had planned when he had led the horse to the farm earlier that evening with his offering of strawberries. He had imagined that Faythe would part her sweet lips just so and that he would kiss her gently. Faythe would be trembling just a bit, fearful of the implications of the kiss, what it might mean. She would be oh, so shy, and she would blush, no doubt. All of this would be especially true since surely she had never been kissed before.

But it had been nothing like that. Faythe had taken complete control of the situation, he now recollected ruefully. She had kissed him back very strongly, even passionately, and put her tongue into his mouth. *Where did she learn to do that?* he wondered. Had she felt his erection through their clothing? The thought made his face go hot with embarrassment even though he was alone. The very thought of it brought on another erection, and he had to adjust himself in the saddle as he rode slowly along in the half-dark.

He relived the kisses all the way home, knowing that what he would do to himself that night was a sin. But there was no way he had been able to help himself—not that night nor any night since.

This was quite a woman he was courting. At first he was really happy and even exhilarated. The girl he liked had kissed him passionately. But in re-examining every moment of their encounter, every word, he had to be honest with himself. When he professed his feelings to Faythe, she had not said she felt the same way. He realized with concern that she had not said "Yes" when he asked permission to court her. She had turned the conversation into a kiss. What did that mean?

Tommy longed to talk it over with his mother, but first he wanted to know whether Faythe would have him in the first place. What would Jane Carlin say? Would she conclude that Faythe was not a good match for him, that the Wentworths were too poor? Much as he hated to admit it, Tommy could not go against his mother's wishes on something of this importance.

Over the weeks that followed that first kiss, Tommy gradually let Jane know of his longing for Faythe, testing her responses, getting her used to the idea. And before he knew it, he was sounding his mother out about his plans for Faythe.

"So, Mother, what do you think?" he asked, for probably the tenth time in the past week. "You haven't said much about this, and the rest of my life is at stake."

"It's not a matter for such theatrics," said Jane Carlin.

"Very well. I'm hereby discarding theatrics," responded Tommy. And then before he could help himself, he added, "But what do you think about Faythe?"

His mother sighed. "I think she's a nice girl ..."

"But ... ?" continued Tommy to prompt her.

"But I'm sorry to point out the obvious—her family has little more than the dirt of their farm. They're the nicest people, but they've got nothing at all. I can see you have feelings for the maiden, but you can't live on those feelings."

"Mother, I'm in love with her. I can't think of anything else."

"Does she love you?" asked Jane.

"I—well, I'm not sure about that. But I hope she does."

Jane Carlin slowly nodded, a bit reluctantly at first, and then she raised her chin and looked her son in the eyes. She smiled.

Tommy knew his mother had known real love, so he glowed with happiness.

Jane Parsons had married Joseph Carlin when they were very young, she fifteen and he seventeen. They were both from farming families in Hinkapee that jointly gave the couple a small farm to work. After several years of farming and several vicious Indian raids, in one of which the family barely escaped death by Joseph hiding in a pile of hay, with Jane and infant Tommy hidden in the cellar below, Joseph needed little urging to relocate to North Hinkapee when Thompson Downing approached him with a generous offer of land—plus, of even greater interest, the absence of conflict with the Indians. Since at that time North Hinkapee really needed settlers, there was no talk of working the land under a lease. Thompson just gave him the farm.

So the Carlins sold their farm in Hinkapee and moved to North Hinkapee. With the proceeds from the former farm plus the free farm in North Hinkapee, the Carlins prospered and had three more children. Unfortunately, two passed in infancy and a third died at age three. Tommy, as an only child, was tenderly loved and nurtured.

One day Joseph, working on the roof, fell and broke his leg. Despite Dr. Alderson's costly ministrations, a slow infection settled in and Joseph died that winter, leaving Jane alone with her then-twelve-year-old Tommy, who became the "man of the house" and did all he could to rise to the occasion.

At first, Jane hired outside help for the planting and the harvest, and to take the harvest to market, but when Tommy was fourteen, he was running the farm himself, and, like many a young man in those times, he moved into adulthood very young.

Jane was an attractive widow and did not lack for suitors. But she turned them all away. No one could replace Joseph in her heart, and she was suspicious of the motives of her suitors, as she was a woman of some means, thanks to the Carlin family's hard work over the years. She was also worried about a fractious interaction between her son and a new husband.

Although mostly her existence after the passing of her husband was uneventful and peaceful, albeit saddened, she had been spared one particularly dangerous circumstance, different versions of which had filtered through from gossip to legend over time.

(ALMOST)
A WITCH'S TALE IN
NORTH HINKAPEE

A certain Christopher Smith liked the frontier nature of the town of North Hinkapee, which largely allowed him to do as he pleased. He roomed at the Towne Tavern when the weather was inclement, and otherwise slept in the woods in a makeshift shelter, by arrangement with the Downings. He traded and prospered in his rough way.

When Joseph Carlin passed away, Smith concluded that the widow Jane would be a perfect match for him. Her young son Tommy wouldn't be much trouble, and he could work the farm, which was free and clear. The economics were perfect. So Chris Smith went a-courting.

"He was unwashed, unkempt, uncouth, and foul of mouth and temperament," said Jane Carlin, on the rare occasions she would discuss the matter. "And those were his *good* points." She turned him down flat.

Smith went to Minister Brown to ask his advice, and he got right to the point: "Minister Brown, I know you know about these things. I have my eye on Mrs. Carlin. She would be a good wife for me. She's fine to look at and has a good farm to boot. She'd be a great match for a man like me."

"And what would you have me do?" asked Minister Brown, who had had his own eye on Mrs. Carlin. The economics of her situation were quite excellent and he agreed that, despite being in her mid-thirties, she was indeed still fine to look at.

"I don't know what you could do," answered Smith. "But don't you know how to handle these things, you being the Minister and all?" And then he blurted out, "You might support me in wondering if she's a witch. Maybe that would convince her to be with me as a better choice, if you know what I mean?"

Minister Brown winced. One just didn't just say things like this out loud, so obviously. It was so easy to set Smith up, so he said, "I can't of course say I could support anything like this, but if I were you and I were going to do something like this, I would let the cat out of the bag at the Towne Tavern and let nature take its course thereafter."

Smith nodded eagerly. "I will do that," he said, and he indeed did exactly that and with great embellishment and lack of tact.

"The first time I came to court her, she was getting off a pole she'd been flying on," he said to his "friends" at the Tavern.

"Second time, I saw her in the woods chanting and singing with a bunch of others."

"And the third time she waved her hands to the barn, and her two cows just kind of walked out together, like they were bewitched."

"No wonder she turned me down," he said, pretending to be disconsolate about it.

Smith was talking to his friends but made no attempt to lower his voice, and he was overheard by Handel Lewis.

Handel was an enormous man, probably over 250 pounds. His daily work as a blacksmith involved pounding steel sometimes for ten hours a day. He was completely muscled and a scary sight, his bald head adding to his aura of power.

That very night, Chris Smith was awakened from his woodsy bivouac by a rustling in the bushes. It was none other than Handel Lewis coming to visit.

"Hello," said Smith, in wonderment, after he realized that Handel was not an Indian nor a preying animal. "Handel, what are you doing here?"

"It's time for you to leave," said Handel quietly.

"Leave where?" asked Smith.

"Leave North Hinkapee."

"What do you mean? I live here."

Handel was not a conversationalist, and their meeting in the middle of the night was short and with few words, but right to the point. Essentially, Handel made it clear to Chris Smith that if he was seen again in North Hinkapee, Handel would snap him like a twig.

Handel might have given Chris a slight example of what would happen, just to encourage his departure, but since no one else was at the meeting, no one knew that for sure. But it was certain that Chris Smith was never seen again in North Hinkapee.

At this point, Minister Brown determined that launching his personal plan for Jane Carlin might not be the best idea after all, so no one actually ever knew about that part of the story.

Handel only told his closest friends Robin Stone and Perkin Massey about his late-night meeting with Chris Smith and his liking for Jane Carlin, but he politely asked them to keep it confidential. They were almost extraordinarily poor choices as confidants and, accordingly, there were few in the town who didn't know at least the outlines of the story. And there were even fewer who weren't aware that Handel Lewis had a fancy for Jane Carlin.

And yes, Jane Carlin herself had heard the tale and was well aware of Handel's infatuation with her. But that was where things were left.

TOMMY PINES
FOR FAYTHE

Tommy had risen to the occasion of being the man of his mother's farm, a respectable young man, and a good-looking one, too. Working hard from such a young age had given him a lot of muscles, and the young women in the town invariably found him irresistible and flirted with him constantly. Tommy, however, was quite shy, and his response to female flirtations usually was to look away and smile awkwardly.

But Faythe didn't flirt. She was just herself, and that drew him in more than did all the giggles and flouncing of the other young women. He was smitten, and he wanted his mother to approve. Tommy loved Jane and respected her as well. After all, she had kept things together after his father had passed, which was not easy for a woman on her own.

Jane had told Tommy that nothing in life could replace the feeling of wedded love such as she had known with Joseph Carlin, and she wanted that for her son. Her blessing meant a lot to him. He stood up and gave her a short and somewhat embarrassed hug.

Now if only Faythe would cooperate just a bit, thought Tommy. Maybe he could try again at the midsummer party coming up.

DINNER AND A BLACK CLOUD AT THE JONESES'

Not far from the Carlin farm that beautiful evening, Sheriff John Jones came in for dinner with his beloved wife, Betsy. He was pleased with the state of the town, for there were no real difficulties right now. The one cell in the small jail was empty and had been for some time. There was no sign of Indian trouble in North Hinkapee, nor in the surrounding towns. Perhaps the beautiful weather and strongly growing crops were encouraging everyone to keep peace with their neighbors. There was actually little for a sheriff to do but enjoy his little homestead and his sweet wife.

Betsy Jones caught her husband studying her.

"What is it, my dear?" he asked. "You seem preoccupied."

"Not at all," she said, giving him a wan smile. "I'm just a bit weary."

"It's something. I know when aught is bothering you."

She sighed. "Sometimes I wish I had a house full of children. That's all."

He nodded. "I know. God has not so blessed us. At least not yet."

"But we have each other," she said, rising and going to stand behind his chair with her hands on his shoulders. "That's more than most people have."

Sheriff Jones let his mind wander back to his past and how they had come to where they were now.

John Jones had come to North Hinkapee at the invitation of Thompson Downing back in 1677, after the Sagawanee attack that Jones had resolved would be his last. Thompson Downing, like Jones, had desired an end to the brutality on both sides, and he'd had an idea, which was simple yet daring; namely, he would create a separate peace with the warlike Sagawanee Indians. A peace would permit both Whites and Indians to prosper and build, perhaps not as friends, but at least not as enemies.

But to build his town, Thompson Downing needed a sheriff to help establish it and give credence to the idea of peace and order.

Thompson Downing had been in his grave now for over a decade. Much of his vision had been realized and somehow most of what he had envisioned was now an incredible reality. North Hinkapee was not yet legally a separate municipality; however, it effectively functioned as one—out on the far frontiers of the colony of Massachusetts Bay.

Now Miles Downing was the titular head of the Downing family, but Betsy had intuited quickly that it was really Martha Downing who set the pace and was secretly in charge.

Sheriff Jones had made clear when Thompson came-a-courting, as he thought of it, that the law had to be a hundred percent respected and, accordingly, that no quarter would be given the Downings for any legal transgressions, and that no matter how much the Downings ran the town, the sheriff's office would not bend to them.

"Sounds like we have a deal, then," Thompson Downing had said to Sheriff Jones those many years ago, putting out his hand.

"We do indeed," Jones had replied, shaking the hand of a man he knew would keep his word.

And this pact had endured now for many years.

It was especially noteworthy that the pact applied with equal vigor to Matt and Pat Downing. Indeed, Sheriff Jones went out of his way to spare no punishment of either of the two when they were out of line.

At first Sheriff Jones had been surprised at the way Miles and Martha handled these situations. He had assumed that it would be the father who would be pushing for stronger punishments and the mother who would shrink back, but instead it was the other way around. Martha realized that her boys running rampant would not be good for the Downings in the long run, and could eventually result in the township resenting the Downings' governance. So she hoped that perhaps the sheriff could tame her boys; from her perspective, the stronger the consequences to their misbehavior, the better.

Along these lines, Martha was wise enough to know how important it was to the Downings' control of the township that law and order had to be respected in the town of North Hinkapee. Indeed, that was a powerfully important factor holding the town together.

So, while most would expect the Downings to be above the law—as they were above everyone else in other respects—The Law, in the form of Sheriff Jones, was the only thing that was above the Downings. That was a relief to everyone.

Although it was unfair to some of the other very honorable townspeople, Sheriff Jones had earned the nickname of "The Only Honest Man in North Hinkapee."

Sheriff Jones gazed up at his wonderful Betsy standing behind him. *I would do anything to give her a child—perhaps God will bless us in this*

manner someday. He crossed his arms to place his hands atop hers on his shoulders, then he stood and turned to face her full on, uncrossing his own hands to keep hold of hers. She looked back at him.

"Maybe we can work on it later," they both said in unison, and they laughed, she stepping closer to nuzzle his neck.

Although Betsy Jones knew their neighbors in other households were also enjoying the fragrant breezes stirring that night, at peace among themselves, Betsy felt the dark cloud coming to North Hinkapee. She felt it strongly, and she suspected that she was the only one who did. Trouble was coming. She wished she could do something about it, but if she tried—even if she knew what to do—it would only make people suspect she was a witch.

Am I? she wondered idly.

A FARMER
BUYS HIS FARM

In those balmy summer days, the people of North Hinkapee were reveling in their promising harvest. The spring onions and greens from the root crops, berries, and cherries cheered everyone with their abundance, and the young flocks and herds flourished. Carts and wagons filled with excess produce would soon head off to Briarcliff and beyond to be sold in the markets, and the young men were eager to man their families' wagons and thereby have an adventure beyond their sleepy town.

The Wentworths' neighbor Brian Harris and his family had even more to celebrate than the promising early harvest, for he was about to finish all his payments to the Downings and own his farm outright. Peter Landon had paid off his farm next to the Harrises two years before, providing an encouraging example to the Harrises and Wentworths. Landon, now a relatively successful farmer in his own right, had thrown a party to celebrate the occasion. Full of triumph with his own ownership, Brian Harris had determined to do the same and thereby establish a tradition. He would make that final payment in the morning and have the party in the afternoon. The Harrises had invited the Wentworths and the Landons and a few other families. Robert Wentworth had only one year left on his own contract.

The mid-June day dawned with mist and a hint of rain, but it turned fine and then quite warm by late morning. Brian Harris got on his horse and rode to the Downing farm, his pockets stuffed with money. He arrived and asked for Miles as he tied up his horse.

"Out by the stable," a stable boy told him, and Brian walked over.

Miles was just coming out and grinned when he saw Brian. "Do you have something for me?"

"I do indeed," said Brian, with a corresponding grin.

"Well, come on in the house, then," Miles said, and the two men went inside to conclude their transaction.

There was some solemnity in the office where Miles's lawyer, Earl Carver, was having a snifter of brandy. Brian had met the sandy-haired, dark-eyed Carver five years before when he had signed the lease. The lawyer stood up to shake hands with Brian. "I see that congratulations are in order," he said.

"Indeed," said Brian, who liked that word and used it a lot.

Miles invited them both to sit with him at a fancy carved wooden table. Indeed, the opulence of the whole house was a great contrast with the simplicity and roughness of the rest of North Hinkapee. Brian was intimidated in spite of his determination to be a man of means himself someday, with that beginning today.

Earl began the conversation. "So, to conclude this business, what we need to do is have you make your final payment and we will tear up the lease. Is everyone in agreement on that?"

"Don't you need to also give me a deed to the farm?" asked Brian.

"Oh, of course, yes," said Earl. "Sorry, I forgot about that." He chuckled. "So, let's sign up the papers."

Earl brought out the Downings' copy of the lease and placed it on the table, and Brian had his copy, which he also placed on the table. Earl also placed a deed on the table. And Brian placed there the final payment in cash.

Earl continued. "Let me go over what is going on here. We will each write 'cancelled' on the lease, which means the lease is over. Miles will take the money and sign up the deed, which means the farm is yours, Brian." He looked up from where his head was bent over the papers, peering at Brian to be sure he understood the importance of the moment.

"Also, as per the lease, the Downing family will retain the right to hunt on the farm for the next seven years. Also, as agreed, the deed has an agreement called a 'reverter' in it that says that if you don't make your Village Payments or you don't comply with duly ordered Village Rules, the farm will revert to Downing. This lasts for three years."

"Come again?" said Brian, flushing. "I thought the farm's mine outright. What do you mean they can hunt on my land or he can get the farm back if I don't do what I am told?"

"That's what it says in the lease," said Earl. "Right here," and he pointed to the language.

Brian, who like many, couldn't read very well, said, "I didn't know anything about that. You didn't say anything about that when we signed the lease."

Earl looked exasperated and shrugged. "I don't remember that far back, but that's why people sign things up, so that no one can later try to change the deal. And that's what it says here, I assure you. Now, do you want to conclude this transaction or not?"

Brian looked at Miles, who stared back impassively, without speaking.

Miles Downing's stomach was burning with acid, but he kept staring at Brian Harris, holding his expression as quiet as he could, as his father had long ago instructed him to do in times of stress. Miles was decidedly unhappy. Brian Harris could never, from this moment, be his friend, and in fact, he would probably hate him.

Martha had insisted that, since these provisions were in the original lease form, outlined by Thompson Downing years ago, that Miles put these provisions in the deed and warned him not to drop them if Brian objected. So Miles kept his mouth shut, even though he felt like a churl. He also felt terribly lonely.

"This is needlessly unfriendly," Miles had said to Martha a bit pleadingly when he'd seen the provisions.

But Martha had responded firmly. "Everyone has to know who is boss. Your father, God rest his soul, was clear about that, in both word and deed. This set of provisions is a simple and minor way of making your authority crystal clear."

Miles sighed. Martha always got her way when they argued, especially if she played the Thompson-as-the-brilliant-patriarch-and-visionary card, and this had been one of those times. This felt wrong to him, but he had reluctantly made his peace long ago with the fact that his own instincts, although good at heart, would eventually be the undoing of the Downings' hegemony.

Miles sighed, as Brian reluctantly signed the document and struggled to copy the word "cancelled" across his lease. Then Miles signed and took up the money, and Brian took his copy of the cancelled lease and the deed.

Miles offered his hand. Brian had a tight-lipped momentary hesitation, then shook Miles's hand and left without another word.

After Brian was gone, Earl studied him. "Miles," he said, "why did you do that? You don't hunt much and you don't even care about hunting on his land in the first place. If you take his farm back over his not making the Village Payments, then you'll have trouble finding any other men to make a deal to farm your un-cleared land in the future. Why cause bad blood for nothing?"

Miles said woodenly, and a bit sadly, "It's important for him to know who is in charge here." He could hardly admit the real reason—that his wife had put him up to it. He remembered Thompson telling him many times, including on his deathbed, that when he was in doubt, Miles should follow Martha's advice even if it felt wrong to him. He told himself that in doing what his wife said, he was really following his cherished father's unerringly intelligent thinking.

FARM PARTY

Brian rode back home, seething at first, but after about a mile he started to feel a lot better as he thought about things. He knew that Miles Downing was the boss, so that was hardly a revelation. And now he owned his own farm. So what if one of the Downings shot a deer now and then on his land? It really didn't matter that much, did it? And obviously he was going to make the Village Payments anyway. In fact, there was no reason to mention any of this to his wife, or to anyone else, for that matter. There was a party waiting and it was time to celebrate his freedom.

The Wentworths arrived early with offerings for the party, setting down two dried-fruit pies to join some berry pies and all manner of food from the leftover winter stores and from the early harvest, with chickens, ducks, and whatever fish and small game had been taken in the past day or so. Chester Walker would bring his flute and Peter Landon his lyre, and there would be some music and cheerful but orderly dancing. It would be a great time. Faythe kept looking around for Tommy. She was starting to realize how difficult it was going to be to be in love and not have thoughts of marriage to make sense of it all.

And Tommy seemed to be pretty eager, too, because he was almost rough in his haste helping Jane off the horse, and he kept looking over his shoulder toward Faythe. Jane tapped his shoulder in blessing to release him to his yearning, then watched with bemusement—as did Lucy—as Tommy made a beeline for Faythe.

As the mothers greeted one another, Faythe worried about their conversation. Likely their smiles were their blessings on what was possibly to come between their respective children.

"How about we take a walk?" asked Tommy, instinctively slipping his sweaty hand into hers, then withdrawing it as perhaps too hasty. "I've much to tell you," he added in a low, serious voice.

"All right," said Faythe. Tommy seemed to have more confidence than when he'd left that barn, bewildered, after their kisses. But Faythe found herself liking this wooing personality.

"Chloe," Faythe said to her sister, always her shadow, "how about you help Mum with the pies? They need cutting, I think." Chloe scampered off and Faythe smiled brightly at Tommy. Now they could be alone.

As they walked away from the party and into the woods, Tommy announced, "I'm pleased to say that I have my mother's blessing."

"Blessing on what?" asked Faythe.

"Well, blessing on—well, you know what I mean."

"Blessing on what?" said Faythe again, although she suspected easily enough. "Please let me know what you are blessed with?"

"Well, then … I have my mother's blessing to … well … to court you formally."

"And what makes you think that I want you to court me?" said Faythe, daring to pull off her cap and let her black hair cascade over her shoulders.

Tommy gulped. "I … I … thought. Well, you kissed me, and I thought …"

"Just because I kissed you doesn't mean I want to marry you," said Faythe. But at the crushed look on his face, she was ashamed. She didn't want to hurt his feelings.

"Tommy," she said, "I like you. I like you a lot. But to be honest, I'm not sure I want to marry anyone … ever …"

Tommy stammered: "I-I … d-don't understand."

"Please don't be vexed with me," Faythe said, "but I can't say I want you—or anyone—to court me right now."

Tommy looked even more stricken, so Faythe added, "But I can tell you I want you to kiss me again … if you want."

Poor Tommy. His confidence had drained away like water out of a bucket with a leak in it. He was obviously confused, standing there looking around him, rubbing his hands over his thighs. He just didn't know which end was up.

"Stop thinking so much, Tommy," said Faythe. "Just kiss me."

Tommy obeyed and once again they found themselves caught in the flow of their mutual desire, even stronger than last time. Faythe explored his mouth with her tongue, offering a thrust and receiving his, sharing the taste of the strawberries. She clasped him to herself and pressed her breasts against him, rubbing a little against his erection. At first he pulled away, embarrassed, but then he followed her example of boldness and pressed harder against her, his tongue playing in her mouth and filling it.

Faythe was blessed, for the present, with not having confusion ruin her enjoyment. Instead of wondering if this were love or something different, she was experiencing new waves of passion she had not felt with him before in the barn. She longed for Tommy to put his hand inside her bodice and even "down there," but that was a bit too much, even for Faythe. So she contented herself with the thrills of the moment.

After a while their embrace ended, Tommy's visible excitement calmed, and they walked back to the party, not speaking, each with their own thoughts.

Everyone noticed that Tommy and Faythe were together, although no one spoke to them of it, giving the young people their privacy.

"How does it feel?" Peter Landon asked Brian as he joined him and Chester and Robert, the two farmers who would be the next to be free of the Downings. Each man sat on a stump with a plate full of food.

"It feels a blessing," said Brian. "A great weight has fallen from my shoulders. I'm feeling free for the first time in my life." He conveniently forgot the codicils in his agreement with Downing; the annoyance and embarrassment were rapidly fading away.

Robert extended his hand as if sharing a blessing himself and said, "I'm heartily happy for you, my friend." Peter and Chester said the same and raised their ale cups to their host.

As he finished his food, Brian set aside his plate and cup and picked up his lute and said, "Well, men, how about some music?" Soon Chester and Peter were playing their flutes, and the guests set aside their plates and formed up in lines for the dance. The young ones ran around and played, and though Chloe was wanted in the dance with the adults, she ran around in circles with her arms outstretched like wings, as if she could fly …

INTERLUDE

NUNUNYI AND MENON

Gilbert Menon had grown into a quiet, satisfied householder tucked away in the woods with his beloved Nununyi. For a decade, he and Nununyi had enjoyed their union of two cultures, and the seclusion of their home enabled that. Menon had occasional excursions for hunting and trapping on the northern rivers, and Nununyi learned the White Men's cookery and housekeeping to which she brought the wisdom of her own people. She, too, sometimes slipped away for days, restless to wield her bow, and inevitably returned with game of all types, ranging from small rabbits to antlered or bushy-tailed deer.

Gilbert Menon was the happiest he had ever been in his life. Love had changed him from a mercenary fighter, and he knew it was a gift from God that Nununyi had favored him.

Nununyi was a creature of pure physical poetry in her oneness with her bow and arrows. They were not possessions for her, but an extension of her being. Menon was a practical man, not given to aesthetics, but watching her shoot an arrow with such incredible power and precision brought actual tears to his eyes, especially as he experienced her joy.

Most days he would wake up wondering why God had given him such a gift. *I surely don't deserve her,* he would think.

After climbing into Menon's bed that day many years before, Nununyi had come to enjoy basking in the warmth of Menon's adulation. At first she tolerated him, and then she grew to like him. Before she understood her own feelings, she was seduced by his deep affection, and in the end she loved him dearly. This sinewy bear of a man, who fattened each fall and grew lean each spring, she knew had been a dangerous warrior, but he was tender to her. His twinkling blue eyes and rosy cheeks captured her imagination—he was a being of another sort from her, yet with deep longings and affection, too.

The one thing that bothered Nununyi was that she really didn't have a plan for what to do if Menon left her. She was dependent on him and fearful about this. And fear was an emotion she truly hated. *Warriors are not fearful. Is it fear I have no plan or is it fear I will have lost my love?* She thought of Katakuk fairly often, wondering about what might have been. But the thoughts turned from a sharp pain, at first, to more of a far off feeling like one has for a loved one long since passed away. Sometimes she wondered whether someday she might return to her people—like her time with Menon was temporary, after all.

But so far none of this had mattered, as Menon was as devoted to Nununyi as she was to her bow and arrows, and Katakuk and the Sagawanee Indians were far away.

In the end, their unusual beginning, fighting on opposite sides of a brutal war, had given birth to soulmates. It made no sense, and thus it made perfect sense. They were like a wolf come upon a wild dog that was part of a chasing pack yet somehow bonding together to hunt, and in the end contrary to nature they became dear companions.

Menon put his arm around his half-sleeping mate, who snuggled contentedly against him.

All was right with the world.

1692, NORTH HINKAPEE

THE DARK CLOUD
DESCENDS

Matt Downing woke that morning with an erection so strong it actually hurt. He could scarcely control himself. Throughout the day he could think of nothing else but going to the blind to look out and see Chloe and then do, well, do whatever happened.

Pat watched his brother anxiously. Something bad was going to happen that day for sure. He considered one last time speaking to his father or his mother, but he rejected the thought for the same reasons as before.

By midafternoon all the work and chores were done, so Matt left. He took Pat along, of course. Pat tried to resist his brother but, as always, he went along in the end.

They got to the blind and sat down.

"Maybe they just won't show up," Pat suggested in a whisper, but even as he spoke, Matt clamped his hand down on his brother's arm and pointed. Instead of settling where the brothers could see them in a nearby clearing, the girls were walking further down the trail, away from the blind. Matt couldn't hear their conversation anymore but could see glimpses of their clothing through the trees.

"Come on," he said. "Let's go."

"Where?"

"Hunting," said Matt, and he climbed quietly out of the blind and crept along the trail, crouched over, knowing Pat would follow.

"What would it be like if you married Tommy?" Chloe asked, braiding some long grass together with clover in a garland as she leaned against a tree.

"I don't know," said Faythe, "but I bet it would be like with Mum and Dad. We would be happy every day, and you would be with us always. You would be like our daughter, and you would have two sets of parents, and his mum, too."

Chloe smiled at the thought. "That would be nice," she said. "I like Mistress Jane."

Faythe shook herself out of Chloe's fantasy. *I can't build up her hopes like that!* "But, Chloe," said Faythe, "don't tell anyone, but I'm not marrying anyone … ever … I don't want to get married at all."

At the sight of Chloe's changed expression, her eyes filling with tears, Faythe quickly added, "So we can always be together!"

Chloe looked at her wide-eyed. "Really? Just like this?" She hugged herself and twirled, and Faythe mirrored Chloe's smile and wrapped her arms around her.

"How about a game of Rescue?" Faythe asked suddenly, not knowing why she suggested it. They hadn't played that in quite some time.

"Sure!" said Chloe, always up for games that brought her back to her earlier childhood. "We need a story, though," she said, and Faythe knew her next move in the game.

"Well, that's easy," said Faythe. "You are carried off into the forest by Indians. They want to take you to live with them. But you want to stay with me and Mum and Dad. I will be tracking you and you will leave behind little pieces of your fairy rope"—she nodded at the garland Chloe had draped around her neck—"so I know where you have gone. Now be off."

Chloe scurried off the way they had come on the trail.

Pat was watching it all unfold slowly in just moments. Chloe was coming right toward them and she was all alone. Her strong sister was quite far off.

He couldn't believe that this was about to happen. Matt, beside him, was actually trembling with anticipation. How many times had they spied on women bathing at a stream, Matt growling to Pat what he'd do if he got hold of one of them? And the time he'd groped Mistress Barker—Mother and Father had had a terrible time getting the sheriff to back down after the woman's complaint—Earl Carver had had to get involved.

And now they were alone in the woods with a girl right there that Matt had been slobbering over—telling his brother all kinds of plans he had for her body, until Pat himself grew hard in spite of himself and squirmed at the vivid sensations Matt conjured up in his mind.

I have to do something!

Pat almost shouted out a warning to Chloe to run, but no words came. It was perverse. He was helpless, and he did not know why. His spirit died within him.

Just as Chloe trotted by, Matt leaped up out of the brush, tackled her, and clamped a strong hand over her mouth before the girl could scream. He dragged her into the thicket where Pat was crouched.

"Come on, stuff the cloth in her mouth!" Matt commanded.

Pat did as he was told.

"Now hold her arms." Again, Pat did as he was told, as if his limbs moved of their own accord.

Chloe was thrashing but she was no match for the two boys. Matt slapped her across the face, and when she still thrashed around, he punched her pretty hard on the side of the head, stunning her somewhat and leaving a huge red mark. That mark would no doubt become a bruise and mar her sweet face, Pat thought with regret. Then, as Pat watched, stunned himself at the spectacle, Matt ripped off the girl's draping white collar, then dug into her bodice and then her shift, pulling them off her shoulders and the arms Pat released, until Matt had uncovered all her upper body.

As Chloe lay there, now paralyzed and silent with fear and shame in her nakedness, Pat and Matt saw her body revealed to them. Those young breasts were now bared and as beautiful as Matt had imagined. The breasts were big and round, with large pink nipples. Surely no man had ever seen this beauty before the brothers did. It was all Matt's dream, but it had become Pat's as well.

Pat was mesmerized, watching as his brother grabbed each breast and squeezed it. Matt was certainly the first to touch them, and as he did, Chloe began thrashing and fighting again.

"Hold her down!" Matt commanded through gritted teeth, and Pat mechanically took those slender arms in his hands again and pinned them above her head on the ground. Matt straddled her, squeezing her legs between his knees, and jerked her skirts up around her waist as she twisted back and forth. She wore nothing underneath! Her beautiful white buttocks gleamed up at the brothers as she turned on her side to escape, and then as she twisted he got a glimpse of the golden thatch of hair at the front. To think that she had flitted up and down those trails, scampered around town, even gone to meeting with nothing covering her privates!

Matt pushed her hips flat against the ground and both brothers stared at that golden glory—they were blond themselves, but not down below!

With her knees more firmly pinned between his, and her arms held by Pat, Matt opened his breeches, revealing his enormous red erection. He put one knee between hers while holding her legs with his hands and spread her legs apart, more fully revealing what was hidden there. Pat was fully stiff himself at the spectacle—*Is this really happening?*

After just staring for a moment, Matt braced himself over her body and tried to enter her, but it didn't work. Chloe was fighting and rolling around harder, using every bit of her strength to close her legs. Matt used his fingers to figure out the way inside, grumbling, "Damned virgin," and Chloe moaned loudly at the pain. He slapped her in the face again, harder than before.

"Shut up!" he growled. "Make another sound and I will snap your neck, you little tramp."

Chloe began to lose strength, her face going slack.

Is she fainting? Pat wondered. If so, that might make things easier. He was deep-down ashamed to be thinking of it, but then he realized it was indeed better that way.

Matt was fumbling with frustration, on the brink of achieving his goal but hindered by the resistance he found between her legs. Finally, he spat on his hand and rubbed it on himself, then spat again and rubbed it on her.

This time his hard cock went right in after popping past the obstruction. Chloe revived a little at that and screamed behind the cloth stuffed into her mouth, and Pat clamped his hand over it for good measure, looking around wildly to see if Faythe had come near.

In a matter of seconds, with a few thrusts, Matt gave a high-pitched sigh and collapsed over the girl's body, then rolled away panting, his cock wet and shrinking.

Chloe lay still.

What had he done? What had Matt done? What had Pat done? Pat's heart hammered in his chest while his erection still strained against his breeches.

"Now it's your turn," Matt said.

Pat shook his head. "No," he whispered.

Matt looked at him and laughed. "You say no, but your manhood says yes. Don't be a weakling. Be a man and do what you want to do."

When Pat still hesitated, Matt added, "If you think you might not get in trouble with the law over this, you're wrong. You've already done as much here as I have—as if you'd had her, too. It's already done."

Matt pointed at Chloe's closed eyes—she had passed out. "She'll never even know," he said. "Go for it!"

Pat let go of Chloe's limp arms and switched places with Matt. In just a few seconds he'd relieved his urgent desire. Then he, too, rolled away, and he couldn't even remember if it felt good or not. He just did it. And then the nausea began to grow in him. *What have I done?*

Matt had gotten to his knees again and put himself between the girl's legs.

"No!" said Pat. "That's enough—we've got to get out of here!"

"Yeah," said Matt, "but maybe one more time ..."

"No," hissed Pat. "We'll get caught. You got what you wanted. Let's go."

Just then they heard Faythe calling to her sister. "Chloe, I'm giving up! Where *are* you?"

Her call brought Matt to his senses, and for once he listened to his brother. "Let's get her covered up first," Matt said, pulling down her skirts. Pat put her arms at her sides and then through the armholes of her shift, then he tried to arrange her bodice and drape the collar over her shoulders again.

With another call from Faythe, the brothers looked at each other and sneaked away, further into the woods, leaving Chloe lying there rumpled and quiet.

Faythe was getting quite concerned. It had never taken this long to find her sister. Then, out of the corner of her eye she saw movement deep in the woods. She looked more closely, then ran toward it. After a moment she caught sight of Matt and Pat. She called out, "What're you boys doing here?"

Matt kept going like he hadn't heard, but Pat turned back and looked at her. Their eyes met for a second. And in that second Faythe knew everything. Pat dropped his gaze and ran after his brother.

Faythe immediately whirled around and went back to where the boys had come from. "Chloe," she whispered and then called out louder. "Chloe, where are you?" She was crying at this point, terrified of what she would discover. "Chloe, darling, where are you hiding?"

At last she heard something like a muffled whimpering and discovered her sister lying where the boys had left her. She knelt down. "Chloe, sweet girl. Chloe, it's Faythe. Are you well? Are you hurt?"

But Chloe couldn't speak. She couldn't say a word. She didn't even seem to know her sister was there. Her mind had left the world.

Faythe was about to weep over her sister and just sit there crying out her grief, but quickly she concluded that there was no time to waste—weeping could wait till later. She sat Chloe up, then bent and picked up her sister, which was no easy task. Even though Chloe was only twelve and Faythe seventeen, and though Faythe was used to carrying heavy loads, she struggled with Chloe's limp body.

Faythe carried Chloe all the way home, without stopping, although her muscles ached and screamed with pain. She noticed that she was not crying. She felt like she was another person watching herself as she carried her sister out of the forest to their home.

She reached the house at last. "Mother!" she cried out. "Mum, come quickly! It's Chloe!"

THE PLAN

Lucy knew the instant she heard the call that something terrible had happened. Every mother knows—and dreads—the sound of a voice calling that something has happened to a beloved child. Her heart broke immediately, and then she stepped outside to see Faythe coming up the path to the house, holding Chloe's broken body in her arms.

Faythe carried Chloe into the house and laid her on the bed the girls shared. Lucy set about feeling for Chloe's heartbeat, covering her cool limbs with a blanket, and determining she was just in a swoon and could be left a few minutes, perhaps to recover.

"Those boys, they ..." Faythe could not continue, but Lucy didn't need her to say any more—it was all so obvious.

Faythe's account of the last hour came tumbling out, and it did not take much examination for mother and sister to verify what had happened. Chloe had marks on her face where she had been hit. And her womanhood was torn and bleeding, her skirts sodden down there. And still Chloe lay quiet, beyond them. Both Faythe and Lucy knew that the Chloe they knew was gone. Blackness settled over them. The dark cloud was everywhere now.

"How could you let this happen?" asked Lucy, sinking onto the bed beside her unconscious younger daughter. But she regretted the words as soon as they left her lips. "I'm sorry, Faythe. I didn't mean that. You have done everything for this girl. No one could have cared for her better than you. This was the work of the Devil himself."

Lucy's comforting words ran through Faythe, settling deeply in her heart. Faythe was indeed fully responsible. Her task in life was to look after her little sister, and she had failed at it—utterly. Her sister's life was now effectively over, and it was because of Faythe's negligence. There were no two ways about it.

"No, Mum, you're right. I'm to blame. I never should have let her out of my sight, knowing those boys might be around."

"How could you have known they would be about?" asked Lucy.

Faythe related what had happened some weeks before when the boys had burst out and surprised them. "I *did* know that they might be there. I don't know what I was thinking, playing that foolish rescue game with that threat about. It was like my thinking was clouded."

"Oh, Faythe," said Lucy, "don't go down the road of musing that this is to be laid at your door. It is not. It was those … those … horrible, awful boys who did this. No one else should feel the guilt … . She choked back a sob. "I-I cannot lose you, too." She reached out for Faythe, pulling her down to sit in her lap, and despite Faythe being full grown, it felt right.

Faythe nodded, limp in her mother's embrace, completely miserable and sickened to her core. "What do we do now?" she asked. She assumed Lucy would say, "We find your dad and bring him in from the fields to take some action," presumably with the sheriff.

Lucy held Faythe at arms' length, looked at her, and took a deep breath. "We bathe Chloe, cleanse her of this filth. We fashion a story that we both can set to memory. We tell your dad this story. We summon the doctor and hope he believes the story when he sees her. And then we do nothing at all."

"What?" exclaimed Faythe. "We do nothing? We just let them escape this?" Her eyes blazed. She stood up, furious, and began pacing through the room.

"Very well, then," said Lucy calmly, wiping away a tear. "Let's consider it differently. What do you think we should do?"

"Well, first we tell Dad what happened. Then we get the sheriff and have those boys arrested." But Faythe's mind was going to where Lucy's must have already gone, and a sickening sadness came over her. "That will not do, will it?" she asked, looking at her mother.

Lucy shook her head. "If we tell your dad, he'll not be able to restrain himself. He'll confront the Downings. One way or another it will go badly for us; indeed, they might even kill your father. Not to mention—our lease likely has something in it that allows the Downings to take this farm if they please. Horrible as it is, we will do best to conceal this from everyone … and hope that Chloe recovers. I'm so sorry, my dear daughter." She closed her eyes.

Two thoughts came to Faythe at once. First, it was clear that her mother was right. There was no other immediate plan that made any sense. And second, there was no chance that she would just let things lie—there was simply no way those boys would get away with what they had done. She would make them pay for this crime if it took a hundred years.

"So, what will the story be?" asked Faythe, with her mind made up.

"You agree?" asked Lucy.

Faythe nodded slowly. "We do need a story," she said, thinking with terrible sadness that the last story she had told would probably be the last story she would ever tell Chloe.

"How about we say that she fell running in the woods?" suggested Lucy.

"Is that to be believed?" Faythe asked. "She runs in the woods all the time and falls all the time. She doesn't look like that after she falls.

"How about she fell off the horse?" suggested Lucy.

"And the horse kicked her in the head after she fell—a slight kick," added Faythe.

Lucy nodded. "Please take the … the … horse and get the doctor. I'll see to Chloe, so she is ready." Faythe nodded in understanding and left the little house to fetch Dr. Alderson, likely at home sipping whatever it was he sipped in the early evening.

THE DOCTOR VISITS

Doctor Philip Alderson arrived with Faythe an hour later and dis-covered Robert Wentworth pacing and agitated, looking like he had been shot with a musket and simultaneously stabbed through the heart. He was a shaken man and a broken man as well. Before he even greeted the doctor, he gave Faythe a crushing embrace, though his arms trembled. But the girl was dry-eyed.

The doctor examined the girl on the bed and found the marks on her head didn't seem to have been made by a horse. He was sus-picious of Faythe's story, which her mother reinforced. But Robert Wentworth himself wasn't telling that story, just allowing his wom-en to do so. *Suspicious.* What were the women lying about?

As he ran his hands over the limp body, he found scratches and the marks of fingers on the breasts, and that led him to examine her more thoroughly. As he suspected, he found the girl had been raped—and brutally so, her genitalia swelling and bleeding, though she'd clearly been bathed. *What a shame*, he thought. *Such a pretty and sweet thing. Who could have done this?*

And then he knew.

He looked up and met the mother's tortured expression, her eyes red-rimmed and haunted.

The girl just lay there on the bed, her eyes now open but with a vacant expression, staring at nothing. Her soul seemed to have fled her body.

What can be done about this? he wondered. For now, in any case, it made sense to publicly agree with the women's story. More could come later—if it must.

He concluded his examination and gestured for Lucy to go ahead of him back into the main room, where the sister and father waited for his report.

He cleared his throat. "This is not good, I'm sorry to say. Your daughter has sustained a dangerous blow to her head and—and bruises elsewhere." He cleared his throat again. "I don't know when it will heal."

Dr. Alderson reached into his bag and brought out two small bottles that he set on the table. "I'm prescribing these medicines and asking you to make sure she has a spoonful of each of these three times every day." There was no call for bleeding, though many thought it helpful. He would spare them that. Besides, the Wentworths couldn't afford that service.

He looked at the floor respectfully. "I'm sorry," he said. "I'll certainly pray for her." He shook Robert's hand and inclined his head to Faythe and to Lucy.

He left pensively, wondering when he should take his next action, the obvious action. Thinking before acting, especially thinking with the help of a brandy, was generally preferable to acting before thinking, so he went home.

OTHERS VISIT

Word of Chloe's "accident" started to spread through North Hinkap-ee, and everyone felt for Lucy and Robert and Faythe. The Went-worths were generally liked and respected about town, and no one had a bad word to say about Chloe. Gifts and visits poured in from gracious and sympathetic neighbors. The Harrises, the Walkers, and the Landons came—and of course the Carlins.

Chloe's condition did not change over the days. She was breath-ing and even eating and drinking a little, and following gentle com-mands to turn or sit or even stand, but she no longer engaged with anyone, not even her beloved Faythe.

Tommy shared Faythe's heartbreak, knowing how much Chloe meant to her, and of course he liked Chloe, too, for his part. He offered to fill in for Robert in the fields while Robert composed himself, and Tommy otherwise acted as a second man around the house. Robert was so crushed that he hardly remembered his man-ners enough to thank Tommy for the help.

Betsy Jones came, too. Her healing arts might be needed, so she brought jars of ointments and aromatics she gave to Chloe to smell. They had no discernible effect on Chloe, but they seemed to ease the misery that had settled upon Faythe and Lucy. Betsy also tasted a bit of Dr. Alderson's medicines and determined they would do no harm, although likely no good, either.

Ever since she had felt the dark cloud, Betsy had known she would be called upon very soon. She had suspected that the dark cloud would show itself as an Indian attack. Instead, it was the destruction of a young girl. It melted her heart to see that Chloe was the victim the dark cloud had taken. She knew immediately that Chloe had not fallen off a horse, and her intuition arrived at solid knowledge very quickly. *Oh, how very awful,* she thought.

The second morning, Miles Downing himself paid a visit to express his sympathy to his friend Robert—or would-be friend, when he fully owned his farm. Miles drove up with a wagon loaded with a crock of soup and loaves of bread from his cook, and gifts of sympathy from his wife's abundant flower garden. Martha was not with him.

"Heard the news, Robert," he said as he stood on the stoop offering his hand. "This is a terrible thing. All I could think to do is bring you a few things and hope it helps. I am here to help more if I can. A terrible thing." He shook his head sadly.

Faythe stood behind her father at the door and at first seemed to be a distraught sister thankful for neighborly comfort, but then a quick look of fury passed over her that she tried unsuccessfully to hide, and then she turned away. Miles, surprised, was taken aback.

Lucy took her place just inside the doorway, smoothing her apron and slowly lifting her head with dignity before she spoke.

"Why thank you, Mr. Downing. This is so good of you. We're all shaken and it's good to have neighbors like yourself when things go poorly."

Miles was not tough, but he was intuitive. He picked up on the awkwardness from Faythe and Lucy immediately—and wondered about the fury in Faythe's quick glance. *Something is quite wrong here*, he thought. It would have been inappropriate for him to invite himself inside to see the girl, so after some brief and even more awkward conversation, Miles went on his way—as pensively as the doctor had. He was considering paying a visit to the doctor—maybe he had some thoughts.

Meanwhile, there was no change in Chloe's condition. She was breathing and functioning somewhat, but she wasn't improving.

MILES AND MARTHA
—AND THE DOCTOR

It turned out there was no need for Miles to visit Dr. Alderson, because when he got home, Dr. Alderson was sitting on his front porch waiting for him to arrive. Martha was there with him.

"Hi, Doctor," said Miles. "It is good to see you. And to what do I owe the pleasure?" Miles was already starting to suspect what it might be, and he had a sinking feeling.

"Hi, Miles," replied Dr. Alderson. "Good to see you, too. It might be a good idea for us to go inside to speak."

Miles—his heart darkening—nodded acquiescence. The two men went inside.

Martha stood immediately to follow them, knowing that that was a conversation she should be party to. Why on earth was the doctor visiting them, and so soon after Chloe's accident? Her mind had quickly sped to the conclusion that now roiled within her bosom. She prayed she was wrong but she knew she wasn't. For some reason, her mind flickered back to that moment in the meeting house when she had intuited Matt's attraction to Chloe Wentworth and quietly kicked herself for not paying more attention to it. *Now where is this going to lead?* she wondered.

She followed them into the house and quietly took the chair Miles held for her.

Dr. Alderson got right to the point. "I went to visit the Wentworths yesterday."

Miles nodded nervously and said, "Yes, I just came from there."

"I'm not really supposed to tell you about my patients …"

Miles nodded again, and Martha as well. It was concerning but gratifying that Alderson was going to violate his obligation to confidentiality for the sake of the Downings.

"The women said Chloe fell from a horse and the horse kicked her in the head. Hence, she cannot speak and just lies there … But that's not what happened." He looked up to see if they were prepared for more. Miles looked down nervously, but Martha held the man's gaze.

"So," Dr. Alderson continued, "I'd like your promise, Miles and Martha, that what I'm going to tell you never has its source traced to me. And whatever you may do, I will not be party to it."

Miles said, after a brief glance at Martha for her confirming nod, "You have my word on it," and Martha nodded assent.

"She was raped—pardon me for my frankness, Martha," said Dr. Alderson. "And violently so. The women are lying about what happened. I spent some time wondering why they would lie about something like that and, well … I thought you might be thinking along the lines I am …"

Miles looked stricken, and Martha felt herself go white at the reality of it.

"Before you say anything," he continued, "our confidentiality includes my own. I will not reveal this to anyone else."

Miles finally said, "Doctor—Philip—I thank you for this. And I won't forget it." He stood up and went to the window to look out, and Alderson stood, too, as it seemed that the meeting was over. He saw himself out, leaving Miles and Martha sitting in the semi-dark study.

Martha stood and crossed the room to stand by her husband, twining one arm through his and patting his hand in comfort. She could feel his panic rising. This was the worst thing that had ever happened to him, and she knew he didn't have the strength to deal with what would be coming.

"What will we do, Martha?" Miles asked her, almost choking on the words.

But after her moments of quiet acceptance, Martha began to think of what to do, what Thompson might have done in such a case. The tighter the situation, the faster her mind raced, even to a truly horrible plan to put into action if need be. She shuddered at what might be its consequences and hoped to avoid it. But if there was no choice, then she would whatever was necessary. Her purpose was to protect the Downing clan, and that was what she would do, whatever came of it.

But there was no need to further upset Miles just now. She needed him as calm as possible to help keep things from spiraling out of control.

When Miles asked again, almost pleadingly, "What should we do?" Martha replied immediately and reassuringly, "Nothing at all."

Miles looked incredulous and Martha explained: "The girl can't speak and the women are hushing it up. We will follow along with that. We have no more to do but hope that story holds."

Miles croaked out an "All right."

PAT AND MATT
AND MILES

Pat was wandering through his days in an oppressive cloud of guilt and doom. Since the fateful event, he had not slept at all. His staring eyes were set in dark hollows when he caught his image in a mirror, and he felt possessed. He had committed not only a sin, but a sin so deep he knew it must be unforgivable. Was he so wretched a creature that he could have done this thing?

Part of his intense misery was plain guilt, but part was confusion at the power of the situation. What had come over him? What had clouded his judgment? What had stopped him from calling out to warn Chloe as she wandered innocently along the trail? It felt like an outside force that had taken up residence in his heart. Was it indeed the Devil? He had always been skeptical of Minister Brown's preaching about the Devil, the silly ghost stories, but maybe there was a God—and a Devil—after all, and maybe this was what it was all about.

He tried to pray but immediately rejected that idea. God wouldn't want to hear from him. He had a fleeting thought of going to see Minister Brown, but that was ridiculous—even if the man took him seriously, he preached about a different kind of Devil than the one Pat felt he now knew intimately.

His stomach was burning with acid. His heart was beating wildly, erratically. He panted and gasped in panic, and his head was spinning. He was dying, he was sure of it. But then that would be a relief … Didn't the Scripture say that Judas had wandered wild as Pat now felt and finished by hanging himself?

He kept wondering, *What's going to happen now?* Such evil wouldn't just lie there quietly.

He had tried to speak to his brother, asking, "Matt what're we going to do?"

Matt was not concerned. "Whaddaya mean what're we going to do?" he said, as if the question were already answered. "We aren't going to do a blessed thing. The women are scared and telling everybody she fell off a horse, and the man of the house is going along with that. That's the end of it. We're free. Stop looking like you saw a spirit or something—you'll give us away! All we got to do is keep shut and that'll be that."

Nothing ever worried Matt, for he wrangled his way out of everything, just by being a Downing. And even when they did get caught, Matt was stoic, no matter the punishment. He seemed to have no normal affections, so nothing bothered him.

But Pat was consumed by guilt, and as Minister Brown might have said in one of his sermons, he was "burning in hellfire," or the first taste of it. He shuddered at the thought.

"There must be a way out," he thought, and after more hours of intense mental suffering, finding himself cut off in every idea of escape, he finally felt such powerful anguish that he came to a decision. There was a way out, and he knew what it was.

In the barn, he found a rope, a good, thick rope. He didn't know how to make a hangman's noose, but he did know how to make a slip knot, and he did that, then looked around for the right beam. This was really the only way out, and even if he committed this great sin to the peril of his soul, his soul was already forfeit. It made no difference.

Miles walked over to the small farmhouse where he and Martha had begun their marriage and where Matt and Pat lived now. Their youthful carousing was not in keeping with the decorum Martha wanted in her house, and she preferred not to know all that they were up to. So this had worked out well for all concerned. Further out into the fields was yet a third house, where the farmhands and house staff lived when not needed by the Downings.

He walked in without knocking to find Matt lying on his bed and just staring at the ceiling, whistling to himself with his fingers interlaced on his chest.

So satisfied with himself, Miles thought with disgust. How was this a son of his?

"Hi, Pop," he said. "You should knock before—"

"What in God's name were you thinking?" said Miles, cutting him off.

"Whaddaya mean what was I thinking?" Matt roused himself a little and propped himself up on his elbows, pretending to be only slightly challenging and maybe a little questioning at the same time.

"Cut the horseshit, son. This time I may just take a horsewhip to you, like I probably should have done long ago. Where is your brother?"

"I don't know, Dad," said Matt. "Around somewhere, I guess."

Pat wasn't really the problem—just a hanger-on who didn't know how to rule himself nor his brother. Matt was the one to question. "Why couldn't you leave the girl alone?"

"That farm girl? I didn't go near her. She fell off a horse—her mother says so," said Matt. He was sitting all the way up now, his legs swung over the side of the bed.

"Don't lie to me, Matthew. Your mother and I are going to have enough trouble cleaning up the mess you made. I need honest talk here. And where the hell is your brother?"

"I don't know. He looked kind of sick an hour ago. I think he went out to the shithouse."

Miles automatically turned to look out the window, suddenly alert with the idea that something bad was happening with his other son. "How long ago did he leave?"

"I guess about a half hour ago ..." Matt stood up and looked out the window, too.

"That's a long trip to the outhouse," said Miles. "Let's go find him and get to the bottom of this. There's gonna be hell to pay."

As Matt crowded in front of his father going out the door, Miles smacked him on the back of the head, and Matt rubbed the place.

They looked around but saw no sign of Pat, and the boy feeding the pigs said he hadn't seen him.

"Pat!" yelled out Miles. But there was no answer. "Let's check in the barn," he said, feeling a strange sense of dread as they walked towards the barn and opened the door.

In the fading light Pat was silhouetted in the dusty space, hanging in front of them, his legs kicking involuntarily. Father and son stared for a moment and then rushed over.

Pat was grasping at the rope as he was choking to death and trying to save himself, even as he kicked them away from him, twisting on the rope as he did.

"Grab his legs!" shouted Miles, and Matt grasped them in his powerful arms, hoisting his brother a little to take the pressure off his neck. Miles ran for a ladder and leaned it against the beam and climbed up to release the rope.

Together they were able to get Pat down and untie the rope from his neck. Pat was gasping for breath and writhing in the straw, sobbing as soon as he got his wind back, kicking and snarling at them both, and then collapsing finally into exhaustion, his face in the dirt.

Another minute and my son would have left this Earth.

Miles was horrified. Things had been so good for so long, and he'd thought that if he could just get the boys to adulthood, they would see their blessings and take on their legacy. But no, the goodness had fled, and both his sons were destroyers—one of an innocent young girl and one of himself. He had almost lost both sons in just days.

"Let's take him inside," he said to Matt. "Not a word to your mother, or anyone …"

As they slung Pat's arms over their shoulders and supported him back to the boys' house, Miles realized that he might tell a story of Pat falling off a horse …

Soon they were inside and Pat on his bed, his brother and father standing beside it.

"Very well," said Miles, "tell me everything. Every blessed thing. I need to know everything if I am to have a prayer of handling this matter. I especially have to know who knows what happened."

Pat couldn't speak, so Matt did the talking, and it seemed that he told the truth, because it was too horrible not to be the truth. Every bit of it. At least he said that they'd gotten away without being seen. Pat, still struggling to breathe, rasped out a few details to add to Matt's.

It was clear to Miles that those who knew of the horrible deed now included Faythe, Lucy, Matt, Pat, Martha, Dr. Alderson, and Chloe herself, if she ever woke up to tell the tale. That was a lot of people the Downings would have to manage.

With disgust and contempt in his tone, Miles asked Matt directly, "Boy, what were you thinking?" Then he turned to Pat and said, "And don't you dare try an easy way out again."

Then, not knowing what else could be said for now, Miles stood up, left his sons alone, and went for a very long walk. For he had some real thinking to do. This was going to be very difficult to deal with, and even though he knew Martha would make the necessary decisions, he still wanted some time to think of what Thompson would do in his place. Miles was the proclaimed "king" of North Hinkapee, but a king could be deposed very easily if the people decided he was unfit to act in such capacity. He wondered if he should just tell the sheriff the truth about what had happened and let Matt suffer the consequences, but that wouldn't do. Of course, neither he nor Martha could not permit the sure execution of their son, especially because Pat would be swept up in the retribution and then they would be childless. That would not fulfill Thompson Downing's will for the clan.

Perhaps the deal with Sheriff Jones that his father had made might not be able to be respected. He sighed heavily, blowing air out of both cheeks, as he walked along one of the trails leading from his farm.

As Miles returned home after many miles trudging through the Downing lands, he concluded that Martha's original advice to him was indeed the wisest course of action. They must do nothing at all. Thompson had once said to him that sometimes, especially when one already held power and position, the best advice was, "Don't just do something—stand there!"

Miles and Martha sat in quiet conference on their porch that evening, watching the sun go down over their lands. Miles had related to Martha everything Matt and Pat had told him—though he held back the detail of the barn, and she cocked her head at him as if she could tell he was leaving something out. And then she seemed to have something she was withholding from him as well.

Well after midnight, Martha got up quietly from the bed, careful not to disturb Miles, but he was aware the second her breathing changed, for he could not have slept that night for all the world. He said nothing, though, guessing at what she might be up to. He feigned sleep.

MARTHA AND LIGGETT AND MATT

Quietly Martha put on a cloak and walked barefoot out the door, carrying her shoes, which she slipped on her feet on the porch. She went out to the barn and was glad to see Liggett's strong and masculine form there already, a shadow in the moonlight. When she'd spoken to him earlier, he had tried to protest, but she had held her authority with him, as she always did.

Together they went into the barn and Liggett pulled out a heavy stick and horsewhip that he held out to show her. She nodded, then told him to wait while she went to fetch her son.

Martha crept into her old house and peeked into Pat's room, where he was, as she would have expected, wide awake in the torments of guilt, of hell on Earth. Martha looked at Pat with pity and sadness, but he was oblivious to her as he studied the ceiling, as if searching there for an answer to his anguished questions. Her broken boy, her sweet son, shouldn't have been mixed up in this. Matt had led him to a place he shouldn't have, and indeed Pat couldn't have gone there by himself. But grieving for Pat would have to wait.

She went to Matt's room and shook him by the shoulder, and when he opened his eyes, Martha said quietly, but commandingly, "Come with me."

Matt knew that when his mother commanded something, she meant it, and it was best not to argue, so he got out of bed, pulled his breeches over his shirt, and stuffed his feet into his shoes and followed her out the door to the barn.

Matt would expect to get a strapping, as he had in the past when Martha and Miles knew not what else to do to curb his wildness. He had done wrong and would know only by the blows that it was wrong that ought not be repeated—Martha knew he had no conscience. He usually just kept saying "Sorry" until Miles tired of hitting him. And Miles's strappings were never severe.

As soon as they stepped into the barn, Matt halted, not seeing his father as he usually did in these nighttime sessions. For it was important that the servants could never see a Downing lose his dignity, so Matt's strappings were done in private, at night. When Matt stopped, Martha closed her hand around his arm in warning. "You are not to move," she hissed. And then she stepped away.

Before Matt could figure out what was going on, Liggett whacked him on the back of the head with the stout stick, and Matt staggered forward with a cry, his hand flying to the back of his head. He whirled to berate his father—*That hurt!* And then he saw Liggett, the biggest, strongest man on the Downing place. Matt turned wild eyes toward his mother, who had closed the barn door and stood holding high the lamp she had brought with her. She wanted Matt to know by her providing light for the beating that she approved it.

Matt began to blubber, but before he could get louder, Liggett rammed the stick into his belly, knocking the wind out of him and sending him to the floor. The big man was silent, just setting himself up for blow after blow, though Matt cried and begged him to stop.

Martha found it harder than she thought it should have been to watch when Liggett crossed to set the stick against the barn wall and take down the horsewhip he'd coiled there. Matt yelped in fear, and Martha braced herself. *Despicable as he has been, he is still my son, and always will be.*

The whipping began and continued for longer than Martha could bear, but she could tell Liggett held back enough not to do him permanent harm. She watched, her face set in stone, until Matt lay on the floor of the barn bleeding and bruised, likely with broken ribs and cuts that would need stitching. He was crying like a baby.

Martha didn't say a word, nor did Liggett. He coiled his whip and hung it again, left the stick leaning against the wall, and walked out of the barn, Martha following without looking back. Matt would have to drag himself back to his bed on his own or lie there all night.

We should have done this years ago, Martha thought. Perhaps that would have forestalled the disaster they now faced. *But we will have no more of this—I hope I've seen to that.*

She trotted ahead a few steps to catch up to Liggett, placing a hand on his arm and looking deeply into his eyes in the moonlight. He had raised another kind of lust in her ... and she wanted him to know it.

When she slipped back into bed, she lay stiff on her back considering what must come next, and then she curled herself around her husband, who moaned sleepily and reached behind him to cup his hand around her beautiful bottom. Entwined like that, both Downings went to sleep.

FAYTHE AND TOMMY

Sometimes you just can't keep a secret, Faythe thought. *Sometimes you just can't do it.* She was bubbling with a hatred that had never been in her before, a hatred that had settled into her bones, aching there. She needed sleep, but she wasn't tired. She was fueled by fury, and that strengthened her, but she knew she would soon collapse.

So Lucy had told her to look for the good in people. *What virtue is in that?* she wondered, finding herself for the first time angry at her good mother. "What good is that?" she muttered through gritted teeth, and Robert looked sharply at her, stirred from his own brooding.

Faythe had watched her father move through his own torment in the days since Chloe's ordeal, and she wondered how he could have borne it if he knew the truth. Robert Wentworth knew a heartache that would never go away, but like Job, he had accepted this misfortune as coming from the hand of God. After all, death was near to all of them in these times—from hunger or disease or accident. And he hoped aloud in his prayers that somehow Chloe would recover—that she would open her eyes one day and say, "Dad, I've missed you. Have I been sleeping a long time?"

If he only knew it was the Devil himself at work in this thing! Faythe thought, determined to protect him from that knowledge. If Chloe had just been kicked in the head by a horse, she might recover, but if she ever woke and relived the nightmare of her attack, she would surely slip away forever.

Several weeks went by and Chloe could walk around a little, eat if someone fed her, or even make her way out to the outhouse if led; they had some hope. She would do as bidden, remembering old habits of braiding her hair or snapping beans. But her mind was not present with them. It was as if her body were still on Earth, but her mind had moved beyond. "To a happier place," Lucy had quietly confided to Faythe.

Tommy was spending a lot of time with the increasingly morose Faythe, trying to cheer her up as she sank deeper into gloom. She had pushed aside her anger, and gloom was all she had left. Tommy just couldn't understand that his attempts only served to irritate her. But that irritation stirred up her anger a bit and gave her some life.

One afternoon, he persuaded her to get away for a while to pick blueberries at his farm, and as they dropped the first berries into their pails with satisfying plunks, he said, "Faythe, you have to find your own spirit again. You can't mourn forever."

"You may say that plainly, and sensibly," said Faythe bitterly. "But it isn't your sister!"

Tommy said, "I know how you feel—"

"How could you possibly know how I feel?"

"Well, I ..."

Faythe went on. "I was supposed to protect her. I was supposed to stop things like this from happening. I knew what could happen and I failed her. And now look at her. Poor thing." Faythe started to cry great heaving sobs, tears of combined anger and pain.

Tommy asked in a puzzled tone, "How could you protect her from falling off a horse? No one can avoid something like that. It just happens."

"She didn't fall off a horse!" said Faythe with such rage that her trembling made her drop her pail, and the berries spilled out.

Tommy looked at her with fright. "Then what really happened?"

"I can't tell you—it will just make things worse." But Faythe knew she had to tell him, and finally the story burst forth.

As Tommy listened, his heart sank. Faythe's pain and misery were blowing through him like a storm.

"Now I have misgivings about our pact," Faythe said, biting her knuckle. "How can we just allow this to go on, this crime to lie unanswered? I have to *do* something. I'm going to tell the sheriff after all."

Tommy said thoughtfully, wrapping an arm around her shoulders in sympathy, "Faythe, let me think about how to handle all this. It's too much for one person. Don't be hasty ... just yet. Let me talk to my mother—you know she has wisdom."

Faythe nodded, but in hopeless misery. How Tommy longed to comfort her, to carry away her burdens!

The next day Tommy found Faythe hanging out the wash and said straightway, "My mother agrees that your mother's plan is best, though we can all agree it's against all good. You're like a lamb fallen into a crevice, scrambling and frantic to get out."

Faythe bridled. "Many thanks for telling me nothing useful."

Tommy, finally tiring of Faythe's adamant self-absorption, after he'd spent weeks near her elbow, listening, comforting, fighting against his own ideas to let her have her own, finally spoke up.

"Faythe!"

She looked up, startled, her brow furrowed.

"That's enough," he said more gently but still firmly. "I'm trying to be helpful. I did not cause this situation, you know. I'm here to help you, though you have hardly noticed me all these weeks, and I remain though you won't even allow me to court you. But I'm still here—because—because—I-I'm in love with you."

Faythe's eyes went wide with pity, then filled with tears that spilled down her cheeks. She wiped them away with the cloth she had been pinning on the line. "Tommy, I'm so sorry. I have fallen so low I just want someone to be low with me, and I've brought you down into that valley with me. I'm not even scrambling to get out anymore. I don't know why you haven't just found another to be your intended by now."

"Never mind that," said Tommy. "I wanted you to know how things stand with me—towards you. Let's consider some possibilities." He helped her finish hanging the wash, then led her into the woods, where they walked and talked for a long time. They considered every possibility, including an anonymous note to the sheriff, confronting Miles and his evil sons in worship, cold bloodedly murdering Matt and Pat—Faythe balled her fists and grew more energetic at that idea—and numerous other plans. All seemed to lead to worse outcomes than would Lucy's plan.

It was clear there was no urgency, and well-considered planning was likely to lead to a better result than would rash action. When they had walked miles into the woods, Tommy stopped and said again, taking her hands in his, "Faythe, I want you to know that I love you, and I'll always love you. I'll give you my best advice, but the decisions will be yours to make. And whatever you decide, I'll be steadfast beside you." He dropped to his knees, looking up at her. "Even if it costs me my life, I will not desert you."

Faythe looked down at this fine man looking up at her, a man whose devotion she did not deserve. She could not—at least not yet—return his hopes for a future as husband and wife, but she could give him what was in her spirit to give. She dropped to her knees as well, and then pulled him down to sit beside her on a mossy root.

She gently laid her hand on his jaw and turned his face to look fully into her own, then she put her arms around him and kissed him. This kiss was less heated than the last time, more slow and loving. Tommy kissed her back eagerly, and she laid one hand on his thigh and stroked it up toward where his breeches were bulging. She knew how they divided in front and she slipped her hand in and found his hardness and warmth. At first he jumped with a start, but she felt him press toward her almost immediately, clearly overcome with the sensation. She looked at the smooth pink flesh in a state she had seen in the stock animals before, but certainly never with a man. She stroked his penis as she expected he would like, and it seemed he did, for he murmured encouragement when she circled the shaft with her hand, enclosing the top. She answered his pressing rhythm with her own and suddenly his tension reached a peak of throbbing and released warm wetness all over her hand and onto the ground. He relaxed at that, and Faythe hoped he had received this gift as the reward she intended it to be.

But now she needed her own release.

Tommy covered himself again and put his arms around her with murmured thanks, seeming to expect that that was the end of things, but Faythe drew his hands to her own body, first cupping them against her breasts, then unlacing her bodice and inviting his hands under her shift as she pressed toward him. It excited her to have her breasts exposed out in God's green world, before a man who longed for her body. As he tentatively touched them gingerly at first, she waited for his confidence to grow as she whispered "Yes" to encourage him. And then she drew his hand down to her knees and parted them as she invited his hand up her own thigh as she had drawn her hand up his a few minutes earlier.

She felt herself grow trembly and warm as she had at the first kiss in the barn, but with the actual touch to enhance the feeling, it grew and grew, until she was urging and pressing as much as he had earlier. *So perhaps we feel the* same, she thought, and then as he touched her most secret places, she reached to guide his hand just where she wanted it, where the waves of warmth pressed against her like flood waters against a dam, building to a painfully pleasant height that called her yet higher, urgently. Then when she thought she could not bear it anymore, the beautiful pain peaked and thrummed through her like when a dam is released and the waves of the river wash over the banks and finally settle in a foaming roar that leaves the riverside dripping and calmed. She had no seed to spill as his had shot out strongly, but she was damp and slippery and felt that on his hand when she pulled it away from her, unable to bear another touch as her climax ebbed away.

Both sat there in a stupor, spent, both a bit embarrassed, but at the same time very pleased.

Tommy looked at her with a keenness that suggested he knew she had received as much from him as he had from her. Both had long heard of women enjoying more than their husbands the activities of conjugal love, to the point that men should even be encouraged from the pulpit to please their wives. But Lucy had hinted to Faythe that she very fully enjoyed Robert's love and expected a well-matched couple of any sort might enjoy the same. *So perhaps we are well matched*, Faythe thought.

They kissed again one more time and then Tommy accompanied her home and left her at her gate, whistling a tune as he set off to his own farm.

Faythe looked after him, knowing her affection for this young man was growing into the kind of love her parents had. *Why must things twist up into such a thorny tangle?* She wondered.

THE DARK CLOUD GETS DARKER

Close to two months had now gone by since the "accident," and there was still no change in Chloe's condition. She seemed to hear people if they spoke to her, and she complied with gentle instructions, but she was not personally responsive, unable to connect with others. It was unclear whether her mind was still just in hiding or her spirit had just left the Earth and, as Lucy hoped, gone to a better place.

But there were other changes that at first only her mother noticed. Her breasts were larger, although that could be explained by the fact that she was still maturing. But of much more significance was the fact that Chloe had ceased to have her monthly flow. Lucy realized, with even greater distress, if that were possible, that her daughter was pregnant.

At first, Lucy just wanted to lie down and cry herself away once she was sure, but then she realized with a start that Dr. Alderson was coming by for his weekly visit, and it would not be good for him to come to the same conclusion. Not at all. But what excuse could she give to keep him away? Perhaps that they couldn't afford the care … But even as she mulled over these ideas, she heard a horse in the farmyard and then his voice wishing a "Good morning" to Faythe outside. Lucy would just have to brazen it out.

"Good morning, Doctor," she said, mustering a brave smile as she stood at the door. "Thank you for coming out here again."

"Of course," said Dr. Alderson. "It's my calling to look after all of North Hinkapee, and especially those who are ill. I'll be pleased to examine Chloe—how is she faring?"

"There is no change, I am sorry to say. She eats, and she does what she is told, but she just doesn't engage with anyone, not even her sister, and they were always very close. Faythe has tried to tell her stories, an old pleasure of theirs, but Chloe just seems not to be present in her spirit, if you know what I mean."

The doctor nodded. "Well, let me have a look at her, then."

Lucy hesitated almost imperceptibly and then assented and stepped aside, welcoming him into the house. The doctor went and sat down at Chloe's bedside. The girl was lying there staring up at the ceiling, with eyes as vacant as any living person's might be.

"How are you, my dear?" he asked. Chloe stared on.

He passed his hands in front of her eyes, but she maintained a fixed stare off into the distance, or into the ceiling, blinking only as her eyes dried and closed of their own accord. There was no reaction of her perception. He pinched her wrist, and the girl drew away but otherwise did not react. "So she can feel external stimulation," murmured the doctor, "but she does not respond to others. Makes perfect sense …"

What makes perfect sense? thought Lucy, in alarm. Surely he could not tell what had happened to her …

Then Philip Alderson noticed the girl's increasingly swollen bosom and a slight rise in her abdomen, despite her wasting in the limbs from her many weeks in bed. With a hand to her abdomen, he felt the characteristic swelling with just that particular placement. He tried not to wince. *The girl is pregnant.* There was no doubt about it.

This is bad for the Wentworths, he thought. *Very bad. And it will be bad for the Downings, too. This is just bad, bad, bad.* He shook his head in despairing sympathy and then checked himself.

Holding his expression impassive, he looked over at the mother. Lucy Wentworth knew what he knew. A mother would pick up on that even more quickly than a doctor. In her expression he read that not only did she know, but she hoped he would not yet realize it himself.

He smiled at Lucy, a grim and wan smile. "Well, there's no improvement, that's true," he said. "But she has gotten no worse, either, apart from perhaps"—and he held up one of the girl's thin arms—"some wasting from her time in bed." He stood up and faced the stricken woman and offered, "Perhaps it's a good thing that nothing has changed … for the worse. I suggest that you continue the medicines I've been giving you."

He started to pull out some bottles from his bag, but she held up her hand.

"Thank you, Doctor, but we cannot afford them any longer—they come too dear. At this point, her father and I would like to put her care in God's hands."

"As you wish," he replied. They were wise not to waste their meagre resources, and he had no confidence the medicines had been a help.

"Well," he said, closing his bag, "I'll be on my way, then. I will certainly pray for your daughter's recovery, as I have been doing."

"Thank you," said Lucy, already standing by the door to see him out.

As he climbed onto his horse, Philip Alderson needed no more time for deliberation—he had mulled over this possibility many times in the weeks since Chloe Downing was injured. He knew where he was going, and right away.

As he came out of the lane from the Wentworths', the doctor saw the blacksmith Handel Lewis coming from the road that led back to the Downings', his pack of tools on his back. The men nodded to one another. Handel restrained himself from giving Dr. Alderson an odd look; for some reason something didn't make sense, but it didn't really concern him, so he didn't think more about it at the time.

THE DOWNINGS AND DR. ALDERSON—AGAIN

Martha was strolling through her gardens at the entry gate of the Downing place when she saw Philip Alderson on the road. She waited at the gate as the doctor approached, then greeted him and asked if she could be of assistance.

He dismounted and held the reins in his hands as he explained he had a matter of importance to discuss with Miles—and with her, if appropriate.

Martha summoned the servant girl who had been carrying the basket of flowers Martha had chosen for the house and sent her scurrying up to the house to find Miles.

"Have him wait for us in the study," she said. Then she strolled along the path to the house, making small talk while a storm brewed in her mind.

At the house it was clear Miles was worried, as he hurried down the porch steps and out to them as they drew near to the house. In a poor attempt to disguise his anxiety, Miles composed his face with brightness and offered his hand to the doctor while a servant took the horse to the stable.

"So, Doctor," said Miles, "what brings you out here?"

"I've some news," he said, "but it's best discussed inside."

The three of them climbed the steps with some effort, as if each carried a burden within, and passed soberly into the study. Once the door was securely closed, since Miles and Martha remained standing and did not offer him a chair, Philip Alderson spoke.

"As was the case last time, I need your oath of secrecy, as I am sworn not to disclose these matters ... though I believe they touch near to your family ... to your responsibilities to North Hinkapee."

Martha's heart sank deep into her bowels as she felt her face go white and hot at the same time. She briefly fanned herself to gain composure—she knew what was coming next.

Miles impatiently snapped, "We've already told you we are prepared to keep silence—what is it?"

"Very well, very well!" said Dr. Alderson, holding up a calming hand. "I'll get right to the point, then. The girl is pregnant."

Miles bent over as if he had been kicked, then sat down heavily in his desk chair. Martha held herself very still.

"This is not good," Miles said.

Meanwhile, Martha's creative and inventive mind was running down different roads all at the same time—with each road uglier than the one before it—her thoughts burbling and swirling.

"Is there anything that can be done?" Miles asked of both Martha and Dr. Alderson at the same time.

"Well, not that I can think of," said the doctor, wondering what on earth Miles was even asking.

"Does anyone else know of this?" asked Martha, sharply.

"I'm sure the mother knows. Mothers always know."

Martha's conscience warred with her for a moment, but she envisioned Thompson Downing's face and his warning about the clan and her future. Martha *must* do whatever was necessary, no matter the pangs of conscience. The Downings must endure if she were to have her place in this better world. She spoke up, quietly, looking straight into his eyes: "Do you have medicines that can … do away with the complication?"

"You mean abort?" asked the doctor, his face betraying both shock and fear. "That's a sin against God, and possibly worse for me, for my oaths."

"I'm not asking about sinning," said Martha, impatient to get to the point. "I'm asking if you *have* such medicines." The brothels in Briarcliff surely had them, and her father had spoken of how the places kept the women available for custom by use of these potions. And surely they were not the only women who might desire to rid themselves of unwanted children.

"Well, maybe—I am not sure. I don't …"

"Come now," said Martha, determined to be practical and clear away the niceties. "I'm sure you've had occasion to perform this service in the course of your care over the years."

"Well, whether or not that is the case, I can't do that in this situation."

"Why not?"

"Well, for one thing, Lucy Wentworth has called an end to my care—I'm sure they cannot afford it. So I've no more reason to visit the family."

"You could do this service without charge, as—as a charitable endeavor," said Martha, waving her arm in a gesture demonstrating the idea of generosity.

Philip Alderson gulped, and beads of sweat stood out on his blanching forehead. "Miles … Martha … you know I'd do anything for you. And that's why I'm here now, so you know where things stand, but I can't do this. I just can't."

Martha stared at the doctor as she considered the possibilities. Then suddenly he stopped squirming under her gaze and pulled himself together, as if coming to a solution.

He cleared his throat and spoke in a low voice. "These medicines"—he tallied them off on his fingers—"pennyroyal, tansy, savin, and some others—they don't always work. Sometimes they do nothing at all, and sometimes, if the dosage is too high … " He paused. "The woman dies."

Martha kept her eyes on the figured carpet but glanced up enough to see Miles kept his eyes firmly fixed on the papers on his desk. The doctor was likely looking down, too. The moments marched by.

Finally, Miles stood up and came from behind his desk, offering his hand. "Doctor—Philip—thank you for coming out here to let us know. Your confidence in us is much appreciated. Let us think on what we should be doing here. And of course—for heaven's sake—say nothing about our conversation."

"Of course," said the doctor, taking the hand.

Martha went to the door and opened it. "I'll show you out, Doctor."

She accompanied him down the hall to the front door and then—despite the surprise he showed in his curious sidelong glance—walked him all the way to the stables for his horse. As he was about to mount up, Martha touched his arm, and when he turned to her, she spoke very quietly.

"Perhaps it might make sense," she said, "for you to come by later today—to give me these medicines, with instructions on how to use them."

"I thought … that … Miles said you were thinking about what to do next."

"Yes, he is thinking about it," said Martha, "and I have thought about it already."

The doctor looked around the stable, pulled at his collar, fidgeted with the reins.

Martha read his mind. "Doctor—Philip"—she laid a hand on his and stroked just a couple of strokes with her finger on the tender flesh between his thumb and forefinger. It was an intimate gesture she hoped conveyed a subtle but very *personal* intent. "There's nothing to think about," she said simply. "You'll go home now and bring those medicines back to me. You'll tell no one about it, including my husband."

"What if I'm seen here?" he asked.

"I'm feeling quite poorly, it seems," responded Martha without hesitation. "I will need your services later today. Understood?"

"Yes, ma'am," said the doctor with an effort. He turned again to mount his horse, but Martha once again put her hand gently on his arm so he turned back to her, a question in his eyes.

"One more thing, Doctor," she said. "These medicines. I'm wondering, can the likelihood of the death of the woman be predicted, based on the dosage?"

Dr. Alderson looked puzzled for a second, so she continued. "What I mean," she said, annoyed at having to spell it out, "is this: if you give too high a dosage, does that make it more likely that the woman will pass away from the medicines?"

"Yes," said Dr. Alderson, who escaped by mounting the horse and giving her a wide-eyed look as he kicked his heels into his horse and swiftly left the stables.

INTERLUDE

JONES AND MENON DEFEND NUNUNYI

It was a fine fall evening when Sheriff Jones received a letter from a long-time and beloved old friend. "I'd like you to meet my wife for a second time. Can you come to Bearminster Inn this Tuesday? GM."

Sheriff Jones smiled. Of course he would go. "Betsy," he said, turning to her. "It looks like Menon's Indian woman is now his wife. I'm going to meet her. I'll be gone just a couple of days."

Betsy smiled at him, pleased at her husband's delight at the chance to reunite with his friend. She well knew the story about how Jones and Menon had spirited the Indian girl away from the camp where the battle had occurred, and Menon had taken her to his secluded forest dwelling, where they had dwelt for many years afterward.

"Well, Nunu, tomorrow I'll be reintroducing you to my oldest friend. You don't remember meeting him last time, since you were fast asleep."

Nununyi wasn't sure about this but smiled reluctantly. She could hardly pour cold water on Menon's eagerness to introduce her to his friend.

Jones wouldn't be arriving until near the end of the day, as he would no doubt have left North Hinkapee in the morning for the day-long ride to The Inn at Bearminster, while Nununyi and Menon had only a quick three-mile ride from their farmhouse. So they set out late in the afternoon and arrived shortly before dusk.

Although it was unusual for a man to bring an Indian woman into the inn, the proprietor, Paul Josephson, knew Menon quite well. "Why, come in, come in, old friend," he said.

Menon shrugged a hello. Josephson pretended false intimacy with everyone he met, and Menon kept up the charade as best he could, with a forced smile. "We'll not be staying the night, but my friend John Jones will be here soon, and I am sure he will want a room. We will wait for him in the main room, if you don't mind."

"Of course," said Josephson. "Come right in. I know John— Sheriff Jones—quite well. He is a good friend for many years." Then he added, turning to Nununyi, "No weapons in the inn," gesturing to her to leave her bow and arrows at the door. She did this quite reluctantly after Menon's nod indicated it was safe to do so, then she followed Menon and Josephson into the main room.

As soon as she got there, all eyes went to Menon and the Indian woman. Nununyi's premonition that this was not going to go well heightened even more, but Menon seemed too eager to see John Jones to take much notice.

The room was relatively full, she noticed. There were five or six tables, each of which was occupied by two or more men. There were two women clearly in charge of serving food and drink. And there three—no, four—other women, dressed both shabbily and seductively, who were there for another obvious purpose.

One of these women had very large breasts, Nununyi noticed. She caught the woman's eye, and to Nununyi's surprise the woman looked back in a friendly way. *Is that sympathy?* she wondered.

At one of the tables two very large men fixed their eyes on Nununyi and Menon, and in a very unpleasant manner. Nununyi could read disgust in their expressions as they surveyed the newcomers. Nununyi and Menon found a table in the corner, and one of the men stood up and walked over to them.

Menon and Nununyi sat down, and the man towered over them. Abruptly, he said, "How much?"

Menon looked up at him, surprised but unafraid. "How much for what?"

"For her"—he gestured at Nununyi. "To have her suck my cock."

Menon flushed, but he restrained his temper. "She's not for that. She's with me." He noticed that the other man at the table had joined his friend. Now they were both standing in front of the couple, menacingly.

The room had quieted down, as it seemed like trouble was about to ensue. And it was.

"You like fucking Indian girls," said the second man, "but you won't share. She looks like a good time to me."

Menon dropped the pretense of politeness. He had dealt with tougher men before. "You'd best be off," he said, "before you regret your big mouths."

The first man put his hand on Menon's chest, warning him to stay seated, and the second man grabbed Nununyi by the arm, half-pulling her to her feet.

As quick as lightning, Menon grabbed the hand that had been on his chest and twisted it extremely hard in the wrong direction. He heard an internal cracking sound and thought—hoped—he had broken the man's wrist. The man winced and shouted in pain as crumpled to his knees and then rolled away. Menon gave him no further thought and was up and out of his chair, turning as he rose to shove hard at the other man, who still gripped Nununyi's arm.

Menon shoved him as hard as he could, and the man fell backwards. Menon was now moving forward, his hands lethally and brutally attacking the man now reeling away.

Suddenly there was a hard knocking sound and Menon fell to the floor like a sack of bricks. There was a third man Menon hadn't yet noticed. Perhaps he had been at the bar or perhaps he had just come back from the outhouse. He had hit Menon over the head, hard, with a tankard. Menon was out cold before he hit the floor.

Now the three men stood over the small woman and the unconscious man, none of them paying the slightest attention to Paul Josephson ineffectually saying, "Fellows, there is no fighting in the inn. You must take this outside. This will not do."

"Bastard—I think he broke my wrist," said the one Menon had man-handled, holding his arm in pain. He kicked Menon hard in the ribs, but Menon, unconscious, felt nothing.

After just a split second of shock, Nununyi made for the door. If only she could reach her precious bow and arrows, this battle could turn around. But it was not to be.

"Where you going, you Indian slut?" yelled the man who had clubbed Menon, dropping the now-bloody tankard and grabbing Nununyi by her hair, whipping her around and dragging her back.

Now Nununyi, perhaps a shade over five feet tall, was surrounded by three giant men. Without preamble, one of the men grabbed her deerskin jerkin and ripped it down in front, exposing both of her breasts and at the same time revealing the scar from many years before, when she had been shot with Harrison Keep-Safe's bullet.

"Nice set," said one of the other men. "And look at that scar." He ran his hand over it, looking at Nununyi in the eyes as he did so. "I wonder where that came from." But he turned his attention to the rest of her exposed flesh, grabbing at her breasts and squeezing them hard. Nununyi made no movement. She wouldn't give them the satisfaction of struggling. There was nothing she could do at that moment, except burn into her consciousness exactly what they looked like.

"Strip this Indian bitch down," said the man with the broken wrist, and the other two set to work removing the rest of her clothes.

"You want to do her right here?" asked one of them. "I mean, with everyone watching?"

"What—are you ashamed of your cock?"

"No, but ... ." He didn't finish his sentence as he was startled by the sound of a shot and a bullet that whizzed past his ear and lodged in one of the logs in the wall.

"Put your hands up, all of you," said a voice that would have been familiar to Menon had he been awake.

"I don't miss, and I don't ask twice," continued the voice, with such authority that it was clear that it should be obeyed, and quickly too.

Six hands went up in the air as Sheriff Jones strode forward, looking at his friend on the floor, bleeding from a wound that Sheriff Jones hoped would prove not life-threatening after he was revived. He looked at Nununyi as well, seeing in an instant that she was unhurt.

He nodded to her, the nod indicating that she should re-clothe herself and step away from the men and behind him.

"I could ask what is going on here," said Jones, "but it's pretty clear."

One of the men began, almost by way of pleading explanation, "We wondered why he was bringing an Indian into a respectable tavern, and he up and attacked us. We meant no harm and were teaching them ..."

"Save it," said Jones. "Sit. Over there." The three men hastened to obey and sat at the table Jones gestured to. "Face the wall, and don't move around too much or I might have an accident that would result in me shooting off part of your face."

He turned to Paul Josephson, saying, "Get a damp cloth and some water and see about reviving my friend there." Josephson hastened to do exactly this, and it wasn't long before a groggy Menon was sitting in the chair he had been in before the altercation. His head hurt understandably, and the room was spinning a little, but he had a warm feeling that his friend John Jones was there with him. *He always watches my back.*

Things settled down. At Sheriff Jones's direction, the three men were tied up with strong rope that bound them to their chairs in the corner. They would spend the night in that situation with Jones on guard. And the next day they would be put out on the road. Since they weren't in North Hinkapee and Sheriff Jones was not sheriff in Bearminster, and with all the other difficulties that would ensue, it seemed to make the most sense to just let them go with a warning that if they were seen around Bearminster again, it would go ill with them.

Finally, Menon had recovered enough to continue his beer and have the reunion with his friend and introduction to Nununyi that he had sought in the first place. Menon said with a flourish, "Nununyi, I would like you to meet my friend John Jones. As you well know, he was instrumental in your rescue. Without him we wouldn't be here together today."

Nununyi nodded at Jones, but she was impassive. The evening's events had not put her in the best frame of mind, especially towards White Men.

"And John," continued Menon, turning to Jones, "I would like you to meet the woman who is by all respects my wife and my greatest love. This is Nununyi."

Jones, reading Nununyi's thoughts after she was almost raped, stood up and bowed to her. "Ma'am," he said courteously, "it is my honor to meet you. I am sure you haven't the highest opinion of us men just now, which opinion I respect. However, I am at your service and hope you will see me with different eyes."

Nununyi looked at Menon. And then looked at Jones, who had rescued them from a difficult situation. She nodded politely. She wanted to muster some warmth for the man who had now saved her twice, but it was difficult. Jones looked at her with understanding and didn't press the point.

The three talked for quite some time, although virtually all of the conversation was between Menon and Jones, while Nununyi looked on, muttering a yes or a no if asked a direct question. If anyone had been watching carefully, they would have noted with surprise that Nununyi did not look at the three men who had attacked her. Not even once did she look over at them.

Finally, Menon and Nununyi retired to the room they had acquired for Sheriff Jones. Jones insisted that he would stay in the common room to watch the three men carefully, including to be sure that they would be off at first light of day. He bade Nununyi and Menon good night.

Menon slept peacefully, knowing that his good friend had his back, as always.

Nununyi did not sleep at all.

1672–1692, BRIARCLIFF AND NORTH HINKAPEE

WHO IS MARTHA DOWNING?

Martha Scrabblestone grew up on the outskirts of Briarcliff, in a house that spoke of the family's humble means. They were not paupers, but they were not well off, either. Martha had seen the rich folk driving by in their fine carts and with their fine clothes. Even as a little girl, she knew that she wanted to be one of them, and she resolved to do whatever was necessary to achieve that status, one way or another. After all, her mother's dawn-to-dusk-and-later labors didn't make for a comfortable life—and Martha's hopes and plans were for something quite different for herself.

Although most families in New England had many children, Martha was an only child, for her mother, Kristen, had suffered a large number of miscarriages, and her "almost-brother" was stillborn. Martha had watched her mother weep over the tiny grave whenever her father was away and would not see. Eventually her mother could not conceive again.

The Scrabblestones were to outside view a respectable household. On the one hand, they stayed together married for many years and fulfilled all the expected responsibilities. On the other hand, Gus Scrabblestone was not a decent man at all. He was brutal to his wife, and Martha was forced to witness all that went on in their house beyond earshot of any neighbors.

Gus's brutality was not typically physical in nature, although it fell to that level at times; instead, he treated his wife with contempt and assumed that Kristen had been created to service his every need—or whim. Whatever Gus wanted, Kristen provided.

As a young child, Martha feared her father and felt close to her mother; however, over time she, too, developed a contempt for her mother, who never defended herself. How could Kristen be a person of worth if she allowed herself to be abused?

Martha's feelings gradually moved from affectionate dependence upon her mother when she was a small child to questioning her mother's character and value as the woman absorbed the insults and scampered to meet Gus's demands. Finally, when Martha was just transforming into womanhood herself, one terrible day it all became settled and locked in Martha's final judgment. Martha had peeked around the bedroom door that afternoon, knowing somehow deep down that there were mysterious things going on on the other side. Her mind filled with swirling alarms when she saw Kristen kneeling on a stool, facing her, her bare breasts swinging, while Gus crouched behind Kristen, his eyes closed and his face twisted into some mixture of animal rage and glee, slamming himself against his wife over and over again, digging his long nails into her naked shoulders. Martha saw in an instant that her mother was crying and her father was enjoying himself at the woman's expense. Kristen caught her daughter's gaze for a moment, then turned away in shame, and Martha melted back into the hall and escaped outside for fresh air. Neither Martha nor her mother ever spoke of this event afterward, though Martha often saw Kristen with red-rimmed eyes and walking and sitting gingerly.

Martha concluded that in this world it would be better to be Gus than to be Kristen, and she so comported herself. Although it hurt her, sometimes deeply, she set her heart against her mother, for she felt that she must be strong to create and maintain her strength, so over time she joined Gus in mistreating Kristen. It could be little things like Gus chastising his wife for the meal that she had worked hard on. Martha would add her criticisms rather than keep silent or praise the food. This would egg Gus on, and pretty soon they would both be abusing Kristen, who kept contrite and just let tears sneak down her face.

Martha found that the more she abused her mother, and the more her mother allowed it, the more Martha began to despise her. Things came to the point that when Gus struck Kristen, Martha would conclude, out loud, that Kristen must have deserved it. She even used her father's pet name for Kristen—"Dishrag"—a time or two. Gus once winked at Martha after slapping Kristen so hard on the backside that she shrieked in pain. Martha—before she thought about it—winked back. Then father and daughter smiled at each other.

Martha wondered sometimes why she was entering this conspiracy with her father, and at times even fancied confronting her father to stop the abuse of her mother, but each time she almost did this, she didn't follow through.

It was certainly wrong, and on a deep level it was troubling to her, and indeed at times she wanted to comfort her mother. There was that one time when she had muttered "I love you, Mother," under her breath. Even though she didn't look her mother in the eyes at that time, she knew by the stiffening in her breathing that Kristen had heard her. Sometimes, when she knew she was being especially unbearable to her mother, the memory of that one time came to her and she hoped somehow that her mother knew her real feelings were more positive than her actions.

Overall, Martha forced herself to push those thoughts far down. In the end it was safer to be on the stronger side than on the weaker side. The benefits of the approval of a strong man were both material and immaterial—Gus began giving Martha ribbons and fabric from his trips to town, so that she might better adorn herself. "Gotta show those stallions what this filly has to offer!" he'd crow.

And Martha had him twisted around her finger.

She became manipulative to get what she wanted. If a tantrum would produce the necessary result, she would throw a properly timed tantrum. If a sweet "I'm Daddy's little girl" would do it, then she would fawn all over him. And Kristen was so cowed that she lost all her maternal power over Martha, no threats necessary and no flattery required. Everyone was a pawn on Martha's chessboard.

Martha became accustomed to men chasing her, and she discovered she liked to lead them on and then, when they thought they were getting somewhere, shut the door in their faces. She liked the triumph of it.

At first this was a game to Martha, but at some point she realized that she was a strong sexual being herself. She made sure that it wasn't going to end up being a game where Martha, the ultimate temptress, would, like the Sirens of mythology, call men to their doom. Instead, Martha realized that she herself could easily become the doomed if she let herself go too far.

At first these were just dalliances, wondering how far she might go, both to feel some power over a man and at the same time please the lustful self she was growing into. Kissing and heavy petting—through-the-clothes stroking of excitable body parts—was as far as it went.

But then one summer afternoon she took a further step and led a particularly attractive one of these young men into a cool, dark barn. She hitched up her skirts and climbed a short ladder into the hayloft, leaving him below to look up past her stockings as she climbed. As he scrambled up after her, eager, she untied her apron and let it fall to the ground, then unbuttoned her waistcoat one button at a time, biting her tongue as if it were difficult work, moistening her lips and looking up from under her lashes with a smile. She could almost see his knees go wobbly at such an ordinary thing done with just the right flair. Stepping out of her skirt, then her drawers, she stood before him in her gauzy shift, letting him see—or imagine he saw, in the shadowy barn—the rosy spots of her nipples and the dark mystery below.

Martha enhanced the effect by smoothing her hands down her breasts, holding the fabric tight against them, then to her waist, and around her hips until she braced her hands behind them and thrust out her chest, tipping her head back as if she herself were overcome with the lust the man could hardly restrain. And she felt her own passion grow within her so that she not only felt incredibly wet down below but hotter than ever before through the rest of her.

But as wild as she was being, Martha Scrabblestone knew that there was a point further to which she should not go. She would give this man his pleasure enough that she might take hers equally.

And so she invited him into her arms, to kiss, and to guide his hand down her body as she had done to herself, and then she guided that hand up under the hem of her shift and left him to explore her cool, smooth flesh as he would.

All the while she was kissing him deeply, thrusting her tongue deep and receiving his deep thrust in return. She bit his lip a little, with a groan, and ground her hips against him, finally inviting his hand between her legs as she leaned back against the hay. But she would not recline fully, for she would not let him pin her. No, she stayed on her feet and kept him on his. And at the man's touch of her slippery womanhood she climaxed almost immediately, for she had aroused herself that far already.

Once she had recovered after the waves of sensation she craved, she helped him withdraw his hand, let her shift drop between them, and began to fumble at his crotch as if she didn't know the way. His penis was stiff between them, impossible to miss, and she grasped it in her hand.

Like she might hold the handle of a churn to dash it up and down, she enclosed his penis in her slender fist and cradle his testicles with her other hand, mewing with feminine wonder as his eyes rolled back in his head. Just a couple of pumps of her hand made him explode, gasping, his breeches sodden.

Although she realized that successful pleasure would need to be a two-way street or it wouldn't be able to happen, Martha had decided that to protect herself, she must be sure to arrange things in ways that would ensure that protection. She had learned that she was probably cleverer than everyone else she knew. Sometimes, though, her brilliant thinking was also her weakness—she knew no one she respected, so she could not benefit from the advice and thoughts of others.

As a young woman, Martha found herself to be fearless and calm under pressure, for she had learned to be so even when she was a child. When Gus was brought home one night beaten almost to death by men who had robbed him, Kristen descended into shaking fits. Martha, only nine years old at the time, took charge. She got Gus to bed, applied rudimentary first aid, then arranged to get the doctor and took charge of her father's care. Truth be told, Martha felt little affection toward Gus, but she knew the family would be in financial straits if he didn't recover. Fortunately, he did.

In the early 1670s in Massachusetts, it was clear Martha could not achieve her goals on her own. She needed a man. She found her man in the person of Richard Stanfield, who had about the same financial wherewithal as did the Scrabblestones, but he had several characteristics that made him perfect for Martha.

First, Richard was financially ambitious, as was Martha, though he did not perhaps share her social ambitions.

Second, he was easy for Martha to manipulate. Richard wasn't that sharp to begin with, and it was easy for Martha to turn him in whatever direction she wanted. She would be the dominant player in the relationship, albeit not the way Gus dominated Kristen, for then Martha would have had contempt for Richard as Gus did for Kristen.

Third, and finally, Richard was hopelessly in love with Martha. Hopelessly and completely, as much as anyone could be. Other young men drooled around her, leered at her, elbowed one another over her. But Richard was almost on one knee to propose as soon as he had a chance. Clearly, he worshiped her. And though they enjoyed many secret pleasures together, Martha made exceptionally sure that nothing occurred that could lead to a pregnancy.

MARTHA MEETS MILES

Richard was just perfect until Martha got a glimpse of the Downing family carriage, the likes of which she saw only rarely in Briarcliff. She and her parents were at the market when she spied a well-dressed young man alighting from the carriage and strolling among the tables and booths in the market.

She could see immediately that he was not a local, and she set about crossing his path several times that afternoon—catching his eye a few times with a smile and a demure turning aside. One time she positioned herself several paces ahead of him, turned sideways to set off her bosom to best effect, and stretched herself side to side with her arms overhead—alluringly, she knew.

This had the desired effect, so quickly that even Martha was surprised. Almost at once, the man rushed up to her. "Miss, might I help you carry that basket? It seems it has fatigued you."

"Why thank you, kind sir," she said in her surprisingly deep voice that a smitten youth had once said reminded him of rich maple syrup. She fell into step next to him, but a half a pace ahead, so that he might gaze upon her. "I have only to walk to the blacksmith's up there. My father, Gustavus Scrabblestone, will be waiting for me."

To Martha's surprise, she could tell that the young man seemed unsure of himself—*Not what I would expect*, she thought.

He said, "Well, Miss Scrabblestone, let me introduce myself. I am Miles Downing, of North Hinkapee some miles southwest of here. My father founded the town."

"Oh, is he the mayor, then?" she asked. *He certainly is prosperous, to judge from the clothes and carriage.*

"Oh no," Miles answered. "He finds it best to let others manage those kinds of things. He is a man of vision," he added with a note of pride in his father.

"Are you, too, a man of vision, Mr. Downing?" She held her head tipped inquiringly, as a robin might do, for her instincts told her he would appreciate the more delicate and girlish aspects of feminine nature. Miles looked down quickly and then raised his head to her in an almost rueful smile, and shook his head as if to acknowledge, *No I am not.*

Before they reached the blacksmith's, Miles pulled up short and quickly handed Martha her basket, muttering a hurried "Pardon" as he took two steps up the courthouse steps. There he met a man who was coming down, a bandy-legged man with a long nose and a distinct resemblance to … a rat? The man was clutching papers to his chest and looking around suspiciously.

That can't be his father, Martha thought. Miles spoke to him, and the man looked at him and then up and down the street again, continuing down the steps and leaving Miles to follow.

Miles was different, and physically impressive—tall and well-built, with gentle blue eyes and long, rich brown hair tied into a sleek knot at the back. *Not the Puritan roundhead fashion,* she thought. *Interesting.* But why was this Miles Downing so anxious? He struck her as being cautious in everything, unsure whether he was in the right or in the wrong. That was puzzling, as she assumed that a rich man's son would be much more self-assured.

Ah, well, it was worth a try, she thought. She walked to the blacksmith's to find her father, and then they collected her mother, who'd been selling plain goods from a basket on a street corner. Kristen stitched carefully but simply, so handkerchiefs and shifts and shirts were all she ventured to make for sale. After Gus growled over the few coins she'd earned while he saw to his own business, he gestured to her to gather it all up, and he set off home, leaving Kristen to follow, holding out an elbow so his beautiful blond daughter could trip along at his side swinging her basket, which wasn't so heavy after all.

Several days later Martha happened to look out one of the low windows of her rude home and saw her mother at the clothesline, dipping her head humbly as a man—*that same rat man!*—held his hat before him, fingering the brim. Kristen nodded a couple of times, and even stood a little straighter as he seemed to speak respectfully to her.

When she came into the house, Martha eyed her to see if she would say anything about the visitor, but Kristen kept as silent as she usually was. *What was this about?* Martha wondered.

Over the next two days, Martha deliberated whether to push her mother into telling about the man or whether to keep quiet and watch what developed.

Then, on the third day later, a Sunday, the family walked to church as they usually did—for all good Briarcliff families did the same. To Martha's surprise, she thought she saw that sleek caramel knot of hair at the back of one head a few pews up from theirs. For the Scrabblestones knew their place and sat near the back with the others not so well-to-do.

No doubt Martha's father was impervious to the words of the sermon, for he attended church only to keep in good stead for his little business here and there. Once the blessed end to the hours of service had come, Martha stood and craned her neck to see the people in that pew file out into the aisle, and it was as she had thought! Miles was dressed in his Sunday best, enough to make clear he was a man of significant means, and though a visitor in town, a visitor who took time to go to church.

"Why, hello, Miss Scrabblestone," said Miles with an air of confidence as he walked up to her.

He seems quite different this time around, Martha thought, and she was almost annoyed with herself for being startled at that, so she replied, "Why hello to you, sir. Do I know you?" *That might throw him off a bit.*

"Not very well, miss, though I did introduce myself to you last week, and carried your basket in the market. I am Miles Downing, at your service." He gave a slight bow of his head, like a true gentleman, and that was a thing not often seen in Briarcliff, or at least among the people the Scrabblestones knew best.

Yes, this did turn Martha's head, as she was not used to men showing courtesy to her. Most just stared at her bug-eyed and some even slightly open-mouthed with their hopes and intentions obvious. Richard was different, of course, as he was always good to her—almost worshipping in his devotion

Miles seemed to recall himself then, and he asked if he might meet her parents. So Martha turned aside to reveal her mother sitting quietly in the pew, and saw that her father had left from the other end of the pew. They'd have to find him outside.

"This is my mother," Martha said, adding, "Mother, this is Miles Downing."

Kristen looked up, startled, and blushed as she quickly stood to meet the fine young man. He bowed to Kristen and did not venture to put out his hand—Martha had seen that was how a mannerly man of means showed he did not presume the woman would offer her hand to him.

"I am honored to meet you, Mistress Scrabblestone." Then he said to Martha, "No need to find your father for me—I saw him when I came in, and perhaps I will find him outside." And then he was gone.

Martha was a bit unbalanced by that very brief meeting. *Would he come all this way just to go to church, and then be gone again?* She walked all over Briarcliff that afternoon and on Monday, looking for some sign of his fine carriage, but there was no hint of it anywhere. *Did he come just to meet me again?*

He must have, for Miles now made a habit of making the two-day journey to Briarcliff at least once a month, and sometimes twice a month, each time to call on her, without announcing a formal courtship. And Richard began to show his alarm at the competition. Martha enjoyed the alternating encounters with one and then the other as both sought her hand. And even though she felt genuine affection for Richard, she was developing the same for Miles as well. Could she really love two men?

Martha deceived herself that she was weighing her options and, to her own surprise, asked her mother about it. Kristen also surprised Martha and probably herself by giving her some very useful life advice, wistfully and sadly.

"You know," Kristen said, "it's just as easy to fall in love with a rich man as a poor man ..."

In those moments Martha realized that her mother was not just a drudge for her father, but had her own feelings, and wanted a better life for her daughter than she had made for herself with her poor marriage to Gus. How poorly Martha had treated her mother, who still loved her despite her behavior. In a flooding flash of feelings, Martha was ashamed of herself. She wanted to embrace her mother and thank her and tell her how sorry she was, but she couldn't bring herself to do it. Instead, she said only, "Thank you, Mother." And she gave Kristen a meaningful look that she hoped conveyed her feelings without the necessity of overt action. Would Kristen remember that look? Martha hoped so.

Kristen looked back at her daughter, and their gaze held for a few extra seconds, but she said nothing more.

For the sake of appearances, and to make herself more attractive to Miles, Martha put Richard Stanfield and Miles Downing on equal footing in their courtship; however, the outcome was never in doubt.

MARTHA
AND THOMPSON

In the days to follow, Miles brought his parents, Thompson and Comfort Downing, to Briarcliff to meet the parents of Martha Scrabblestone. The Downings were polite and respectful to just the right degree. Impolite would have been condescending, making too plain that there was a dramatic social order difference between the two families. Too polite would have made it just as plain, but more subtly. The Downings dressed well enough that they were not hiding their wealth, but not so well as to make the Scrabblestones feel inferior. And their temperament at dinner with the Scrabblestones was just the same.

The evening was a great success for everyone. Kristen had had Martha's eager help in the kitchen for the first time in many years, to put together what was for them a magnificent feast and for the Downings tolerable. Comfort Downing seemed not to be subservient to her husband, but at the same time not particularly interested in the Downings' businesses. Comfort seemed to respect her husband and his effective genius for growing and governing, and she did not meddle. She kept to her role running the household.

The two families got on very well, with the women speaking lightly together in the kitchen and the men laughing heartily over third mugs of ale at the table and talking until late in the evening. Martha was pleased that Gus was behaving himself—she'd well prepared him to do so. All appeared completely well.

Then Thompson took Martha aside and requested a quiet walk and talk outside.

"My son fancies you," he said, as an opening gambit once they were strolling through the kitchen garden and then beyond to the trees.

Martha smiled and looked down, saying nothing and trying to look coquettish. She knew that this was an important conversation and would play it out appropriately. She expected a typical encounter with a prospective father-in-law, though she had never met anyone like Thompson before. He was clearly Miles's father, to judge by his looks, but there was clearly much more substance to him.

"I care greatly for my son's happiness," Thompson said, and Martha assumed he was going to ask if she would be a good wife, so she could make the appropriate "Oh, sir, yes!" response. Instead, he said, "But I care even more for the Downing legacy."

Martha nodded, trying to look knowing, but despite her belief that she was wilier than everyone else, she was only nearing twenty years old and had not yet realized that for the first time possibly ever, she was way out of her depth. Indeed, she had no idea where Thompson was heading.

"I would like Miles to find a wife who'll help him lead the family in North Hinkapee, a woman who will support my—*our*—vision. Are you that woman?"

Thompson looked at her directly, and now she could see that his eyes were a much more dangerous blue than Miles's eyes. This unbalanced her. She blushed—flustered—it was an uncomfortable feeling that she distinctly disliked.

There was an obvious answer and Martha gave it. "Yes," she said, once she'd regained her composure, and looked Thompson in the eye as unflinchingly as she could. She realized that Thompson had the upper hand in this conversation, and probably would in future conversations as well, but she resolved to do as well as she could after saying the one-word answer. "Yes," she repeated, then said nothing more, sensing that silence might seem stronger than more words.

Thompson looked back at her penetratingly. "I know you have to say that, but I think you mean it as well."

He paused for a bit, giving her a very long stare, intending to be disquieting—and succeeding. "Martha, let us be honest with each other."

"Yes, Mr. Downing."

"You can call me Thompson."

"Very well … Thompson."

"I intend to live a while longer. Then I will pass and leave my son Miles with everything. If you marry him, you will be very wealthy, as I am sure you have noticed."

"Well, of course," said Martha, "but that has nothing to do with—"

Thompson cut her off. "As I said, let's be honest with each other. Of course monetary considerations are paramount for you. They would be for any woman, but for you in particular, this is what you have angled for all along."

Martha now realized she was outmatched, and it wasn't even a close match. She concluded that the only way to play it was straight up, so she said only "Yes."

"I intend to pass everything to my son; however, my will will make very clear that nothing will ever pass to you under any circumstances. When Miles dies, the money, the property, and everything else will go to his offspring or others in the Downing clan. You'll never get anything of your own.

"However, I will also provide that you will live well, and extremely well, as long as you are married to my son and supportive of the Downings in North Hinkapee."

He added, knowing that her mind would have raced to this conclusion, "And I will also provide that if my son pre-deceases you, as long as you are married to him at the time of his death, you will be well taken care of in that case, as well."

Martha looked at him quizzically, so Thompson continued. "If I do this, then you will have no motivation but to protect, grow, nurture and take care of the Downing clan, because its strength and power will be your safety net."

Martha made to speak, but Thompson silenced her with a raised hand. "Let me conclude. I think you've figured out my son pretty well by now. Is that right?"

"I don't know what you mean," said Martha.

Thompson fired up a bit and said, "Martha if you're not going to be honest with me, then I will not approve this marriage. Do I make myself clear?"

"Yes, sir," she said, realizing that, sharp as she was, she was no match for Thompson, and probably never would be. "And yes, I've figured out Miles very well." Martha was now completely humble, which was a new feeling for her but one that, to her complete surprise, she was enjoying. It was a strange thing, but something about Thompson was comforting—it was good to have someone around she did not feel intellectually superior to. She shivered, despite the fact that the evening was not cold. Then she came back to the present with a start. Thompson was speaking …

"He's not strong. He's a sweet and good man. If he marries you, he'll quickly become your puppet, will he not? And indeed that's one of the reasons you want to marry him. Answer truthfully."

"Yes, sir," said Martha.

"I can't have that, can I?"

"Can't have what?" she said, flustered.

"I can't have my son become your puppet, can I?"

Martha paused and said, "I suppose not." She felt a clutch of unnatural fear—was Thompson going to disapprove of her?

"But I will, anyway," he said.

Martha looked surprised.

"Look. I've accomplished much, but even I can't change a person's basic nature. I've set up North Hinkapee as the best place for the Downings, but I know that my son is not capable of running it. Within ten years after my death it will all fall apart as things stand. I do need someone like you after all."

"So, as I said, I'm going to set things up so that you can have everything only if you do what needs to be done for the Downing clan." He left that thought lingering on the breeze as he pulled out of his pocket a beautifully carved ivory pipe, filled it with fragrant tobacco, and struck a spark with a flint to start it. Martha found herself mesmerized by the ritual, then enchanted by the rich smoke that spoke of what wonders awaited her in the company of this man.

Thompson blew two rings of smoke that rose and dissipated in the night air, and then he spoke again. "I just said those things so you would understand me, and at the end of this conversation I will ask for your word that you will do as we agree.

"In return, while I'm alive, I'll teach you all that I know. About power. About how to run the clan I will grow with your help. About how to bend people to your will. About—well, everything."

Martha felt like a little child again and could only stare at him, wide-eyed.

"And in return you will do everything in your power to make my son the happiest man alive, will you not?"

Martha shook off the spell and started thinking fast. Even for her nimble mind this was coming at her in a rush. After a pause she looked Thompson in the eye and said, "Yes. I agree to every single thing you just said. And I promise to be completely honest with you on everything going forward."

Thompson smiled and, with the same aplomb he must have used whenever he sealed an agreement with a man, he extended his hand to Martha. "Then I guess we have a deal, don't we?"

"Indeed we do," said Martha, relieved that she had survived the most important meeting of her life.

Back in the house, they found that Miles and Gus had run out of things to discuss, but Comfort and Kristen were chatting companionably by the hearth.

Yes, it's been a successful evening, thought Martha, relieved and excited at her prospects.

Martha wanted to avoid the painful and unpleasant duty of gently breaking the news to Richard Stanfield before Miles's official proposal, before the banns were announced in church to set her new life in motion. She thought it best to do it quickly and coolly, but she found the conversation difficult; indeed, it was more difficult than any conversation she had ever had before.

After she met with him, for once she found herself with tears in her eyes. Richard had received her words as if she'd slapped him across the face—he crumpled in pain, just moments after his eyes had shone at her in love.

She found herself trembling at what she'd just done. Sometimes, she realized, there was a cost to even the best choices.

The next day in town, Martha noticed frowns and people turning away from her, shaking their heads. One old crone hobbled out into the street and pointed a bony finger at her: "Mark my words, you temptress—you have destroyed one life, but that is likely only the first. Shame be upon you!"

Martha turned and rushed home, wondering what had happened, how the news had spread so quickly about a simple broken courtship. But then when Gus came home that evening, he made it all plain.

"Now you've done it, girl," said Gus, shaking his head with rare fatherly disappointment. "You made that boy do away with himself! They found him by the river, a musket ball right through his head."

Martha searched her conscience as she lay awake in bed that night, eyes dry and sore—finished with tears, but certainly shock had flooded through her at the news. She wondered if she could have handled things better—for example, by not leading Richard on so long, giving him hope of a chance even while Miles was courting her at the same time.

So Martha Scrabblestone—still a virgin in actuality but certainly not in spirit—married Miles Downing before the magistrate in Briarcliff. Miles proudly brought her in what was now sort of her carriage to what would be her new home, and Martha beamed at the North Hinkapee villagers who awaited them after their wedding journey.

As the Scrabblestones died within several years after her marriage, Martha truly belonged in North Hinkapee from then on. Miles called his a "modest farm," and so it seemed, next to Thompson's enormous farm estate. But still, the farm was as fine as Martha might have ever imagined might one day be her home. It was a good place to sojourn—a temporary arrangement—as they waited to take over the much bigger estate one day.

MARTHA AND MILES IN NORTH HINKAPEE

Over the coming years Martha had frequent conversations with Thompson and eagerly absorbed his unquestionably brilliant advice. Thompson was not afraid to be frank with Miles in Martha's presence, for she knew his weaknesses and had come to love Miles as her husband, too.

"Miles," Thompson said one day, as the three of them were sitting outside on a wooden bench not far from the main building. "Sometimes a man has to be strong in the face of adversity. Sometimes a man has to do what has to be done even if he is afraid to do it."

"Yes, Father," said Miles.

"Sometimes a man just must be in charge."

"Yes, Father."

"And that's not you, is it, son?"

"No sir," said Miles with a sigh. "I know I'm letting you down, but I think I'll let everyone down if I pretend to be what I'm not."

"Son, I'm impressed," said Thompson. "It is rare that people are capable of being straightforward with themselves about their own shortcomings. But we have to do something about this. Otherwise, the Downing clan will be at risk ..."

Martha knew that this is where she came in, why Thompson had drawn her into his dynasty. She trembled with excitement at the possibilities, as Thompson continued to speak to his son, giving him sage advice.

"Miles, if you're feeling like you are weak or don't know what to do in a situation," Thompson said, "then just don't say anything. Just be quiet and nod knowingly. Trust me, people won't know what to make of it and will assume something strong and ominous. Nothing is more frightening than a person with perceived power not saying anything."

Then turning to Martha, he said, "And as for you, Martha, you will be the strong one here, as you both know. But this has to remain private, as others will not accept a woman leading. They will do what you say at first, but eventually they will become restive. So, for all public purposes it must seem that Miles is in charge."

Then he looked at the two of them. "Alone, each of you will have troubles, but together you will be the right team to lead and grow the Downing clan in North Hinkapee."

Martha and Miles, entwined in each other's arms, looked back at Thompson and nodded agreement. Everything seemed to make sense.

As the years passed, Miles was content to read books and to cultivate friendships, leaving the business of the estate to his wife and father, though he was careful to know and understand everything that was happening. Oddly, but maybe not really oddly, he found himself developing a friendship with Ahanu. *We are both outcasts*, Miles realized from time to time.,

Miles's biggest issue over time was loneliness. It was hard for him being in a place of authority in North Hinkapee, because there were no other men of his station that he could be friends with. His father had insisted that they maintain an appropriate distance from the people they governed—though the visible government seemed not to be in their hands—and that left Miles often quite alone. More than anything, he wanted a man for a friend, a man to hunt with, to shoot with, to talk about books with, to smoke and drink with, and to take long walks with through the rich holdings of the Downings.

Both Miles and Martha learned many lessons from Thompson, but the greatest was that loyalty to the family—the clan—had to always be the paramount consideration. That loyalty would build the strength of the clan, and without the clan, and what it represented, there was no power. And without power there was no ability to protect what they had built. Thompson drove this lesson home repeatedly, making things clear to both of them with exacting words and by his actions as well. Both his son and his son's wife would have a part in this dynasty to come.

For Thompson, Martha immediately became the missing link—they were kindred spirits. Martha basked in his approval and absorbed his life energy into her own being. But she could always tell he held back with a little caution, as if she were not fully worthy of all his ideals. And it was true that—clever as she was—she occasionally completely missed his meaning, took something too far, or was just flummoxed at what he intended.

Thompson was truly a great man—a visionary—and indeed a genius. Martha, although brilliant, was not his equal and was intelligent enough to understand this. The comforting feeling she had felt at the first meeting, to have someone smarter than she around, never left while Thompson was alive. She knew that after he passed, she would have to manage things the best she could.

Thompson continued to remind her that although Martha could—and should—be the effective power behind the throne, no one would accept a woman in an obvious position of authority. Accordingly, it was important for Miles to continue in that role publicly. Martha would be a critical advisor and even mover of key events, but as far as North Hinkapee was concerned, it would have to appear that Miles was "the man in charge." Some might eventually suspect the truth, but there would be little advantage in discussing such a matter, for no one would want to cross the Downings. The people of North Hinkapee would likely keep their thoughts to themselves.

Martha knew that Miles utterly loved this arrangement. He knew his father's affection for him and he knew he was not suited to the more unseemly and occasionally more ruthless parts of the work that Thompson did. Miles didn't want to run things and make tough decisions. When his father passed on and was no longer "in charge," then Martha would take over.

Miles fancied a big family and Martha wholeheartedly agreed. They got busy conceiving, which was happy for all concerned, at least at the beginning of the business. Miles was a normally randy young man, and Martha an amazingly attractive woman, with a huge bosom contraposing her otherwise thin and supple figure, and with a sexual appetite to match her appeal. She also remembered her promise to Thompson to make his son as happy as she could. Martha certainly had a great capacity for making a man happy behind closed doors.

Though Martha became pregnant seven times, the first two miscarried. The third time, she gave birth to twins—Matthew and Patrick. Then there were two infant deaths, despite the earnest ministrations of Betsy Laurents, the talented young midwife they'd brought in from Hinkapee, who later married Sheriff Jones and became the established midwife of the village. Two more miscarriages then followed, and in the end Martha and Miles had just the two sons, born in the second year of their marriage. Those two would be the hope for the dynasty Thompson Downing had in mind.

While Thompson was alive, he made many plans. When he brought in the former Indian-killer John Jones as sheriff when the young couple were busy raising Matt and Pat, it was clear that Thompson was establishing a power structure to carry on what he had begun. Meanwhile, Martha was completely content in her place. She had a perfectly good husband who adored her, and whom she could bend to her will as needed. She had two growing sons. And she was learning how to rule a kingdom from one of the greatest visionaries the colonies had yet seen. Eventually she would in fact rule this kingdom, one small step behind her genial husband, knowing that was her purpose in life.

Thompson Downing died in the early 1680s, content in his eighth decade, surrounded by his wife and son and promising daughter-in-law and his son's sons. Comfort died soon after, and then it was time for Miles and Martha to take over the estate Martha had longed to inhabit for a decade. For the residents of North Hinkapee, it was a seamless transition. They had other things to worry about than who was running things. In this frontier town, the priorities were being fed all year, staying warm in the winter, and keeping safe from Indians. Then it was important not to fall prey to illness. And finally, as they considered their souls with the help of Minister Brown, the people of North Hinkapee were well cultivated in their fear that the Devil, or witches, might enter the community. These things were more likely to occupy their thoughts than were township political issues.

Things were going extremely well for the Downings, but nothing good lasts forever, and the seeds of change had been planted; indeed, from the fruit of Miles's very loins, trouble had been born.

As the Downing boys—Matt and Pat—grew, they began to get in an almost non-stop heap of trouble. Sometimes it was scrapes with the law, and sometimes scrapes that did not involve the law—it was all the same. Matt was the instigator, and Pat followed along. Sometimes Martha wondered at an ugly expression or a small cruelty from Matt that reminded her of her father. *Does he carry Gus's blood so strongly?*

And these were to be the next generation of Downing rulers— Pat as ineffectual as his father and Matt as cruel and degenerate as his grandfather? This was a problem for Martha to solve, and it would be without Thompson's guidance.

INTERLUDE

NUNUNYI STRIKES

"Three dead," said the man Josephson had hired to keep the peace if unpleasant events broke out at The Inn at Bearminster. It was odd that the man hadn't been around when needed the night before, though.

"What do you mean?" asked Josephson.

"Those three men who were here last night. That man right there"—he nodded to where Sheriff Jones was dozing in a wooden chair with his head against the wall—"ran 'em off this morning. They're dead on the road."

"Where?"

"About half a mile down."

Sheriff Jones overheard the conversation and roused himself, then ambled across the room. "What is this about?" he said.

The three men hurried out of the inn and down the road to where a wagon stood, its horses quietly in harness, waiting for instructions. It was pretty obvious what had happened.

Three arrows were present.

One arrow had hit one of the men in the back with great force, piercing him through the front so that he lay on his side in the wagon bed, the arrow holding him in position.

Another arrow had hit a man in the chest and pierced through his sternum with enough force to come out of his back. That man was on his side on the ground, presumably having fallen from the bench at the front.

And the third arrow, most gruesomely, had gone through the eye of the third man—the driver—and lodged in his skull, and he was slumped over the seat, held somewhat by the reins still tangled around his hands.

All three were dead, of course, and after further examination, Jones, Josephson, and Josephson's man loaded them into the back of the wagon, turned it around, and drove it back to the inn to figure out what to do next. There was no particular law in Bearminster, and Sheriff Jones was not in his own jurisdiction.

When they arrived, Menon was in the main room, still dizzy and groggy but hungry as a bear and about to plow into an enormous breakfast. Nununyi sat quietly by his side.

"Hey, Jones," said Menon, half rising, as the men came in, the innkeeper and his man babbling about what they'd found.

As Sheriff Jones sat down, waiting for black coffee to be poured, he relayed the morning's events to Menon in more detail. "I wonder who did this?" he murmured, looking pointedly at Nununyi.

"I guess you know as well as I do," said Menon quietly.

"I guess I do," said Jones. He remembered how arrows had whizzed from the underbrush in that battle many years before, cutting down fighter after fighter. There was no doubt in his mind what had happened. Apparently, she had acted on her own, awakening quietly while Menon slept, creeping outside, dispatching the three evil men, and sneaking back to their bed before Menon arose.

"What are you going to do?" asked Menon.

"Me?" said Jones. "Why do I have to do anything? I'm not the sheriff here. I'm guessing that this is a matter for the good Mr. Josephson. I have no real thoughts nor evidence to give in a court of law here. I would guess that the three men were waylaid this morning by Indians or ruffians. I can't say I will rue their passing."

They both stared at Nununyi, who looked back at them, slowly blinking her great dark eyes. It took little effort for her to keep her expression impassive.

They all looked at each other for a bit, one to another, and then Menon chuckled, then a laugh came from Jones. Both were soon guffawing, and not long after, Nununyi could not hold back, either, and her face lit up with a big smile—a smile that was rare and dazzling.

So things didn't go as expected, but it was a merry reunion after all. Sheriff Jones was thinking about how much fun it would be to tell his Betsy what had happened.

1692, NORTH HINKAPEE

LUCY TELLS ROBERT EVERYTHING

"Robert," said Lucy, when he had come in for lunch, "there is something I have to reveal to you. It is a grave matter, a dire one … but I must tell you. Sit down, I pray you."

Robert sat down, setting his hat on the table and wiping his brow with his forearm. The two had known much heartache recently, and his expression showed he was bracing for more. Lucy paced up and down, wondering how she could say it, thankful that Faythe was in the garden and Chloe as far away as if she'd gone on a long journey.

"Please forgive me for what I have done," Lucy said all at once, wringing her hands as she stood before him. "I did what I thought was best—for Chloe, for you, for Faythe, for me, for all of us. But it might not seem so now."

"Lucy, whatever it is, it is—out with it already." His anxiety was making him short with her.

Not a good beginning, she thought.

"It's about Chloe … the story we told you. She didn't fall off a horse."

Robert's eyes widened. "Then why did you say so?"

"To protect you."

"To protect me from what?"

"From yourself."

"Enough of this," he said, rising from his chair and bracing his hands on the table. "Just tell me what happened—the truth this time."

"Chloe was … violated by Matt and Pat Downing." She saw that he was frozen in place, so she continued, all in a rush. "Faythe was nearby but knew not until it was done. She saw the boys leaving and went to Chloe, but it was too late. I knew what you would do—what I can see is now in your eyes."

She raised her hand to forestall his reaction, so she might continue. "I didn't tell you because you'd seek vengeance, and in the end the Downings would kill you, or worse—well, put an end to our family … You know it is no difficulty for them to do so."

Robert was breathing heavily as he came around the table to her. Though he was usually a tranquil man, now he was shaking with rage.

"Woman," he said, low and threatening. "How could you hide this from me?"

Lucy faced him bravely. Never in their score of years married had she endured such a chasm between them. But she knew she had created it out of honor, out of love. She spoke quietly, hoping to gentle his own tone. "I hid it from you to save you. If you go off headstrong now, you will put us all in mortal danger. Every one of us. It was devastation that came to Chloe. I did not want to witness worse."

Robert stood there trembling, fists balled, face contorted as he struggled to master himself. She had never seen him like this. But as the moments passed, he would know that what she said was wisdom, if only he *could* master himself until he came to that conclusion. They must survive these days, and whatever lay between Robert Wentworth and the Downings could wait for a more opportune time.

He looked up, a question passing over his features. "So why reveal this now?"

"Because … because …" The words were sticking in Lucy's throat. "Because Chloe is … with child." She looked down at her shoes.

Robert staggered back at this second blow. Lucy had had time to prepare as her suspicions grew and then were confirmed. But he was learning all this at once, and reeling. She expected he might need to walk, and indeed he made his way past her and strode out the door without a word.

Robert found himself well into the woods before he came to himself. He looked around and began to feel what was lost—ironically, he was on the very trail where Faythe and Chloe had spent so many happy hours together.

And now it was all blasted.

His mind was in a storm, a wicked wind flinging around his thoughts, banging them against one another and tangling them together. His first instinct was to just continue on the trail to the Downings' and kill Matt and Pat with his bare hands, and who would blame him? Another path would take him to Sheriff Jones to demand their arrest. Other whims and determinations whirled in his mind as he tried to settle with the revelation. Even Job had not seen his children destroyed as Chloe had been.

After he had stalked through the woods for what seemed a long time, he thought that perhaps he should pray for guidance. Maybe God would guide him?

Robert fell to his knees on the trail, taking the posture of help-lessness he felt more keenly than any man on Earth that day, he thought. He spoke quietly, his hands empty before him. "Dear God," he said, "I've always been a penitent man when I have known myself to be wrong, a God-fearing man. I've always tried to do what is right and what is good. Please, Heavenly Father, guide me now. Show me what I should do. Please ... Please ..."

He knelt, silent, for a long time, and after a while he felt a quiet settling of peace overlaying him like a blanket on his shoulders. Like a man plucked from a shipwreck, knowing his companions were lost forever, though he chattered yet with life under the care of his rescuers, he knew he must endure. His peace was a stilling thing, a calming thing, though he had lost nearly all. But what remained—his wife and daughters at home—must still be cared for.

He rose from his knees and started the walk back home.

When he arrived, Lucy was there, as was Faythe, both staring at him with fear and pity and question, and he went to them and wrapped his arms around them both at the same time. Then they all turned to Chloe in her chair, staring vacantly at the wall before her.

Whatever devastation had come to their family was not yet over; indeed, it was likely just beginning.

"What are you going to do?" asked Lucy timidly.

"I have no idea," said Robert. "I have no idea ..." He sat down heavily, like a man decades older, and stared into the wood of his kitchen table. He thought back on his life, which, because of Lucy and his girls, had brought him great joy. The journey had not seen progress overall but a series of setbacks, and he had fought against them by dint of character and will. And so he would continue.

He thought, *I do indeed have kinship to Job, and I will take my measure from him. I will never give up on the Lord's ultimate goodness. "Though He slay me, yet shall I trust Him."*

DR. ALDERSON VISITS WITH MARTHA

Philip Alderson arrived later that afternoon at the Downings' farm, for the second time that day. Martha heard him announce to the servant who greeted him that he had been told Martha wasn't feeling well, and he was admitted to her sitting room, where she sat with her feet up, in an attitude befitting her supposed indisposition.

He was carrying his medicine bag and, as soon as they were alone, without a word he pulled a pouch out of it and withdrew two vials of liquid from the pouch.

"Well, then," she said, gesturing toward the vials he held. "How do they work?"

"Pretty simply," said Dr. Alderson. "You combine equal parts of each and give a spoonful to the girl three times, at intervals of three hours. And that should be that."

"And if it would be more ... likely ... that the woman not survive"—she coughed a little and adjusted herself in her seat. "Or, of course one must be sure not to give so much as to cause harm to the woman. How much would do so?"

Dr. Alderson closed his eyes. "The darker one," he said, opening them and pointing to one of the two vials. "If there were too large a portion of that one, the medicine would be more potent and ... survival less likely."

"Thank you, Doctor," said Martha.

Dr. Alderson got up to leave. There was no need for Martha to admonish him to silence. He knew the stakes.

"One more thing," said Martha, as he reached the door. "Tomorrow afternoon it might be well for you to report a theft of some of your medicines .... . these medicines. Report to the sheriff ..."

Dr. Alderson nodded reluctant agreement and left.

Once alone, Martha sighed, feeling a little of the illness her posture in the chair indicated. *Is this the wisest plan?* she wondered, uncharacteristically unsure of herself. She felt grief, too, to her core. What had come before, what was happening now, and what would come to be—at her hand—she could never be proud of. Although she did not feel at heart what so many around her felt in their devotion to God, she knew that He would not look kindly on her actions.

If Thompson were still alive, he would know what to do. Probably not this, she knew on some level. But he had entrusted to Martha to do the best she could. And whatever it took, Martha would protect the Downing clan.

She rang a bell for her Indian maidservant to find Elmer, and then for the maidservant to be ready to help her to bed before dinner. She would be glad to have the excuse of her illness to quell any questions.

Elmer Perkins stuck his long nose through the doorway of Martha's sitting room and she wrinkled her nose at his presence, always sniffing around. He was a necessary nuisance, loyal toward the Downings and unscrupulous otherwise.

"Come in," she called from the dim corner where she'd been thinking hard through all the eventualities, the contingencies.

He jumped a little, her words from out of the shadows startling him.

"There's nothing to be concerned about," she said. "I have a job for you to do."

"Should I wait for Mr. Downing to join us?" he asked.

Martha shook her head. "This is just for us, Elmer. Miles doesn't need to know everything that goes on."

Elmer swallowed hard and nodded agreeably. "Yes, Mrs. Downing," he said.

Martha spoke directly and plainly, but quietly. There was no need to soften things with Elmer.

"Chloe Wentworth is pregnant," she announced all at once, and Elmer raised his eyebrows in surprise. "Elmer, these medicines"—she held up the pouch—"if mixed together, will do away with that burden. Never mind why it is any of our concern. Tomorrow morning you are going to take this pouch to Lucy Wentworth and suggest that she give the medicine to her daughter. If it works, the problem is solved. If it doesn't work, then we're no worse off than we are now. Any questions?"

Elmer nodded agreement and shook his head that he had no questions. This was the sort of distasteful job he often did for the Downings, and even if it was unpleasant, he was always happy to have something of importance to do for the family, who paid him well. "The Rat" was well named by those who whispered behind their hands in town.

Martha said, "You *should* have asked the dosage. Are you paying heed?"

He nodded attentively.

"The proper mixture," she said, is two parts of the darker liquid and one part of the lighter one. That is to be given to the girl in a spoonful every three hours until ... You understand?"

"Yes," said Elmer. He took the pouch from Martha. "I'll be on my way, then."

As soon as he left the room, the Indian maidservant came in, as Martha had earlier bidden her. *Was she close enough to hear that?* Martha wondered. She often had trouble discerning what went on under the woman's stony expression, and she was often surprised to find her quite close by, for she moved so quietly in her Indian way. Well, it was no matter—she was a dull thing, after all.

FAYTHE AND TOMMY
—AND JANE, TOO

After the family mourned together over Robert receiving the awful secret Lucy and Faythe had been keeping, Robert dejectedly went back to do the evening farm chores. What good was there in continuing to muddle over ways of escaping the deadly trap they all found themselves in? But the crops still needed care, so that was at least one worthwhile thing to do.

Faythe took leave of her mother soon after that, as well. Faythe wanted—and needed—to talk to Tommy. He might have no answers for their dilemma; but he would listen and he would take her in his arms. And that seemed a good thing to pursue.

She walked the two miles to the Carlin farm and found Jane Carlin in the barn doing the evening milking. Her three cows were solid evidence of the Carlins' prosperity, as was their fragrant, well-filled barn. Jane gave Faythe a friendly "Hello."

Ever since the tragedy of Chloe's "accident," Jane Carlin had been especially welcoming to Faythe, likely wanting to encourage her son's aspirations to courtship. Though Faythe had perceived this interest for the future and perhaps should not have encouraged it, she had felt so alone recently, and so unwilling to further burden her own mother with her sorrows, that she had gone along with the unspoken idea that she might be Jane's daughter-in-law one day.

Ironically, Faythe thought that, even though not it was not in Tommy's interest, Jane might well be more sympathetic than others to the idea of a woman desiring not to marry. After all, she was widowed and not taking up with her several suitors. Jane Carlin did perfectly well without a husband, and so could Faythe!

Jane said, "I'm sure you are here to see Tommy and not this old woman. He's out in the field setting up a scarecrow. Those birds want our crops just days before we do! Just go down the lane and you'll find him soon enough."

Faythe gave Jane as warm a smile as she could muster and headed off.

Tommy waved to her from a distance and she tried to return his smile, but she could not manage it, and he, concerned, hurried toward her. His care for her brought tears to her eyes and she suddenly longed for the shelter of his arms, his strong chest, his head above her, looking out for what might trouble her.

When they reached one another, she said, without preamble, "Chloe's pregnant," and then she collapsed into his embrace.

"Oh no," said Tommy, and then after a pause, another "Oh no."

Faythe, having drawn strength from his arms, stepped back and explained as they walked side by side further from the house. "Mum figured it out, and it's possible that Dr. Alderson might know, too. I don't trust him. He feigns good will, but his manner is cool. I get the sense that he can tell what ails a person's heart as much as the body, but he may not use that knowledge to the person's good. Mum told Dad—and of course he did not know the truth before about the attack—so it all came at once for him, and oh, how he suffered, Tommy! He loves us so much, and all he could do was go striding out to the woods. He came back hours later, and … oh, none of us knows what to do!" The words were just tumbling out, and now sobs as well.

Tommy made to give Faythe another hug, but she had stiffened herself against her tears and against him, and she stepped away. "A hug won't help," she said.

Tommy said, "I don't know if anything else will actually help, either."

Faythe said, "I don't want a hug. Your arms around me will just make me cry even more, and I don't want to cry now. I want to decide what to do. I have to figure out what to do!"

She started striding furiously, leaving him to catch up. Her fury was growing. She was actually thinking of just shooting Matt and Pat and their father, too, for good measure—for allowing them to grow up to be beasts. She was an excellent shot, as Robert had ensured in another season of her training, and her skill had been honed through the years they'd hunted in this forest.

But Faythe pushed this exhilarating thought away. She wouldn't do that, at least not today.

"So, then," said Tommy. "Let's go talk to my mother, and the three of us can talk together. You know she loves your family, and she is wise—and crafty, too, when she needs to be."

Faythe was running out of reasons to keep things quiet, and because Jane Carlin was as trustworthy as was her son, she nodded and followed Tommy back to the house. One look at their faces made Jane pull out a chair for Faythe and urge them both to sit at the table.

"What is it, my dear?" Jane asked. "How might I help?"

Faythe related the story to Jane as she had to Tommy, and once Jane had recovered from the shock and sorrow, she grasped both Faythe's hands and said, "Tell me what you're thinking."

"Well," said Faythe, glad to have another supporter, "I suspect that Dr. Alderson knows. I just do. Mum thinks so, too, and she's never wrong about things like that. And I bet he told Miles Downing, because, like most everyone in North Hinkapee—or everyone important—Dr. Alderson is beholden to the Downings, who always want to know everything that goes on. So now Miles knows too, probably, as does anyone he cares to tell."

There was silence for a bit. Jane was thinking and Faythe and Tommy were watching her, Faythe hoping Jane's mind could spell her own exhausted one. *Could Jane have a solution?*

Finally, she spoke.

"What matter is it if Miles does know? What would be his gain in telling anyone? Surely he learned long ago what happened to Chloe—he is their father! One way or another he has decided not to say anything, as there's no advantage for him to do so. Now it has become even worse, and it is more important for him to keep his silence. I wager he will do nothing."

"I thought that, too, at first," said Faythe. "But that will not work for him—or for us. A woman—or girl—with child will eventually give birth. And how's that to be explained? No fall from a horse leads to a child."

Jane responded. "Yes, that is true, but I've another thought you may not have considered. You might not like this … but let me set forth the idea."

Faythe was certainly listening. No wonder Tommy had so much faith in his mother—Jane's calm demeanor inspired confidence.

"In a strange way, Miles is our fellow," said Jane. Faythe frowned, but she did not interrupt. "To explain," Jane went on. "Miles would not want this news to be known to the town, either. Otherwise, why is he concealing it?

"He's the most powerful person in these parts, as we all know."

They nodded.

"Maybe he will act in your favor, not because he's a saint but because it is a help to him to do so? He has had his hands full with Matt's mischief for years—and Pat's along with him—and this is the last thing he needs. You have likely noted that Sheriff Jones has given the Downings the same penalties that any other citizen of North

Hinkapee would suffer when Matt and Pat have been found in the wrong. He gets no special consideration, as far as I can tell.

"And the villagers here go along with the Downings being in charge because things don't get out of hand. Everyone has more important things to worry about than who is in charge of what. If people get the sense that the Downing boys can get away with what they did to Chloe, it will make it that much harder to keep the town together. Instead of everyone assuming the Downings run things by leave of the people, Miles Downing would find it much tougher to govern the town."

Faythe considered. She was making some sense. "How could Miles help us?" she asked.

"That I don't know, but having a Miles Downing in alliance, even if in secrecy, would certainly improve your lot. I don't like the man much myself, but he did not himself do Chloe wrong; it was his sons, perhaps just the one—the despicable Matt. No father would want his son so charged—publicly, to incur the possible ultimate penalty. For that is what it would be, to be sure."

Faythe was grudgingly beginning to follow along. She knew her father had actually liked Miles, though until he owned his own farm Robert would remain an inferior. Perhaps Miles Downing was not as bad a person as she had thought. Faythe noticed that she was asking questions and letting Jane do the thinking. That was restful and refreshing. She had been so long in solitary turmoil.

"What help would we ask of him?" Faythe asked again.

"Well," said Tommy in his first contribution to the discussion, "he might pay for the doctor, for a start."

"The doctor cannot help at this point," Faythe answered immediately. "Even before, the medicine he gave was worthless." Then she looked at Tommy's stricken face and realized that she was taking out her frustration on him. "Sorry, Tommy. I know you want to be of help, and I'm dragging that away from you. Thank you for trying ... I've just thought it all through so many times ..."

Jane added, "But wait, Faythe! Think of it this way. To carry on from what Tommy has said, the Downings could give you money to care for Chloe. Perhaps they could even cancel Robert's debt, so that the farm could be his without further payment! It is small consolation, to be sure, but it could be of real help."

"How would her current state be explained?" asked Faythe, musing.

"How about half of the truth?" asked Jane.

"What do you mean?"

"Tell people she was raped in the woods."

"Yes!" added Tommy. "You have no idea who did it—you found her there and lied to your parents about it, since you did not want to distress them."

"And you were ashamed," said Jane, covering Faythe's hand with her own.

"Who'd believe that?"

"Ummm … everyone," said Jane. "I certainly would."

"Are you sure?" asked Faythe. Her thoughts had roiled around so long she wasn't sure of her own judgment anymore. She found it difficult to know what people would think.

"People will *want* to believe whatever Miles tells them, so we must gather him to the cause. Of course, most of the town will conclude that it was Matt, but who will say that out loud?"

"Nobody, that's who," said Tommy with a grim laugh. "I mean, how many call Elmer 'The Rat' to his face or in front of Miles? Has anyone ever really confronted Miles on anything? Too many of the town depend on the Downings for their very homes and food. If you say this is what happened and Miles agrees, publicly, who is going to challenge this story?"

Faythe turned this over in her mind. The great injustice that would be done with this small lie was that Matt and Pat would get away with it. She ground her teeth together at the thought. She hated it with all her soul. She would have her vengeance, she knew, one way or another—she would not be stopped in that. But there was no need to hasten the retribution. Revenge could wait. Meanwhile, her family's pain could be lessened and they might even be able to get stronger together, to thrive. She would wait for an opening for herself.

"Tommy," she said, "until now, I wanted to be with you for your personal qualities"—she playfully ruffled his hair and squeezed his bicep, and all three of them laughed with a little relief. "But now I'm with you also because your mother is so wise. I think we might have a way through."

She turned to Jane and grasped both her hands on the table. "Thank you so much. Our family is indebted to you—or will be when I tell them."

Jane smiled, then winked at Tommy.

Faythe stood up. "I must get home," she said. She had a shred of hope.

Tommy stood too. "I'll walk you—it's dark now and just a sliver of moon."

Faythe knew he was hoping for a kiss good-bye, and he got it when they arrived at her farm.

THE WENTWORTHS
TALK ABOUT OPTIONS

When Faythe entered the kitchen, she could see they had not yet had supper, despite the late hour, and Lucy was bringing Chloe to the table to eat and Robert was washing up.

"Where have you been?" asked Lucy.

"I was with Tommy," said Faythe.

Lucy nodded knowingly and they all sat down for Robert to say grace. He thanked the Lord God for the meal but also prayed, eloquently, for guidance as to "the right thing to do" in their current circumstances. As soon as he said "Amen" and they echoed him—Chloe mouthing the long-familiar word though she knew not what she said— Faythe thought it the perfect moment to outline her plan, and she did.

Lucy immediately liked the plan and nodded as she served the food. Robert immediately hated it and savagely sawed into the tough morsel of meat on his plate.

"How can we do this?" he asked. "We'd be living a falsehood, and everyone would know. And those … those … *beasts* would escape the consequence. How could we live with this?"

"Who else would know?" asked Lucy. "The Downings will want it concealed as much as we do. No one else need know."

Robert shook his head. "Everyone will know. No one will believe the story. As you just said from your own lips, they will pretend to believe the tale because they will fear to challenge the Downings. Everyone will know what those beasts did, and they will know that we—that *I*"—he jammed his forefinger into his own chest—"that *I* didn't have the … the … courage … to defend my own daughter."

All their eyes went to Chloe, who was slowly, absently, spooning mush into her own mouth.

"And that I sold my soul to the Downings," he finished, dejectedly. "We'll be humiliated not just once but for the rest of our lives."

"What if we were to move on?" asked Lucy, and they all went silent. Faythe's father would see that as yet another defeat, and Lucy would bear up under it cheerfully as she always had. But Faythe was surprised at the catch in her own spirit at the thought. Leaving would mean being without Tommy.

But you don't plan to marry him … why would it matter? Faythe shook her head to clear the thought away; things were complicated enough.

"We've no money to do that," said Robert, "and I've put in five years of work and four years of payments here for this farm already. There's just one year of payments to own it. Not to mention the shame of it, we'd be starting all over again, as paupers. It is not much of a plan to run away."

"Miles Downing would surely pay us to leave," said Lucy.

"No," said Robert, with finality. "I'm not leaving here, and that's that."

After a moment, he added, "How about if I just go to the sheriff and let the law do its work? John Jones is an honest man, as far as I have learned. He'll do what's right."

Lucy responded testily, "That just isn't going to work, and you know it. My heart burns to do that, too, to set all before the Lord and His institutions. What my heart really burns for is for you to just settle this with your musket. But we all know you have no chance of succeeding with that.

263

"If you go to law, either nothing at all will be done or—worse—there will be a trial and the Downings will be acquitted. And from that day you will have Miles Downing and his entire clan as angry sworn enemies. Everyone else here will side with them, as you well know."

And then we'd have to leave anyway, Faythe thought, as she knew her parents were also thinking.

After a few moments, Lucy added, more quietly, sadly, "Do you really think anyone will want to ruin their lives to side with us? We will be outcasts, if we're fortunate. It's a death sentence you're proposing for us, albeit a long, slow one. We all want justice, but any kind of justice is just going to make things worse."

Robert looked from Lucy to Faythe, as if considering the merits of their plans, their arguments. He was clearly not ready to agree to anything. "Let's sleep on it," he said.

As Lucy prepared Chloe for bed after the meal, Faythe asked to speak to her father alone, so the two went outside.

"Dad," said Faythe, "I want you to know the whole plan. I did not want Mum to hear it all."

"What's that?" asked Robert, curious.

"I want to carry out the plan we all just talked about, but someday, later, when things are different, and when we are in a better position, I want us to get our revenge. Like you, I have no desire for us to live out our lives here in humiliation. So help me God, the Downings will not escape with this. Not at all, not for long. I wanted to tell you this, just between us, as it may make the plan easier to swallow. For now. The idea of eventual justice is the idea that allows me to consider this plan in the first place."

Faythe felt her father's loving gaze on her. "I'm so proud of you," he said suddenly, realizing he'd said his thoughts aloud. He composed himself. "Thank you for your thoughts. Let's indeed sleep on it. Maybe things will look clearer in the morning."

ELMER IS ON THE JOB

The next day, Elmer Smith waited patiently near the Wentworth farm until Robert was away from the house. He wanted to speak first to Lucy, in case Robert was not aware of the pregnancy, and because the mother would likely be more amenable to Martha's plan. When the time seemed right, he rode up the lane to the Wentworths' modest dwelling.

The daughter was out in the yard and greeted him with an undisguised look of contempt.

"Good morning, Miss Wentworth," he said, tipping his hat.

"Good morning, Elmer Smith," said Faythe grudgingly. "To what do we owe the … pleasure?" The pause before the word "pleasure" said it all. But Elmer was used to that.

"I was hoping to speak to your mother …"

"She's in the house. I'll let her know you're here."

While Elmer got down from his horse, Faythe went into the house and Elmer heard her speak in a low, urgent voice, and her mother reply.

At the door, he called, "Mistress Wentworth, I wonder if I might have a word with you, privily."

The daughter said, "I'll go and keep myself busy" and pushed past him at the doorway and left.

Elmer went in and said, "Do you mind if I sit down?"

Lucy nodded him to a chair and she took another.

"I'm here on very private business," he said, in a hushed tone, with an air of great importance.

She said, "There's no reason to be subtle, Elmer—Mr. Smith. Just get to the point."

He cleared his throat. "So here it is. We have it on good authority that Chloe's situation may have changed."

"What on earth do you mean?" said Lucy.

"I think you know what I mean."

"Really, Elmer, I have no idea what you are talking about. My daughter fell off a horse two months ago, and her condition has not changed since then. As you can see"—she held out a hand towards the girl lying on her bed.

"She's with child, isn't she?" said Elmer.

Lucy colored. "Why would you think something like that and say it aloud? I'm taken aback."

"But it's true just the same, isn't it?" said Elmer. "You can be as 'taken aback' as you want to be, but in a matter of time, you won't be able to hide it from anyone, including your husband. You'll need a new tale."

"I don't know what you mean," said Lucy, "but assuming for the moment that you were correct, why are you here?"

"Well, it's no secret who I work for," said Elmer. "I do the occasional favor for Mr. Downing."

"Really?" said Lucy, in mock surprise.

"I'm here on a commission."

"And that commission is …"

"Assuming your girl there is indeed in the family way, there is something can be done about it." He pulled out the pouch.

Lucy stared at it with eyes as wide and round as he had ever seen, as if she had looked upon a three-headed frog.

Elmer continued. "These medicines will solve the problem quite rightly."

Lucy was truly taken aback. She stopped feigning that she did not know what he spoke of. She truly had not expected this from Miles Downing.

But Elmer just plowed ahead, as he'd been instructed by Martha. "You just take these two bottles"—he held them up. "You mix two spoons of the dark one with one spoon of the light one, and you give it to her every three hours in a single day. If she becomes ill, that is to be expected, and you just give her the next dose anyway."

Lucy had still not spoken, so Elmer continued. "This'll get rid of that baby, for sure."

"Get out!" said Lucy in a low voice, with vehemence, as she stood up from the table.

Elmer stood up, too, in surprise.

"Get out!" repeated Lucy, her voice rising. "You—and Miles Downing—are even more despicable than I'd have thought. You have a despicable plan. It is not only an additional violence against my daughter—and the babe—and against the law, but it is a sin unto death before God. And your master does not even have the courage to come out here himself but sends his—his *creature* to me for this purpose! Get out. And don't return here. Ever!"

Elmer stood up. The meeting had not gone the way his master … or his master's wife … would want. He held out his palms to her. "Very well! I did not mean to offend. I'll go."

Lucy stood with her arms folded, watching him leave. She didn't move even after he had mounted his horse and ridden off down the lane. She hoped never to see him again. The man made her skin crawl. It wasn't until he was gone and she relaxed out of her fury that she turned back to the table and realized he had left the pouch with the medicines.

Now what to do about that? she wondered. She picked up the pouch and weighed it in her palm, thinking about how to dispose of the vile potions, then Faythe poked her head in the door.

"Mum, what happened? And what's that?" she asked, pointing at the pouch.

After Faythe explained and the two women seethed together, Faythe asked, "Should we tell Dad about this?"

Lucy didn't hesitate. "Yes," she said. "I cannot hold back from him again. Once was bad enough, and it brought no good, as you have seen. We must tell him everything, then ponder what should be done."

When Robert had heard their account, the anger and desire for justice that had been pushed down in him for the past day came rushing back. The blood ran to his face, and he declared quietly, "We cannot stand for this. We cannot. The Devil take the consequences …"

"Dad," urged Faythe, "please do not act hastily. Nothing has altered. Instead, it seems that what we wanted—for Miles to be worried about the situation—is coming to pass. That's why he sent his man to us. He wants an end of this, one way or another."

Robert stomped out for another walk, not wanting to subject his loved ones to the storms within him. But as he walked, he continued to wonder about Miles. Robert was rarely wrong about other men, and he was convinced that Miles was not a bad man. Elmer Smith had provided the remedy as coming from his master's hand, but that just did not seem consistent with Miles Downing's character.

But Robert's opinion of Miles did not matter. Before them all was a situation that had to be dealt with one way or another, and soon.

MARTHA MAKES
A NEW PLAN

Upon hearing Elmer's report on the failed meeting with Lucy Wentworth, Martha went straight to Miles in his study. He took his feet off his desk and put away the book he had been reading and stood to greet her, his hands held out affectionately as he crossed the room.

"You look lovely today, my dear," he said, reaching out to tuck a stray blond wisp into her cap. "If a bit flustered."

"Enough of that," she said, waving away his hand. "Miles," she said, "you must meet with Wentworth and make an agreement with him."

She saw the wave of distaste, and fear, pass over his face. Plain talk of unpleasant things always made her husband uneasy, but there was no help for it.

"Isn't there another way?" he asked, as he always did. "Perhaps you could talk with Lucy?"

She shook her head definitively. "No, there's no other way. I have explored all. You are the *man* in the case." She paused as he was reminded. "You have to do this yourself. So you must order your thoughts, and it should not be nearly as bad as you think."

"What'll I say?" he asked.

Martha sat in the chair opposite him and went over exactly what to do and say.

"I'm going out," she told him once she was sure he knew his part.

"Where to?"

"I have to see Minister Brown," she said. "This is all so distressing that I am reduced to the spiritual way. I would like to pray with him for a resolution."

Miles nodded, and might have wondered why, but he was too embroiled in his own worries about the current situation to give it much thought to it, or wonder what his wife was up to.

MARTHA AND
MINISTER BROWN

"Why, hello, Minister Brown," said Martha as she walked into William Brown's small house next to the meeting house.

For a moment, he wondered why she had come to visit him, for it was quite rare that she did so. It was immediately apparent that this was not a social call.

"Hello, Martha … Mrs. Downing," he said, on guard. "To what do I owe the pleasure of your company?"

Martha arranged her skirts as she sat before him, motioning him to sit as well. "You may be tested soon," she said. "I expect your loyalty to the Downings, and I expect you to do as I bid you without delay or disagreement. Is this understood?"

"Yes," he said. "You have my word I'll do as you say." He had never seen Martha this forceful, and he was quite afraid. It must have something to do with the Wentworth girl, as nothing else of importance had transpired in North Hinkapee of late, but his part in the matter was unclear.

Martha looked down for a moment, then straight up at him, her eyes boring into his. "I think Robert Wentworth might be a witch. Don't you agree?"

"Wh-what?" he blurted out, completely shocked. "I've seen no evidence … I mean … I'm not sure why you … I …"

"He does not need to be a witch just yet," said Martha, "but that might change very soon."

"I would need two witnesses—"

"I know," said Martha, interrupting him.

Minister Brown was reeling. He asked Martha plaintively, "Can you tell me what is going on, Mrs. Downing? You know I would always want to help you in any way. I'd just like to know what the matter is."

"You don't need to know more yet," said Martha. "And you might never need to know more. At this point I just want you to gather evidence of witchcraft in case it is needed."

After a few moments of silence, she added, "You need to be prepared for what may be coming. And I warn you," she said, looking at him ominously, "if you let me down, you will not have another opportunity. Leaving North Hinkapee alive will be the least of your worries. Are we in shared understanding?"

"Yes, ma'am," said the minister, quite fearful.

"One thing more," said Martha, standing up. "I came here only for prayer, in my concern for the poor, injured girl. If anyone were to ask. Do not breathe a word of this conversation to anyone … ever. Understand?"

Minister Brown nodded his agreement. Martha looked at him again. "If—I mean *when* you do as I bid you, you will have the reward you crave." She held his eyes, knowing what he could not help himself thinking.

She held his eyes for a moment longer than was appropriate, and then her demeanor changed back to its normal aloof courtesy. In a friendly and louder tone, she said from the doorway, so that anyone passing might hear, "Well, Minister Brown, I do hope you have a fine day. And thank you for praying with me about the poor Wentworth girl—it is our duty to do so."

Then she left, and Minister William Brown stood there shaking and wondering. Whatever was about to happen was not likely to be good. But he had a task. He must find—or create—evidence that the good man Robert Wentworth was a witch.

WHO IS MINISTER BROWN?

William Brown was not always the way he turned out.

As the only child of a wealthy family of the Massachusetts Bay Colony, settled in Boston, William was not interested in his father's trade but longed for the respect, even the awe, that ministers received in the community. He had a knack for language and was willing to study hard, and with his father's blessing and funds, he was able to study in England before returning to Boston, both Browns intent on his eventually becoming the head minister of the Boston First Church, the most prestigious congregation in the colony—or even to take the newly formed Second Church, to make that the premier church. With his father making solid contributions, and William being so conscientious in his studies, his success seemed assured.

But what the Browns valued in education and honor was not quite what the Bostonians were looking for, and it became apparent that there was not going to be a place for him in Boston after all. So, with additional finances from his father, William transferred to the church in Briarcliff, where there was a great chance for advancement as the population—and prosperity—grew. The minister there was set to retire in a few years, and William would have a clear shot.

But in any company, as one rises through the ranks, often talent, skill, and hard work begin to take a back seat to politics, and such was the case in the church, the center of Massachusetts civilization. Although the retiring minister had much influence on the decision for his successor, he wisely wanted support from others, so he was known to be humble, and not renegade, in his thinking.

William was eminently talented in creating sermons and diligent in service, but he had several defects that began to disqualify him from the position to which he aspired.

First, perhaps to his credit, he had absolutely no head for politics. He had no skill in making allies and alliances, and he was consistently outflanked and fooled by others who were better at playing the games necessary. When William tried his hand at making alliances, he was either too obvious or too subtle. In each case he was unsuccessful.

Second, William simply did not have a flair for public speaking, which was an essential prerequisite for the job of a minister. His sermons were scholarly and godly, but his elocution was lacking. Somehow, he was unable to reach the congregation.

Third, it became apparent over time that the young minister just had no backbone. When things were tough, William would take the easy way out. If a difficult matter of principle must be decided, William would attempt to avoid the decision or make whatever decision was easiest. He had a strong will for working hard at another's leading—like the leading of his tutors—but he had no independent vigor for moral decisions.

Fourth, and perhaps most tellingly, another applicant for the Briarcliff position set William, in comparison, at a great disadvantage. Lawrence Mills was a young man whose character held much that William lacked.

Even still, William might have achieved his goal—due to his intelligence and diligence—but for an unfortunate incident. The result was perhaps unfair, and it proved fatal to his goal.

In keeping with his singular devotion to his aims, William tried to be as pure as possible in word and deed. So it wasn't his doing that he found himself in a house of ill repute. He was led there by others and even tried to resist and go home instead of spending an evening with a prostitute. But with too much drink, his will to resist was weakened, and his long chastity had perhaps become too much to bear by that point.

When the woman came over to William and began to murmur and rub herself against him, he could not resist, try as he might. Before he knew it, he was alone with her and the deed was done. When he returned to himself, he was consumed by guilt, and he hurried to escape the place, vowing never to be overcome by lust again. But the memory of that encounter played over in his mind and body again and again, until he began to reason that it was only the lack of a permanent pulpit that kept him from the usual remedy of marriage. Ministers were not required to be celibate in the first place—in fact, they were enjoined to be husbands of one wife—and he was working with all his might to be in a position to be able to take a wife. One sin along the way could not matter that much, could it?

It turned out that it could …

At last, the aging minister was to step down and William Brown and Lawrence Mills were the final candidates to become the chief minister of the Briarcliff Church.

Lawrence Mills was a poor student in comparison to William Brown, neither naturally blessed with the highest scholarly gifts nor particularly interested in the close work of textual study in which William Brown excelled. However, Lawrence Mills cultivated relationships with all of the elders and had numerous friends of both high and humble position. He was a gifted speaker, his tone capturing attention and his simple Gospel message reaching hearts. And, finally, Lawrence was able to make difficult decisions with authority and confidence. The Lord was with him.

Though William was threatened by Lawrence's gifts, he had trouble disliking the man, and indeed he could not help falling into the spell of his friendliness. Lawrence lived with good cheer, the hope of their faith. Notably, he challenged the error that some believers fell into, so that they became severe with themselves and others, calling that godliness. He encouraged people to enjoy their lives, not believing that suffering or avoiding pleasure was a good in itself. "It is one thing," he said, "to rightly call out the false glory of the papists—their gilded icons and jeweled crowns. But we can celebrate true beauty, the true good of the Creation. We are bound not to fall into 'harsh treatment of the body,' as the Apostle Paul has enjoined us."

The retiring minister had been widowed for many years and had not remarried, and the slight reference to his asceticism might have grated on the head minister, giving William a slight advantage over Lawrence for the pulpit both sought. But the old man could set aside those words of libertinism from the seemingly pure Lawrence Mills, for he had heard the whispered suggestion that William Brown might have *actually* violated the required chastity of a minister—celibacy while unmarried. The old man had no patience for those who could not resist carnal pleasures.

Friends of Lawrence Mills encouraged him to report or at least let word escape about William's one-time dalliance, but Lawrence, true to character, refused outright to do this and strongly warned his friends to keep their silence, too. He did not want to "win that way," as he termed it, and triumph through another's downfall.

However, one of Mills's friends, a young man who completely detested William, could not resist. He privately conveyed to the retiring minister the facts about William's one-time indiscretion. And so it was that Lawrence Mills was announced as the next minister of the Briarcliff Church. With the appointment, the new Minister Mills quickly invited William to stay on as a secondary minister.

To say that William was upset is an understatement. He was furious, and at the same time he was a broken man. After all his

hard work, he had been passed over. He assumed the worst and immediately hated Mills for taking advantage of his tiny lapse. The
decision and the response were tragic for two reasons: first, a single
indiscretion should not necessarily have ended William's aspirations,
and second, Mills had not in fact done what William thought he had
done. What made it still worse for William was that he knew full
well that Mills himself had been with women occasionally.

At first, William was so downcast he could not rise out of his
bed each day, and when he did so, he went about with bitterness.
What was the point of all the study? Hard work and being the most
qualified counted for nothing; kissing the right rings and being liked
were all that mattered.

Little by little, William's mind began to take him into places where
it was easier to exist. At first, he concluded that he was done with the
church. He went home to find his mother dying and his father distracted by grief, and then not long after, his father died, too. William
was left alone in the world, with a tidy sum of money but without a
purpose. He went through the money as a determined wastrel, spending it all in drink and debauchery. His desire to take his misfortunes
clear down to hell became so strong that William traded his determination to succeed at all costs for an equally powerful determination to
destroy himself and anyone who entered his sphere of influence.

Part of his debauchery included gambling, and this speedily led
to his losing all of his inheritance. It didn't take long before William
was broke as well as broken. Having landed in hell as he knew it,
William became a beggar for a time.

Finally, he had no pride left and no reason to live. But his bodily
self was hungry, so he went to the Briarcliff Church and presented himself Minister Mills. Poor William was unable to speak as
he stood in the warm anteroom, and Lawrence Mills tried to make
things easier. He genuinely felt bad for William and at the same time
he was aware that others might be impressed with his kind treatment
of a former rival.

"William," he said, "I'm sorry for what has happened to you. The past is now the past. Come now and be healed."

"Thank you," gasped William, unable in his extremity to say more.

Bolstered by prayer and encouragement and decent food and housing, William began to come to himself. When he seemed to be ready, he was sent out to be a minister in the community of New Grammercy, only a few miles from Briarcliff. But there his weaknesses surfaced again, and it was not long before the community had had enough of Minister Brown. He was inebriated much of the time and, to make matters worse, had been seen with women of unchaste reputation as well, on several occasions. He had made advances, some welcome and some unwelcome—he seemed unable to tell the difference—upon certain women of the community. The elders determined this minister would not do.

Strangely, William now felt entitled to his indulgences. If the church promoted others who had sinned, then he should be able to sin as well and still be part of the church. Clearly, he was beginning to lose his hold of what was right and what was wrong, and he began to develop the ability to say one thing and do the opposite. Strangely, his preaching improved. Although he was still not at the truly exalting level, the sermons he gave in New Grammercy were passionate in extolling virtues and condemning sin; yet at the same time he was participating in the very sins he preached against. Sometimes his own sermons so inflamed him that he was doing that which he had preached against not more than an hour after his sermon on the very subject.

The irony was palpable to anyone with wisdom who might have observed it, but not to William. No matter how bad he was, he felt he was still doing the Lord's work, and thus the balances showed in his favor. As he continued to live in two worlds, he grew harder, more violent in his sins. He loved being in charge and was ruthless in his abuse of his power. Indeed, woe betide anyone below him in any pecking order. He was imperious, nasty, ruthless, and worse, and because he was so familiar with the array of sins men could fall prey to, he could easily find someone's weakness and use it against him. He became enraged if he felt challenged in the slightest.

Yet if William Brown were not the authority in a given situation, if someone else was in charge, he was pathetically subservient and deathly afraid of negative consequences. When he was dismissed from New Grammercy, he turned up again in Briarcliff, and Minister Mills gave him yet another chance to clean himself up. William Brown was so exhausted by his depredations that he found it a relief to turn once again to virtue.

After a year of temperance, prayer, and chastity, William was given another last chance.

"William," said Lawrence Mills, "I have been told of a position that could be your redemption—to serve as minister of a newly formed community called North Hinkapee."

To William's obsequious babbling of thanks, the now-irritated Minister Mills said, "This really is your last chance. You'll not get a third try."

MINISTER BROWN AND THE DOWNINGS

William Brown went to North Hinkapee about 1670 and had been there for two decades. When he arrived, he met with Thompson Downing, who showed him the meeting house then being built and served him tea. William badly wanted a fresh start, and what better place than in a meeting house that was so new it would for quite a while smell of freshly cut wood? But then Thompson invited him for a walk outside.

"So you'll be our new minister," said Thompson.

"Yes," said William.

"That's good," said Thompson, "but one thing you should be aware of ..."

"What's that?" asked William, feeling a bit of alarm.

"I have a man—we've looked into your past and I know all about you, including your time in New Grammercy."

The would-be Minister Brown winced, feeling blood rush to his head. He held his breath to hear what would come next.

"I've staked everything on this town," said Thompson. "I can't have a minister who drinks or whores or otherwise acts improperly. It won't help me build this town."

"I won't do that again," said William, very concerned.

"I'm very confident you won't," said Thompson. He then related, in great detail, the story of how he had received his permanent limp, from a beating he had received long ago as a young man.

"I want to be direct with you, William Brown," he said, stopping to face him and look him in the eye. "Your failure here will not result in your leaving town in disgrace. It will result in your leaving town not being able to walk again. It will result in your leaving town to suffer in severe pain for the rest of your life. I want to know—do we have an understanding?"

William nodded—terrified. For all the difficulties of life in Briarcliff or Grammercy or even Boston, they did not include bodily harm, merely harm to one's reputation or livelihood. *This is a further incentive to keep me on the straight road*, he thought to himself.

"Also," added Thompson, "I trust it is clear by now that I am in charge of this town. On my side, in support of me and my policies, is a good and safe place to be. Those who intend to live that way will do very well here. And those who don't … will not be part of the community of North Hinkapee. Do you understand?"

William nodded again—even more afraid. He could feel the power emanating from Thompson Downing and knew to his core that he did not want to be on the other side of it.

"We shan't speak of this again," concluded Thompson. "I am confident you will be my man, and you will be just the man for North Hinkapee. Let's go in for supper."

William had settled in as minister of the growing town of North Hinkapee, and he did not want to risk his future. He controlled his drinking—no more than an occasional pint at the Towne Tavern. If his passions built up too far, he went away to find prostitutes, typically in Bearminster and occasionally in Briarcliff.

When Martha arrived as Miles's wife, and then a few years later, when Thompson died, much stayed the same, though some things changed for Minister William Brown.

First, it was clear that while Miles was a pushover, Martha was the opposite. In fact, Brown heard from her mouth some of the same things Thompson had said to him in the past. Clearly Thompson was teaching her everything he knew. And Minister Brown was one of the first in North Hinkapee to realize that Martha was really in charge, as opposed to Miles, but he said nothing of this to anyone.

Second, he found Martha so physically attractive that he had to literally force himself not to look at her lustfully when they were together. There was something about her that drove him to sexual distraction so that he could hardly think. When he couldn't get to a woman in Bearminster in time, he'd abused himself while dreaming dreams of Martha as his paramour.

Martha picked up on this advantage immediately but did not act on it for some time. But when Matt began acting out in ways she could no longer control, she looked ahead to what might come of it before law or before the church.

So one day Martha Downing appeared at the parsonage in the early evening, apparently to seek advice on a matter on which Minister Brown might be an authority. He was flattered at the idea, and then he was flabbergasted when, without preamble, she began to unbutton her waistcoat. His eyes widened, and then widened even more, and his breath caught in his throat.

Then she unbuttoned her chemise and showed her deep cleavage while unfastening and letting her skirt fall to the floor. She now wore only her chemise—a garment in silk no other woman in North Hinkapee could enjoy—and her shoes and stockings. Little imagination was needed at this point to know what delights lay within these few garments, but imagination wasn't important as, with a look into Minister Brown's eyes, Martha stepped out of her shoes and lifted her hem to show her leg as she slowly rolled down her fine stockings.

She stood before him now with nothing on but her chemise, which had conveniently slid off one shoulder, almost completely exposing her generous breast.

After a pause to let the tension build, she slowly pulled the chemise the rest of the way over that arm until the whole garment fell to the floor and she stepped out of it like Venus stepping out of the sea.

It was no wonder a pagan goddess came to mind, for this woman William Brown had longed for for years, was suddenly in complete power over him as much as a goddess might be, and he was under her spell. William Brown's throat was so dry that if he had tried to speak, nothing would have come out.

She moved into his bedroom and sat on the bed, motioning for him to follow her there until he had drawn close enough to touch her. She nodded, giving permission, and Minister Brown reached out to timidly fondle her breasts, to trace the smooth creaminess of her flesh that rose to firm, rosy points.

As he touched her, she murmured one word: "Harder."

In her thrall, Minister Brown could not assert himself. It was all too clear who was in charge. So he grabbed both breasts with more gusto and she leaned toward him, tipping her head back, her delicious mouth open and panting. Again, she said "Harder" and showed him how to pinch her nipples. He followed her command.

Then she drew his hand down her firm belly to the wetness she spread her legs to display.

Minister Brown was too confused even to wonder what was happening, or more importantly, why it was happening. Martha Downing had never shown him particular regard, yet here she was offering herself to him so freely, so passionately. His dreams were coming true!

To his great wonder, Martha Downing took his head between her hands and pushed it down to the wetness as she lay back on the bed. The whores he had been with never did anything like this with him, but Martha seemed to want pleasure for herself.

It didn't take long before Minister Brown was having the greatest sexual experience of his life. Martha was not only even more beautiful undressed than he had fantasized, but she was imaginative in bed in ways he had never thought about. Through it all, Martha explained exactly what she wanted him to do—with his tongue—and with the rest of his body.

His fantasies were more than fulfilled, and then beyond. To his surprise, he found himself more aroused with this woman than he had ever felt with any other, because she was dominating him.

Afterwards, Martha stood up, naked, before him. He lay exhausted on the bed, staring at her pointed breasts and the arrogant bush that had taken him captive. His mind was a blank, but for his speculation about the time and place of future assignations.

"Minister Brown, I hope it's clear what this encounter means." Her voice was businesslike, not purring as it had been moments before.

"Wh-what's that?" stammered Minister Brown.

"It means that it would not be well for you, should the events of this evening be discovered." She stood before him still naked, holding her clothing in her hand.

"Right, but you ... it was your idea ..." he sputtered, bewildered.

"Really?" said Martha. "Who would believe that?" She paused and added contemptuously, as she pointed one beautiful foot and drew one finely knitted stocking over her silky leg, "And who would care?"

Minister Brown had a strange mix of emotions indeed: fear and passion made a powerful potion. But all he could think of was that maybe, just maybe, Martha would come back to him again for more.

But by this time, Martha had finished dressing herself and left.

INTERLUDE

NUNUNYI RETURNS

Chief Katakuk was proud of his maturing son, the boy Tamawah, who had grown out of being a round-faced child with his mother's great dark eyes and quiet spirit, so that he now tested out his lengthening limbs and increasing strength, running through the land as Katakuk had done as a boy. Tamawah, though gentle of soul, was learning of the warrior within himself, and Katakuk had begun to teach him the battlecraft he might one day need. For even though the Sagawanees had been at peace with the White Men of North Hinkapee for many years, there were other White Men always encroaching on their territory, and with those White Men there was no tacit peace treaty, so skirmishes, and much worse, continually broke out.

Katatuk, with as much of a genius for governance of his people as Thompson Downing had for his, knew that being too much of a peacemaker would eventually be taken to be cowardice from his tribesmen. So he made sure to be overtly and overly aggressive against the White Men who were not of North Hinkapee, so his tribesmen would see him as a powerful leader. Privately, he knew that endless fighting with the White Men would decimate his people. So, carefully, very carefully, he led them by sounding as aggressive as possible but avoiding conflict as much as possible.

In the end, peace reigned between the Sagawanees and the Whites in North Hinkapee, but the Sagawanees were not at peace with other White Men. But whether he found himself in peace or in war, Tamawah would have to learn warfare. Trained by Katakuk, Tamawah might be able to rule his people as well as his father had ruled, and as well as *his* father, Passatan, before him.

From time to time, Katakuk could not help thinking of what might have been if Nununyi had become his wife. Their son together would certainly have needed only rudimentary instruction in the use of the bow and arrow, for with a mother of such prodigious skill with the bow, Tamawah would have come into the world with the archer's glint in his eye.

At such times of reflection, Katakuk would shake off the dream and gaze at his actual wife, his actual son, and be thankful. Out of his despair those many years ago, he had come to embrace other treasures that could be had in this world. And so he had taken his son into the wilds to teach him.

Now the time had come for Tamawah to make his venture alone into the forest for a time, as part of the rituals of manhood.

"My son," Chief Katakuk said from his place by the fire, arrayed in the finery of his rule as all the people gathered around, "on this night you will set out on your own, guided only by the stars and the scents and the feel under your feet of the land you have come to know. The spirits will lead you where you should go and teach you what you should know. You have the tools and weapons you have learned"—he gestured to the quiver hung upon the boy's shoulder, the bow in his hand, the small axe tucked into his waistband, the knife bound along his calf.

The boy stood tall for his fourteen years, his long hair bound back to reveal the sharpening bones of his face, his legs long and strong, his feet firmly planted.

A fine man he is becoming, thought Katakuk in a moment of private musing. Then he returned to the ritual.

"Now go to see what the Earth has for you, what the stars have written for your life. The creatures you meet—or even a man in those lonely places—learn whether they are food or friends or foes, and wield the wisdom you have been taught. When the time is accomplished—and you will know it—return to us here and tell us the new wisdom you have gained, that all might learn of you."

The boy solemnly bowed his head, raised his bow, and turned from the company, from the firelight, and strode off into the forest.

Katakuk had no doubt Tamawah would make him a proud father, returning in confident triumph at having endured alone.

Nununyi was unable to explain how she had found herself called away from Menon's warm cabin at that time, called back to her people's lands, but a day or two after she rose quietly from her marriage bed, she found herself among her people, in a hiding place in the trees. There she had watched the ceremony, remembering not two decades before when Katakuk himself had been sent into the forest to find what it held for him.

I have not known you, Kata, through these years, but I see you in your son.

It made no sense, or perhaps it did, that Nununyi could become for this young man what she could have been for the son she might have borne for Katakuk. She could give this boy some of what the spirits had given her, teach him some of the magic she had with the bow. And maybe thus she could become—quietly, mysteriously—a part of the life of her old beloved. And thus she could return in part to her people.

Nununyi stayed quiet until all had left the fireside for their sleep, and then silently, swiftly, she followed where the boy had gone.

1692, NORTH HINKAPEE

MILES AND ROBERT

Martha wanted a quiet resolution to their current situation but realized that that just might not happen. Perhaps Wentworth would just be too angry and would spoil for a fight. If so, he would get a lot more than he bargained for, but she must hurry to get the timing right.

She felt sick at what she was about to do, about the wheels she was about to set in motion. Almost she wavered, but there was no turning back.

She arrived at the parsonage two days after her previous visit and found Minister Brown in the yard. "We must speak," she said.

"Very well," he said, looking at her warily. "Won't you come inside?"

Martha walked into his spare quarters and sat down at the kitchen table, where he joined her. She told him of the intended meeting between Miles and Robert Wentworth scheduled for that afternoon.

"I will expect you to be in the tavern during the meeting. If an agreement is reached between them, then you will go home and do nothing at all. If not, my next plan will need to go into effect immediately."

She described the plan to him very matter-of-factly, though he blanched. She was confident that he would carry it out, for the leverage that she held against him. But he was a coward, and there were personal risks for him if he fulfilled her instructions.

"Is there no other way?" he asked.

Martha was stone-faced and Minister Brown quickly quailed before her. She was sworn to protect the Downing clan, and she would do what was needed. She knew that Minister Brown would do exactly as she demanded.

As Robert prepared to leave home to go to his meeting with Miles Downing, Lucy asked him, "What are you going to do?"

"I haven't decided yet."

"Shouldn't you have a plan before you go into a meeting of this importance?"

"Yes, I suppose I should," he admitted reluctantly. "I'm just accustomed to dealing with people honestly in the moment, not planning things out ahead of time."

"Promise me that whatever he proposes, you'll tell him you'll think about it," she said. "Then we can all discuss it. Don't react to what he says at the time. Please promise me that."

"Very well, I promise," said Robert, realizing the wisdom of her counsel.

"It will be simple," added Lucy. "You just explain that whatever's decided affects your wife, too, so you want her in on the decision. Or something like that."

"I guess I know what to say," said Robert finally, a little bothered that she thought he needed so much guidance, and he set off for the Towne Tavern. He was dreading this meeting, but at least things would come to a resolution one way or another.

The Towne Tavern proprietor, Perkin Massey, was watching as he entered, and so was Minister Brown, and some others, too.

Do they all know what's going on here? Robert wondered.

Perkin jerked his thumb toward the door that led to a private room in the back. "He's waiting for you in there."

Robert nodded and crossed the tavern and took a big breath as he let himself in through the door. To his surprise, Miles Downing was not alone.

"Hi, Robert," said Miles, standing up and offering his hand. "Thank you for coming. You know Earl Carver, my solicitor."

"I thought this was a private meeting," said Robert, not taking Miles's hand nor sitting down.

"Yes," said Miles. "This is very private indeed. I'm hopeful it will be to the advantage of both of us, so I asked Earl to join us."

"You wanted this meeting, Miles. You sent your servant to ask me to meet with you here in private. Not to meet with your lawyer. He needs to leave."

"Very well," said Miles, holding up his hand as if in surrender, though he seemed a little nervous at a change of plans. He shook his head as if shaking off the responsibility of it all, then turned to Earl and said, "I think you should make yourself at home just outside."

"Surely," said Earl, with a quick look at Miles. He stood up and left, closing the door behind him.

"Sit down, Robert, please, and let's talk," Miles said, holding out his hand again.

Robert was pleased in a small way that he had won the first skirmish, and he wanted to give Miles the benefit of the doubt in that little moment, so he took the offered hand, then sat down.

Miles watched Earl go, thinking, *If Martha were here, she wouldn't have backed down.* But Martha was not here, and Miles must do this thing himself.

"I'll get to the point," said Miles, shaking his head again, looking down at the table to steel himself for what he would say.

He was hating this meeting. Hating everything about it. Hating everything he was doing and might have to do. All because of Matt, who had gotten him into this mess. And Martha, too. *Damn him and damn her!*

"I think we all know what happened," said Miles. He remembered his father's advice that when he felt afraid, he should keep his face impassive and try to say as little as possible, although of course that wasn't really an option now.

"Yes, we do know what happened," said Robert, his own jaw set and he unable to hide his fury.

Robert clenched his fists and spoke low and forcefully. "The animals you raised got off their leashes. They attacked my little girl." He choked for a moment. "They raped her like the animals they are. They destroyed her mind and her womanhood and left her … only … half alive. And we've just learned that one of them got her … with child." He said the word "child" with contempt and pity mixed.

Miles himself choked at the thought unbidden—*actually my grandchild!*

"Finally," Robert went on, "to finish this … this"—he could not find the word. "You sent your … your … rat … to my home. He dared speak to my wife about giving my daughter potions to kill the child. What more would you add to your sins against God and against my family? Is there no limit to where you will go?"

As Robert related Elmer's errand with the potions, Miles was shaken even deeper. *They would have killed the babe?* he thought with a shudder. He had not known of this!

Miles said nothing for a bit as he struggled with the news of Elmer and the potions. Martha must have arranged this behind his back. *What else has she done that I know not of?* The thought flashed through his head that it was probably best that Martha had not told him, as he would have resisted this idea but given in in the end. *I always give in.*

Miles looked at the other man, the other father, with sickness in his spirit, for every single awful word that Wentworth had said was true. Miles's shoulders sagged for a moment, and then he was in the present again. Like it or not, and despite the respect he felt for Robert Wentworth, his own family came first. And whether it was good or ill, he would try his best to do what he had to do.

He exhaled and answered. "I don't dispute what you just said, and I guess it's late for an apology. I've been thinking about how to make things right ... and there's no sense in mere talk. Here's my proposal ..."

Miles pulled from a pouch a folded document.

"I have here the deed to your farm," he said. "It's yours. I've got twenty pounds for you as well. All of this is yours, too. In return, I ask you to say merely that the poor child was taken by an unknown attacker and is with child. Neither of us can be proud of this means of averting disaster, but we will have taken a bad situation and softened it as much as we possibly can."

Before Robert could respond, he added, "I'm not pleased with any of this. I know I can't undo what was done, or make it right, but this is a lot better than my not doing anything."

Robert said nothing. Clearly, he was contemplating it in spite of his deserved and righteous anger.

"If you're willing to consider my proposal," Miles continued, concerned that Robert was not speaking, "please do keep in mind that if this thing explodes publicly, it will not be to my good, that is true. But it will be a lot worse for you. A good deal worse. I know you will rightly hate me and my family, and I don't blame you for that."

He stopped and looked mournfully at Robert. And so he spoke the words Martha had bidden him to speak: "But be mindful, Robert, that I don't have to offer you this, and you have no power to wield yourself."

Martha had insisted that he be tough with Wentworth and make it clear that there was a penalty to his saying "No" as well as a reward for saying "Yes." Indeed, Miles was almost repeating Martha's exact words, which sounded much better when Martha said them than when he said them to Robert Wentworth in person.

But this speech he'd delivered was a miscalculation on Martha's part and had terrible consequences.

Robert was trying to compose himself. He was tempted with the deed and the money. Instead of being poor the Wentworths would, overnight, go to being well off; indeed, quite well off. But how could he do what Miles was saying? How could he do that? It was too awful to contemplate.

Whatever he decided would be terrible. There was no way out of the trap.

But at Miles's last words, which were essentially a threat from an evil man in an evil position, harsh words of response bubbled up in him and came to his lips. He could not control himself—indeed, what other response could a man of honor give to such churlish behavior?

He stood up and said so loudly that it could have been heard throughout the Towne Tavern, "Go to hell, Downing!"

Miles didn't respond but lowered his head, and Robert returned to control of his emotions. His voice moderated to normalcy. "But I will think about it. You'll have my answer shortly. I need to talk to my wife."

And then he left. He walked out and slammed the back-room door behind him. He knew he'd gone pale, and he walked through the tavern saying nothing to anyone. He went through the front door and slammed that one, too. Then he was gone.

Out in the tavern, after Robert Wentworth had slammed the doors, Minister Brown saw that he had to go with Martha's awful next plan. He had no choice.

IF YOU THINK THINGS WERE ALREADY BAD, WATCH WHAT HAPPENS NOW

Robert walked around aimlessly for several long hours after his meeting with Miles, turning over in his mind what was the right thing to do, but there was no "right decision." He had only to choose from among different wrong decisions. His prayers dissipated into the air around him.

Lucy and Faythe were waiting for him, both of them very upset, angry instead of curious. Had they heard what had happened at the Towne Tavern?

Lucy spoke first. "I guess you didn't keep your promise," she said, with her hands on her hips. Faythe mirrored her anger.

"What do you mean?" asked Robert. "I did exactly what you said I should do. He made a proposal to me and I told him I'd think about it, that I needed to speak to you first." Then he added uncertainly, "What's wrong?"

"What was the proposal?"

"A terrible one, but in short, he said to say an unknown attacker took our poor Chloe and got her with child, and we will then receive the farm, plus twenty pounds. All ours."

"That was it?" said Lucy with suspicion.

"Yes, that was it."

"It makes no sense, then," she said, furrowing her brow.

"What makes no sense?"

"The story that's all over town?"

"What story?"

"You'd better sit down," she said. "You have no idea, do you, poor thing?"

"I don't need to sit down. Just tell me what it is."

All at once she blurted out, "You have been accused of consorting with the Devil, pursuing witchcraft, committing incest, and raping your own daughter!"

"What?" exclaimed Robert. "What? It cannot be ..."

Even as he spoke these words, the blood rushed to his head. What trickery did Miles have in mind by luring him to the Towne Tavern, making that offer? Why do that if he was going to spread these rumors behind his back? It was a machination against him!

Lucy grimaced and sighed. "I wish that were the case. But it is very real, the charges are real. The sheriff was already here ... with Elmer."

"Why were they here?"

"Elmer apparently told Sheriff Jones that he had heard that we had special medicines to do away with an unborn child. And Dr. Alderson reported that those medicines had been stolen from him. Of course Sheriff Jones found the pouch here, the one Elmer left with the potions in it. He took it as evidence."

"The bastards," growled Robert. "They'll not get away with this."

Lucy sighed. "I'm not sure what to do. I'm not sure at all. This time I have no plan at all." Uncharacteristically, she started to cry, and her hands hung limp before her.

Robert saw that Faythe, too, was undone, just standing there in shock and dismay.

The new ... good ... plan had failed them all, and they were back where they started; actually, they were much worse off than when they had started to remedy things.

Robert squared his shoulders and headed to the door, shrugging off Lucy, who suddenly came to herself and was trying to suggest that he "think first and act second."

"No, woman," he replied. "Last time we did this we just dug ourselves a bigger hole. The time for slinking around in the shadows is over. It's time for plain action."

And so he walked quickly back to town. He had no plan and knew he was acting before thinking, but at this point it just didn't matter.

He fairly blasted into the Towne Tavern, slamming the door back on its hinges and setting the tankards rattling on a nearby table. He expected Miles would still be there and indeed he was, probably expecting him.

Also present were Minister Brown, the lawyer Earl Carver, Handel Lewis, and the gossips Robin Stone and Perkin Massey, who presided over all happenings in his tavern.

"You bastard!" shouted Robert after he slammed the door, striding straight up to Miles. "You bastard," he said low and menacingly. "You son of a bitch!"

Miles was prepared for this as best as he could, since he had been quietly apprised, by Minister Brown, of the accusations against Robert Wentworth. After hastening to get over his own shock at the injustice and indeed the shocking inexplicability of why this had happened when a deal seemed to be at hand, he had no choice but to steel himself for Robert's return.

Of course Miles was not the villain here, not the one who had spread the rumor. Martha was responsible, in league with Minister Brown. Never before had Martha wielded such deadly power in her efforts to protect the family, and never before had Miles been called upon to front her action for such a devastating move.

Though the people of North Hinkapee had heard of grave sins, of witchcraft and unspeakable crimes of the flesh, those had not come among them in a serious way. But having been prepared by Minister Brown's titillating sermons, they found their minds were open to such rumors.

Such a tragedy, thought Miles Downing, but he now had no choice but to stand up to Wentworth and to support the story.

He recalled Thompson's advice that when in doubt he should listen to Martha, but this time Martha herself had been swept away by misjudgment. *Maybe I should start making some decisions myself,* he thought briefly, knowing that Robert had likely considered his offer earlier that evening. They had almost come to an agreement.

But now there was no more time to think and no real choice. The lots had been cast, and he had to see what they read, whether he liked the message or not.

He stood looking at Wentworth with a disgusted look, even though his stomach was filled with bile and he was afraid of the confrontation. In fact, his disgust was really for himself and what he was about to do.

Robert continued his tirade all in a rush, before these witnesses. "Miles Downing, your boys raped my girl Chloe in the woods. There was a witness—my other daughter Faythe. Chloe is now with child. And earlier today you tried to bribe me to keep this quiet. Now you are accusing me of unspeakable things, that you might hide what's going on. You'll not get away with this." He shook his fist in Miles's face.

Miles Downing was not calm, but he had his thoughts under more control than did Robert Wentworth. Miles realized he would speak not for Wentworth's sake, for Wentworth knew full well the truth. Instead, Miles was speaking to the watching crowd. After Wentworth finished shouting, Downing replied, quietly, trying to control the quaver in his voice, so that everyone had to strain to catch his words.

"It's bad enough, Robert Wentworth, that you couldn't resist your own daughter and sexed her, and apparently against her will. But now you bear false witness against my sons, who are completely innocent of any crime. That puts you as the lowest of the low. Incest, rape, and false witness. The Devil is surely within you."

Miles's heart was racing so fast and his face was so hot that he could barely speak, and the last sentence was almost a whisper; however, it had its intended effect, at least as far as Wentworth was concerned. His red face deepened to purple.

"You accuse me of bearing false witness? You, of all people!" he shouted. Then he raised his fist and struck Miles Downing in the face as hard as he could. Miles fell back but then rolled over, stood up, and struck out at Robert, and the two fell over a table.

Those watching were either enjoying the show—rare for North Hinkapee—or were too shocked by it to do anything to separate the men as they rained blows on one another. But at last Handel Lewis intervened. He waded in between them and put a huge paw on each man's arm and literally pulled them apart, as if he were separating two struggling children.

"I think that's enough," he said kindly, and even gently. "That's about enough of that."

The two men, with no real choice, stopped attempting to hit each other, but they were still shouting, cursing.

Miles composed himself a bit and turned to Minister Brown. "Minister," he said, "you're a man of God. What do you make of this?"

Wentworth went pale at this question, but he could not take the position that the respected minister should not be heard. What could he say?

303

Everyone looked at Minister Brown, who straightened his frock coat.

As Martha would if she were right here to guide him, Miles thought with disgust.

The clergyman threw up his hands and looked at Robert Wentworth.

"How could you do such a thing?" he asked. "'Tis the work of the Devil here. There's no other explanation for the crime of incest and rape of a daughter by a father. And the bearing of false witness only makes it worse. I've heard talk of witchcraft about you before, but I demurred to receive the rumor. I thought it to be a false accusation. But now I see that it's true."

The rest of the crowd was silent. Everyone seemed to have suddenly realized what was going on. They were either with Miles Downing and the Downing clan, or they weren't. There were no two ways about it. Each must choose. Minister Brown's statement had not only made that clear, it had also made clear which side the minister was choosing. That meant that opposing the Downings meant opposing the church as well, opposing the Lord Himself.

The patrons of the Towne Tavern were staring at Robert Wentworth, ready to accuse. He could see it in their eyes.

ACKNOWLEDGMENTS

I want to recognize the people who deserve credit for helping me with this book.

First—I would like to thank my wonderful wife, Ann, without whom, well, things just wouldn't be fun in my life, and without whom I would never have had the emotional strength to write this story. Although my amazing and wonderful wife has many great qualities, one of her best aspects is that she is honest with me. I thank her for giving a solid "thumbs down" to the first draft of this book. It kinda stunk, being honest. So I started over, and it was much better the second time.

Second—I would like to thank my children, Bethany and Kimberly. I told them the story when they were little, and they not only enjoyed hearing it but had real input into the story line. And then as adults they read it and contributed new ideas.

Third—I would like to thank Andrew Clayburn, who read the book as my daughter Bethany's fiancé. He is now her husband. Andrew was good enough to be the first man to read the book, and his input was invaluable in all sorts of ways.

Fourth—I want to thank the Chatham Rolling Hill Book Club. These are my wife's friends who did an amazing thing for me: they read an early draft for their club meetings and took a lot of time to give me comments. These were not just light comments—they were of major and important use. I give them great thanks.

Fifth—I want to thank various friends and family members for reading drafts and giving me their ideas. They include Barbara Stachenfeld (my mom), Haylee Messing, Marilyn and Lynda Frankel, Marcia Wofsey (my wife's mom), Joan Hirsh, and Alex Goldstein.

Sixth—I thank my mother for pushing and shoving me along the many times I really didn't want to be pushed or shoved. I certainly didn't love it at the time, but rules like "No TV on weeknights" inspired me to write my first fiction book at age sixteen. Thanks, Mom!

Seventh—I want to thank my publishing team at Creative Management Partners, headed up by David Wilk.

Eighth—I want to thank my editor, Cindy Rinaman Marsch. Here I need to dwell a bit. Typically an editor, well, edits, and my understanding is that the editor kind of annoys the writer with word changes. Cindy's role here was more dramatic and encompassing than that. Among other things, she revised solid chunks of the story, spiced up the writing in ways I would never have thought of, created interesting plot lines, and contributed her deep knowledge of the Colonial period that was way beyond mine. Cindy's effort and work here was transformative to the excellence of this work and I thank her for it.

Ninth—and finally—I thank God for things I never take for granted—like being born relatively intelligent, and with a fire to achieve great things. Like being in good health despite being over sixty—and having the friends, family, and work colleagues in my life who inspire me to write and to do good things.

ABOUT THE AUTHOR

James T. Hogg is the pseudonym of one of the most prominent New York City real estate attorneys. As a real-life attorney he has published two non-fiction books about real estate and business, one of which was a *Wall Street Journal* best seller.

Girl With a Knife is his first novel, writing as James T. Hogg. The novel is based on a story he told many times to his now-grown children. The goal—then and now—was to create a story that the reader simply cannot put down, even when it is midnight and the reader has to get up to go to work the next morning. That has always been his simple goal—to write a *page-turner,* so that the reader can have a great time with an enjoyable read.

Hogg now lives in New Jersey and has been happily married for thirty-eight years to his soulmate wife. They are blessed to be the proud parents of two daughters.

The author's muse calls from his summer home getaway, where he goes to play loud music and write and write and write.

If you want the real skinny about James T. Hogg—and a reveal of who he is—go to www.jamesthogg.com, where you will find that Mr. Hogg is not a boring New York City lawyer, but actually a very interesting fellow.

READ THE FIRST CHAPTER FROM BOOK TWO, *DEFENSE*

SHERIFF JONES TAKES OVER THE SITUATION

Sheriff Jones banged open the door of the tavern to make a notable entrance and stood there looking over the ruckus that quieted at sight of him. "What's going on here?" he demanded.

Robert Wentworth and Miles Downing both started talking at the same time.

"Quiet, both of you!" barked the sheriff.

The men stood quiet, and the other patrons watched for the drama to further unfold.

Sheriff Jones nodded towards Miles and said, "So you tell me your version."

Miles stammered but eventually recovered, took a big breath, and said with an air of dignity, "I'm embarrassed almost to say this, but Robert Wentworth here had incest with his daughter, even to the point of violence—he raped her. Then when she became pregnant, he blamed my sons, in order to save himself. Then he tried to blackmail me to keep it quiet. It's a pretty ugly tale."

Sheriff Jones turned to bid Robert Wentworth speak, and the man was white with rage.

"This is an outrageous lie before God," Robert said, his voice shaking. He pointed to Miles. "His animal boys raped my little girl and left her insensible. She's gone from the world." His eyes filled with tears. "My beautiful little girl"—his voice cracked. "Downing tried to bribe me not to tell, to hush it all up. I told him … well, I told him …"

Sheriff Jones noted that Robert was uncertain here and awaited his next words.

"I told him I needed time to think of what to do—that was in this very place earlier today—and the next thing I know, it's all over town." Robert Wentworth looked around at his neighbors. "They say I've done something too terrible even to speak of. It's not true. Downing's sons have to be brought to justice."

"Any other views here?" the sheriff asked the surrounding group.

They shuffled uncertainly, and Miles Downing looked at them as if awaiting corroboration of his story.

Robin Stone broke the silence. "'Course we don't know anything for sure, but I can understand the temptation. That little girl was sure a beauty." He looked down at his shoes.

"I didn't want to say it, but I was thinking the same thing," said Perkin Massey, setting an overturned chair to rights.

Handel Lewis still had a massive hand on Robert Wentworth's upper arm and seemed to realize that all of a sudden, so he released it and clamped his hand reassuringly on Robert's shoulder. But he had nothing to say.

Miles looked pointedly at Minister Brown, who took the cue: "'Tis the work of the Devil, for sure," the minister said.

"What's the work of the Devil?" asked Sheriff Jones.

"What this man hath done," he said pointing at Robert Wentworth.

"This is all well and good," said Sheriff Jones, looking hard at Minister Brown before continuing, "but does anyone have any actual evidence of anything?"

"I don't," said Miles, "but I know you do."

"What do you mean?" asked Jones.

"I mean the medicines you took from the Wentworth house just in the past hours—the medicines for doing away with the child."

Sheriff Jones now looked at the man with whose father he had made a long-standing agreement. For many years North Hinkapee had been an easy place to be a sheriff—the law was honored, and the peace kept. But now he looked long and hard at Miles, the son. This man was not Thompson Downing, and for the first time, the law might not sit easy with the Downings.

The sheriff cleared his throat and spoke to the crowd. "All right, everyone, these charges are very serious. A young girl has been abused but cannot speak for herself. We must have a trial, and I'll call for a traveling judge to make an inquest and determine what should be done. Right now I'm going to ask both of you men"—he looked first at Robert, then at Miles—"to leave and go home. But first"—he held up a finger of warning—"I'm going to need promises from each of you."

The men both looked at him, and Jones delivered his orders. "Stay away from each other. No more blows, no violence." Robert and Miles each nodded.

"Don't leave town. Either of you ... or"—he looked at Miles—"your sons." Both men nodded.

"And no more talk about this, either. You'll have plenty of time to talk at the trial. I suggest you prepare for that. Got it?" Both men nodded again.

Robert angrily yanked his hat away from Handel Lewis, who had picked it up for him, and the accused man strode out of the tavern. Miles looked around at everyone and left after several moments.

Sheriff Jones sighed. Open war was now inevitable—and indeed had been declared.

The patrons of the Towne Tavern filtered out one or two at a time. The sheriff studied them and waited for the last, Earl Carver, who was sitting in a dim corner. After a few minutes, the Downing lawyer stood up, paid his bar bill, and walked out.

Yes, thought Sheriff Jones. *Carver will have a lot of lawyerly work to do.*

CPSIA information can be obtained
at www.ICGtesting.com
Printed in the USA
JSHW051937280223
38320JS00008B/78

9 781632 261076